CARRICK GLYNN

TONY URBAN

Copyright © 2021 by Tony Urban

All rights reserved.

No part of this book may be reproduced in any form or by any electronic or mechanical means, including information storage and retrieval systems, without written permission from the author, except for the use of brief quotations in a book review.

For my childhood friends.

PART ONE

"You never think about someone dressing up as you for Halloween."

CHAPTER ONE

Summer

The village had its ways, and Conal knew them all. From his vantage point in Brighid's cottage, he could see almost the entirety of Carrick Glynn and its surrounding lands. Farmers tended to lush fields of wheat and corn, their gardens and orchards bursting with fruits and vegetables. He longed to be out there, working alongside them, but his failing body wouldn't permit it. He cursed his old bones, along with the unjustness of growing useless.

As Brighid stirred the brackish mélange in a copper pot hoisted over her fire, Conal's stomach seized into a hard knot. The smell, a rancid combination of rot and deep musk, drifted toward him while the liquid bubbled and gurgled as if something was drowning down in its depths.

I can't do this, he thought as he pushed the chair away from the kitchen table, the legs scratching against the uneven floor. *No more. Not again.*

The commotion drew the woman's attention. She swiveled her head his way, moving with the speed of cold molasses. Her halting, deliberate motion gave her an uncanny look, like a ventriloquist's dummy or a wax figure with a rusty motor hidden in its torso. Even across the room, he could hear the ancient bones in her neck cracking under duress.

"And where do you tink you're go'n, Conal?" Her voice was thick with a lazy Celtic accent.

"Shouldn't have come this time," Conal said as he pushed his palms against the tabletop and tried to stand. But his body wasn't up for the task. His pain was too much to bear.

"You're 'xactly where you need to be," she crowed, her voice cruelly jovial and high-pitched.

Conal made another attempt at rising. It ended the same way, and he sagged back into the chair, spent from the effort. His chest heaved, and he tasted a ball of bloody phlegm rising in his throat. He brought a hand, gnarled with age and arthritis, to his mouth, spat it into his palm, then rubbed the tacky wad into the parched fibers of the old wooden table.

All the while, Brighid observed him, her body frozen as the reflected light of the fire danced across her milky irises. She'd been an elderly woman when Conal was a boy, and his body had racked up nearly eighty years since then.

How old is she, he wondered, not for the first time. Her age was one of the village's few secrets, even from him.

Her hair wasn't gray or white but translucent. It hung far beyond her waist, grazing the floor, each strand as fine as spider's silk. Through it, her skull was visible. Alabaster skin stretched taught across the bone. Her eyes hid deep in their sockets, dull yet avid.

Brighid's face contorted into what Conal hoped was a smile. Her long, pencil-thin nose crinkled. Her lips, the color of uncooked shrimp, pulled not up in the corners but straight back, revealing nubs of brown teeth which had been ground to nothing but pulp.

"Well past time you came to see me," Brighid said. "Shouldn't have waited so long. You men..."

Shouldn't have come at all, Conal thought again. But another part of him knew she was right. He needed her if he expected to survive another summer.

As if she could read his mind, Brighid retorted, "'Nother month and you'd a been beyond saving."

"Aye," he said with a dottery shake of his head. "I'm here now, so quit harping on me." He tilted his chin toward the pot. "You about ready wit it?"

"Patience." Brighid gave the brew another languid stir.

Patience he didn't have, especially not in this place where the walls were painted with black mold and the floor was thick with animal waste that had laid there so long it had fermented.

A featherless rooster strutted under the table, pecking at his feet. He gave it a quick kick, and the bird moved on, shifting its attention to a laying hen locked inside a birdcage so small it didn't have room enough to make a complete turn. The rooster pecked its mate through the bars. So much for love.

A dozen or more rats, each scrawnier than the next, darted from one side of the kitchen to the other as if in the midst of some game, the rules of which were known only to rodents. Occasionally, the vermin broke from scurrying and attacked each other, their high, pained squeals filling the room before they broke apart and the race recommenced. In between, they paused to devour the assortment of scraps, crumbs, and feces that littered the floor. Their own private smorgasbord.

He'd watched them for only a moment – or so it seemed – when Brighid's voice cooed in his ear.

"Got your nostrum." She spoke the words from a distance so near the humid dampness of her breath prickled his skin.

Conal flinched, jerking away from her. His body screamed

with pain over the sudden movement, and his eyes burned with threatening tears.

Brighid pushed a ceramic bowl toward him. Her fingers were stubby but tapered to yellow, cork-like nails which curved inward at the ends. They reminded Conal of the crochet hooks his wife used to fashion scarves and mittens. Warm attire to get the villagers through long winters.

Memories of his wife brought a different, deeper kind of pain, and Conal directed his attention to the bowl to keep himself from reminiscing. The contents were muddy-colored, chunky, and steaming.

Might not be as bad as I remember, he told himself as he accepted the offering. He considered inquiring about the ingredients, then thought better of it. Sometimes, it was better not to know.

"Hurry it down," she said. "Works best when it's good 'n hot."

Conal looked to the table for a spoon, but there was none. So, he raised the bowl to his lips and tried not to breathe through his nose as he tilted the dish. The concoction had the consistency of rubber cement, and it was slow to ebb into his awaiting mouth.

When it hit his tongue, he cursed having taste buds. The contents of the bowl, his medicine, tasted like rancid cheese. Like spoiled meat. Like pureed death.

He swallowed and swallowed and swallowed again, trying to force it down his throat before his brain could catch on and stop this abomination. But the mixture was too dense, too viscid.

His stomach rebelled, and all that he'd consumed fought its way back up his gullet and out of his mouth, spilling into the bowl where it coagulated with the uneaten contents. Still retching, Conal leaned into the table, running his fingers across his mostly bald dome. Sweat leaked from his pores as if his whole body was sobbing in disgust.

Then he felt Brighid's boney hand on his shoulder. Her nails pressed against his shirt, threatening to puncture the material and skewer his skin if she pushed hard enough.

"Eat," she ordered. "You need this to carry you over until the harvest."

Conal peered into the bowl, where his vomit cohabitated with the original contents. Then he looked to the fire where the cauldron sat among the flames. Where fresh nostrum awaited.

"Can't you give me--"

Her sharp voice severed his words. "Eat what's yours, Conal."

He knew there was no choice, so he brought the bowl to his mouth once more. To distract himself, he again looked out the window, past the farmers and the fields, into the forest.

There, the great horned beast stared back, barely visible amongst the cover of the trees. *Soon, old friend*, Conal thought. *Soon.*

"Eat!" Brighid repeated.

And Conal did.

As he had before.

As he would again.

CHAPTER TWO

OCTOBER

On the fourth and final Saturday of October 1986, I couldn't think of a better way to spend the day than wading through an orange sea with one purpose in mind. Finding the perfect pumpkin.

Farmer Spivey's pumpkin patch was my go-to, but I wasn't above sleazing around and making purchases at a couple of the other area farms if something caught my eye. I drew the line at grocery stores, though. The pumpkins sold at County Market or Riverside weren't even grown locally in Sallow Creek, so buying from them seemed like rooting against the home team.

Not that I had any special affinity for my hometown. It was a downtrodden place that might have been worth something in the fifties and sixties, but by the time I came around, it was already spiraling toward irrelevance.

Sallow Creek was perched high in the Appalachians, far enough north we pronounced them *Ap-uh-lay-shuns*. That means we got the worst of everything. About seven months of dreary, godforsaken winter, followed by a month of incessant rain in the spring. Then came summer, so humid you broke a sweat walking to your mailbox.

If we were lucky, we had three weeks of fall. But I'd be damned if they weren't three glorious weeks.

It was late afternoon, and the air was crisp enough to make me pull the hood of my sweatshirt up and over my head, covering my ears which were always the first part of me to get cold. I'd often dreamed of growing my hair really long - hair metal band long - but my dad would've had a shit fit, so I made do with a shaggy mop and bangs long enough to make me look half sheepdog.

I squatted beside a plump offering. It had nice size to it, but I judged it too squat and broad, almost tomato-ish in shape. The next pumpkin I examined sat lopsided. Also no good to my discerning eye. The third had a broken stem which was entirely unacceptable.

As I continued my search, a gust of wind breathed through the nearby ryegrass, walking through it like an invisible force. On the outskirts of the patch, dry, golden brown corn stalks stretched for acres, whispering secrets. The trees were already barren, nothing but skeletal branches. The leaves had put on a good show, but it was always short-lived.

My hunt dragged on for another half hour before I found a suitable specimen. Tall but well-proportioned. No flat spot where it had laid in the field too long. Smooth skin with no signs of insect-induced trauma or scars. A sturdy stem, five inches long, and showing no signs of decay. It was the shade of deep orange that practically screamed *Halloween*.

I'd been struggling to keep my Halloween cheer after a ludicrous development had rocked fourteen-year-old me to my core earlier in the fall. Due to complaints from old bittys and nosey nebbies who got scared when teenagers wearing masks came to their doors to beg candy on Halloween night, the town of Sallow Creek had taken the draconian measure of putting an age limit on trick or treating.

If that age limit had been fourteen, I might have tolerated it, at least until the following autumn when I surely would have pouted. But the arbitrary number set by our town leaders wasn't fourteen. It wasn't even thirteen.

It was twelve. *Twelve!* What a load of horse manure that was.

Any child older than twelve was banned from trick or treating. Banned from getting dressed up in a costume and going out in public too. They may as well have banned fun, as far as I was concerned.

The announcement had been made on Labor Day Weekend, and, five weeks later, I was still coming to terms with the heartbreak. They might not let me go door to door and fill my little, plastic tote with Smarties and Tootsie Rolls and the occasional full-sized Hershey bar (God, those people were the best), but I wasn't going to let this stupid town ruin what had always been my favorite time of year.

I hoisted the pumpkin, a prize-winner for certain, off the ground. The effort required all of my might. I'd been stuck at five feet two inches for going on three years and barely broke one hundred pounds, even in my warm fall attire. But the exertion was worth it.

I couldn't keep the lopsided smile off my face, satisfied at a job well done, as I locked the pumpkin in a firm embrace, then waddled penguin-style toward a wooden lean-to where the financial end of the day's mission took place.

Angus Spivey, so long and lean that he'd often been mistaken for a scarecrow while surveying his crops, lounged in an aluminum lawn chair with crisscrossing red and white webbing. A brown cigarette dangled from his lips, and smoke ebbed steadily from his nostrils like he was half-dragon. Upon seeing me, he gave a genial smile and rose to his feet.

"Back again, are ya?"

Too out of breath to speak, I only nodded.

"Fourth time in the past two weeks if my memory ain't foolin' me."

I nodded again, finally at the table where the scale awaited. The thing was so rusty and old I was afraid it might break if I looked at it too long, so I sat the pumpkin beside the scale rather than on it.

Then I got out, between gasps, "Fifth, actually."

The farmer rubbed stubble on his chin, which was as pointed as Satan's chin on the cans of Underwood deviled ham my dad kept stocked in the pantry. For some unknown reason, the devil's broad smile and jaunty wave made me feel like my skin was going to creep away from me every time I grabbed a Pop Tart or a fruit roll up. Maybe I owed my trim figure to that leering Lucifer.

But Farmer Spivey was no devil. A transplant from New England with an accent I found fascinating, albeit indiscernible at times, he was one of the nicest adults I'd ever met. Maybe even nicer than Skip Haywood, who ran A&H Video and let me rent R-rated horror movies with a promise of, *My dad said it's okay.* My dad had not said it was okay, but he also wouldn't have cared. He was cool, for the most part. My dad, I mean.

On the whole, I got along better with grown-ups than most of my peers. To most of the kids I went to school with, I was an octagonal peg in a crowd of round holes. Similar, but different.

Kids have a way of homing in on that difference and realizing you're not like them. I didn't have it as bad as some, though. Surely not as bad as the reliefers who lived in the Towers or the welfare kids like the Mayhughs and a dozen or so other families everyone referred to as poor white trash. Those kids get the real shit end of the stick.

I was more of a loner by choice. Or maybe that's what I told myself to feel better. Either way, I was pretty content with my small cadre of allies and didn't need to be invited into any of the cliques to feel like I mattered.

Adults always treated me well, though. Maybe my diminutive size made them feel protective. Or maybe they liked me because I looked at them as *people* and not ancient specimens from a time long forgotten. The way most kids viewed anyone over the age of thirty.

I enjoyed listening to them talk about their lives and tell their stories. Sometimes, I even jotted the best of them down in a notebook, integrating them into the short fiction I wrote in my free time.

The farmer dropped both of his hands, large and covered with seventy-five years' worth of scars and age spots, onto the pumpkin's bright skin, giving it a fond caress. "I must say, you're my best custom'uh, Benjamin. Of course, you're pretty near," those two words came out *pert ah neer*, "my only custom'uh."

"I'm not sure why I like pumpkins so much. Something about them just makes me happy," I said as Spivey lifted the fruit with ease and set it atop the scale. This year, happiness wasn't so easily found, but the pumpkins did bring solace. Solace and reminders of happier times.

Of a time before I came home from school and found my mom missing. *Found* missing. Sounds funny when you think about it. But I didn't find it funny at all.

Pumpkins reminded me of carving jack o'lanterns with her. I always opted for scary faces, whereas her jacks were goofy and fun - mirrors of her own personality. Pumpkins reminded me of throwing sticky seeds at each other when our hands got tired and dad getting home from work to find globs of stringy pumpkin guts glued to the cabinets and refrigerator, then scolding us both over the mess we'd made.

They reminded me of the first time my mom took me trick or treating. We'd been ambling down Listie Road when a stray dog came out of nowhere, barking and chasing us. We ran for our lives, and I lost most of my candy in that mad dash. Even though we thought a hound from hell was going to tear us to pieces, we couldn't stop laughing.

Good times.

Gone times.

The needle on the scale bounced back and forth, back and forth, back and forth, before settling on twenty-one pounds.

"I guess that sounds kind of lame," I added, feeling self-conscious over my love of a glorified squash.

Spivey gave his head a quick shake. "I like 'em too. Like me a good pumpkin pie with some vanilla ice cream on the side even bett'uh."

I looked at the pumpkin, unsure how it transitioned from its current, whole state to pie filling, and considered asking the farmer about the process. Then the sun glinted off the plain gold band on the man's left hand, and I figured the farmer's wife probably handled all matters related to baking. That's how it had worked in my house in an era I now thought of as simply *before*.

"I don't believe there's a better time of year than autumn," Farmer Spivey said, twisting at the waist and popping his spine.

I looked up and examined the man's narrow face, trying to decide whether my leg was being pulled. I would have traded Christmas and birthday presents, fireworks on the Fourth of July, summer vacation and its school-less months, all of those for additional days of fall and its spooky, mischievous glory. But I didn't know many adults who felt that way. Certainly not my dad. Nor any of my friends' parents. It seemed like every grown-up I encountered treated Halloween like a burden to bear. Something tolerated rather than cherished. Something childish and foolish. My mom had been the only person who'd cherished the holiday as much as me, and she was a self-professed weirdo.

But Farmer Spivey's pale, hazel eyes seemed genuine, and there was no hint of sarcasm in his voice.

Once satisfied that my leg was, in fact, not being pulled, I risked spilling my uncensored feelings. "I wait all year long for Halloween. I wish it never had to end."

I grabbed the pumpkin, clutching it the way a younger boy might latch onto a teddy bear or old blanket for emotional support.

"I think that's just fine." Spivey tapped his cigarette against the table, knocking ash to the ground where wind scattered it.

"I really wish I was still allowed to go trick or treating," I added, feeling small and a little ashamed.

"Ayuh. Shame what this town's gone and done." Even though the sign in front of his farm read, 'Established in 1953', Farmer Spivey was an outsider in Sallow Creek. He was *From Away*, and that hadn't changed, not even after the passing of more than thirty years.

As someone *From Away*, he had an unfiltered view of the town and its people that lifelong residents lacked. "Folks 'round here got their heads so far up their own assholes they think it's permanently midnight." After he spoke, Spivey seemed to realize it might be too frank of language to share with a fourteen-year-old boy and backtracked. "Don't you tell your pa I said that."

I smirked, enjoying his candor. "I won't. He says way worse, though, believe me."

Spivey gave a knowing nod as he examined his cigarette,

which was still good for another drag or two. "I reckon he does. But the words a man uses around his own son's altogether different from what a stranger says."

"You're not a stranger, Mister Spivey. You're my friend." I meant it. And not just because of the pumpkins, either. I stopped at Farmer Spivey's fruit stand at least once a week from May through October. On some days, I bought apples or pears or raspberries, but on others, we simply shared the shade of the lean-to and discussed the minutiae of our lives.

As a boy with no siblings, no living grandparents, a father whose successful engineering firm required most of his waking hours, and a mother who was MIA, I cherished those talks.

Spivey's mouth twisted into a mildly shocked smile. "Why, that's kind of you to say. A man can never have too many friends."

I nodded in silent agreement, but my gaze drifted past him, toward the west end of the farm where the sun sagged low on the horizon, fat and full and looking more than a little like a pumpkin itself. Or maybe I had pumpkins on the brain.

"I should probably head home." I didn't have a curfew, but I wasn't crazy about riding my bike in the dark out here in the sticks.

After lugging the pumpkin to the bike, I set it on the rear rack and used two worn bungee cords to strap it down. They held it, but I'd need to be careful not to hit any rocks or potholes during the ride home or else risk my prize pumpkin popping loose and splattering on the road.

I straddled the bicycle, one foot on the peddle when--

"Benjamin?" Farmer Spivey called.

When I turned to look, the man was extending his empty palm. "Ten cents a pound makes that pumpkin two dollars and one dime. But I'll round down for you."

CHAPTER THREE

On my way home, I stopped at a half dozen or so telephone poles, carrying on a rote mission I was beginning to think would continue for the rest of my life. At each pole, I tore off a weathered sheet of paper and used my trusty stapler to replace it with a fresh copy.

The contents of each flyer were the same.

MISSING in thick, black font.

Below the word was a grayscale image of my mother. It became less discernible every time I paid the print shop to run me off a new batch, but I'd lost the original, and it was still the best picture I had of her.

The text below the photo included vital details about my mom; her name, date of birth, height, weight (I guessed low), hair color, and a 1-800 phone number I'd convinced my dad to pay for after her disappearance.

REWARD closed it out.

You might be wondering if those flyers generated any leads. They had, but none had panned out. The best to date came just a few weeks after she vanished. The caller said she'd seen my mother at a turnpike rest stop near Harrisburg. She described my mom to a tee. Even the outfit the woman claimed she wore matched one of my mom's dresses. We gave the info to Sheriff Moland and the state police, but nothing came of it.

For more than a year now, the only calls to come through were of the crank variety. It was so bad that, at one point, dad threatened to cancel the second phone line if they didn't stop.

He thought they had. In reality, we still received several each week, but I always beat him to the answering machine and erased the messages before he could listen and get pissed off, all because some anonymous source had seen my mother riding elephants in India or wrestling gators in the Everglades.

I was pretty sure most of those crank calls were from kids at school. I could tell their ages - or close enough - by their voice. But a disturbing number were clearly from adults. People say there's more good in the world than bad, but I don't believe that anymore.

The Roth homestead, aka my house, was empty, just as it was every day when I got around to completing whatever meandering path I'd taken between school and Clover Hill Road. I was used to it and only darted inside to check the answering machine. No calls. Not even of the crank variety.

While I was there, I took a quick leak, then dropped my backpack in my bedroom. Next, I headed into the back yard, passed the swing set - it hadn't been used in years and served no purpose but to breed tetanus - and plunged into the forest.

I traveled along a well-worn path, crunching through fallen leaves and avoiding the poison ivy that we'd been trying to exterminate for over two years with no luck. After a few minutes, I reached the makeshift ladder of wooden planks nailed into the trunk of a towering oak. It looked about four hundred feet tall if you peered up from ground level.

During the green portion of the year, what those rungs led

to was completely hidden. Now, however, the tree was bare, and my pride and joy was clearly visible.

The treehouse, sitting more than thirty feet above the ground, wasn't Dan Roth's best work, but it was, without a doubt, the best treehouse in all of Sallow Creek. It was also the only treehouse in Sallow Creek so far as I knew, but that mattered not at all.

My dad had built it two summers earlier. The year after my mom disappeared from our lives. He said I'd been moping, so he wanted to cheer me up. It wasn't as easy as flipping a light switch. I was still depressed, still confused, still *moped*. But now, I had a place to do it in private. I appreciated that. I'm pretty sure dad did too.

The treehouse was the place where I could go to escape the realities of life. Where I could write and daydream. Where I could sit and wonder where my mother had ended up and what life she was now living, far removed from her husband and son. Assuming she was living at all.

It was also my *clubhouse* where my friends and I had overnight campouts, played board games, ate like pigs, and held horror movie marathons.

Thanks to two hundred feet of extension cord, the clubhouse had electricity which powered one lamp, a thirteen-inch TV, and a VCR. But, as day shifted to night, I left the TV off and used the light of the lamp to guide me as I whittled away at my newest purchase, transforming the pumpkin into a jack o'lantern.

I'd been futzing around with it for the better part of an hour, using a drywall knife to create a gaping maw full of fangs, when the cast iron bell mounted on an old pulley rang.

Clang. Clang. Clang. Clang.

Four rings meant the ringer was Stewart "Stooge" Decker. Three would have signaled Dwayne Carson. My dad, the only other person who ever came visiting, never bothered with the bell. He preferred to shout.

I set aside the knife and moved to the trap door. A squadron of fruit flies assaulted my face, and I waved them away, squinting so they didn't dive into my eyes as I flipped open the hatch and tried to shoo them out.

"I was on my way to the house when I saw the light on," Stooge called up. He was no more than a big shadow in the burgeoning darkness below.

"Working on a pumpkin," I said, wiping my hands, slimy with pumpkin guts, on my shirt. "Want me to come down?"

"Nah, I'll join ya. But drop the dumbwaiter. I've got Lowboy."

The dumbwaiter was a forty-quart cooler attached to yet another rope and pulley system. It hoisted a variety of goods too big to fit into our backpacks. Goods like pumpkins. Or, in Lowboy's case, Stooge's middle-aged dachshund.

I lowered the cooler, waited for the signaling tug, then pulled it back up. Fortunately, the dog was lighter than the pumpkin as my forearms were still burning. Once the cooler was in the treehouse, I pulled it to the side and set it on the plank floor.

Lowboy hopped out and gave a full body shake, which I took to mean he'd enjoyed the ride. The dog trotted around the familiar terrain, found a stray pumpkin seed, and began to gnaw on it.

A full two minutes later, Stooge, huffing like an asthmatic with a bad smoking habit, made it up the ladder. He paused, upper body through the trap door, as he caught his breath.

"We're gonna need a bigger cooler so you can haul my fat ass up here," he said.

I looked him over with narrowed eyes. Stooge was almost two years older but in the same grade because he'd failed kindergarten - twice. He was a mountainous boy who'd topped two hundred pounds when we were still in elementary school and hadn't slowed down. Currently, he was rocking an epic, blond mullet and a faded AC/DC tank top which revealed his ham-sized upper arms. A silver ring dangled from his nose like he was a stud bull.

"I couldn't lift you one inch off the ground," I said. Even the thought of trying made me ache all over.

Stooge ascended the final four rungs of the ladder and stepped onto the floor, immediately swatting at the flies as they went on the attack.

"Holy Jesus, it smells like Charlie Brown gave the Great Pumpkin an abortion in here." Stooge glanced around the clubhouse where four fully carved jack o'lanterns looked back at him. The oldest, one I'd had carved ten days earlier, was in the middle of a slow implosion and had gone black with mold.

He looked at me, nose snarled, "That's unsanitary."

"So are you," I said.

Stooge plopped to the floor, setting off a quake that shook the entire structure. He grabbed the knife I had been using to carve and jabbed it randomly like he was fighting the Invisible Man. Then he nodded toward my newest, still unfinished, creation. "What's that one going to be?"

I shrugged. "A monster." Aligned, my jack o lanterns would have created something akin to an evolutionary chart of monsters. Sharp teeth, evil, down-sloped eyes, slivers for noses. To me, they all had their own personalities. To anyone else, they were nearly identical scary faces.

"Cool beans," Stooge said. "Want to watch *A Nightmare on Elm Street* again?"

"I had to return the tape yesterday. We need to get some new ones. Skip said he'd give us half off on everything except new releases through the end of the month."

"We should rent *Halloween*," Stooge said. "Watch it on Halloween night."

Compared to trick or treating, watching a movie I'd seen more than twenty times barely compared, but it might have to suffice in a town where joy was contraband.

"We can pause it when Linda shows off her titties. She's got great titties," Stooge added, then he raised his usually deep, gravelly voice to a falsetto and mimicked the character. "*See anything you like?* Hell yeah I do, babe!"

That was less appealing.

I enjoyed female nudity as much as any fourteen-year-old boy but far less than Stooge. Maybe it was the age difference, or maybe Stooge was a pervert (probably both), but any time a woman dropped her top in a horror movie, Stooge broke out the catcalls and wolf whistles and made it beyond awkward.

"I don't know. Maybe," I muttered.

Stooge, usually as observant as a fence post, caught on to the lack of enthusiasm in my voice. "What's wrong, little dude? You love *Halloween*."

"I don't know. I guess." I avoided the question by grabbing Lowboy's collar and steering the dog into my lap. The dachshund rolled onto its back and enjoyed a thorough belly rub. My dad was allergic (or so he said, I had my doubts), which meant pets were off-limits, so I took every opportunity possible to love on the animal who I considered mine by proxy.

"Come on, tell Uncle Stoogie what's the matter."

If I could be honest about my feelings with anyone, it was Stooge. Even though the boy was older, he'd never mocked or looked down on me or made fun of me. He wasn't a big brother figure, but he was a confidant I could trust. Even in a situation where I knew I was being immature.

"This just sucks."

"You gotta be more specific. The world is an ocean of suckitude"

"I can't believe this stupid town says we're too old to go trick or treating. What gives them the right?"

"My dad says they're a bunch of fascists," Stooge said.

"More like a bunch of assholes." My rare use of profanity made Stooge chuckle.

"I feel ya, dude."

"I even had my costume thought up. I was going to be a homicidal lumberjack."

"That would have been rad," Stooge said. After busting the seams of his Spiderman unitard five years ago, Stooge's trick or treat character of choice each and every year had been a Rock Star. The costume was his standard daily attire with a broken electric guitar for a prop.

"Bunch of lame asses around here." Stooge grabbed a can of lukewarm Pepsi from a trunk containing our snacks and drinks, popped the top, and swallowed half the can in three gulps. After belching, he said, "You know, my mom said the Baptists are putting on a thing after church. If you sit through a bible lesson, they'll give you a Snickers."

That sounded like the lamest thing I'd ever heard, but it was better than nothing. Maybe. If the bar was low enough. "Are people allowed to dress up?"

Stooge finished off the pop. "Yeah. But it has to be a bible character. I told Janey to tart it up and go as Mary Magdalene. Mom didn't see the humor." Janey was Stooge's nine-year-old sister and the bane of his existence. "So, she's going as Jehosheba instead."

My knowledge of the bible, or anything religious, didn't extend far beyond the cliff's notes. "Which one's that?"

Stooge flattened the can between his meaty hands. "I dunno."

The more I considered it, the more I warmed to the idea. But I had reservations. "They don't do that thing where they dunk you underwater, do they?"

"You mean baptize?" Stooge asked.

"Yeah."

"I think you need to be a member for that. Or marry Jesus or something."

"Are you going?" I asked him.

Stooge barked a laugh so loud that Lowboy did a full body flip and landed on his feet. "Me? Hell no. I'd burst into flames if I walked into a church. Like a vampire or some shit." He seemed to notice my shoulders sag and my mood along with them. "You should go, though. I know it's not the same as a serial killer version of Paul Bunyon, but you could be like a badass Moses or something. Break a stone tablet over some little kid's head. That would be bitchin'."

"Yeah," I mumbled, trying to decide how desperate I was for a morsel of Halloween.

The answer was pretty damn desperate.

CHAPTER FOUR

After finishing the carving and bidding Stooge farewell, I headed back to the house. Trudging through fifty yards of stygian woods didn't scare me - I'd done it a thousand times - but I always breathed a little easier when I stepped into the relative brightness cast by the floodlight illuminating the backyard.

Once inside, I took two seconds to run my hands under water at the kitchen sink, rehydrating the pumpkin slime, which had dried to a thick crust, then wiped them clean-ish with a paper towel. A cold Big Mac, still in the wrapper, sat on the counter, along with an empty container that had once held fries. Beside it was a note with my dad's perfect draftsman penmanship.

You snooze, you lose.

I didn't care about missing out on the fries, and the burger could wait. More important thoughts than eating weighed on my mind.

I continued down the hall toward my dad's office. The door was closed, but light spilled under it. Led Zeppelin's *Moby*

Dick played on a radio inside the room, but I didn't waste time with a knock.

The room was littered with sketches and building plans and smelled of black licorice and old paper. A pile of drafting tubes filled one corner. On one wall hung a detailed and perfectly-to-scale map of Sallow Creek. On another was a bookcase where dozens of tomes were stacked with no particular rhyme or reason.

Behind his oversized mahogany desk, my dad played air drums with frenetic glee. While Dan Roth was no John Bonham, what he lacked in talent, he compensated for in enthusiasm. Dad was so caught up in the solo that my arrival went unnoticed until I cleared my throat for a second time.

Dad froze, then broke into his own lopsided grin when he saw me standing in the open doorway. He set his invisible drumsticks aside, then spun the volume knob to zero as he beckoned me inside with a wave.

"Fruit of my loins," he said. "I thought maybe you'd run off to join the circus. How's life these days?" The man was nearing forty and not much taller than his pipsqueak son. So slender he shopped in the *young men's* department. He wore an untidy mess of salt and pepper hair atop his head.

I dropped into the leather chair on the opposite side of the desk, looking as beaten down and defeated as I felt.

The mood was impossible to miss, even for a single father who was doing his best but who'd aped most of his parenting know-how from TV sitcoms. I must have looked on the verge of confessing something horrible, like maybe I'd set fire to the school or murdered Mrs. Neri, who lived next door.

"What's the matter, Chief?" Dad had taken to calling me *Chief* within the past year, after auditioning similar nicknames – Ace, Champ, Sport – that failed to catch on. Once, he'd even dropped *Captain*, which was embarrassing for the both of us and was never addressed thereafter.

"Fail a big test? Get caught dealing dope in the school restroom? Impregnate the head cheerleader?" Dad loosened his tie. "Lay it on me, I can take it."

As dads went, I loved mine, but I wasn't in the mood for amateur comedy hour. "Stooge was telling me about some trick or treat thing they're having at the Baptist church. I want to go."

"Trick or treat thing?" Dad asked, losing his smile.

"Yeah. You dress up like someone from the Bible, and they give you a candy bar."

"Oh, that... I remember Wallace at work mentioning something about that. But we're Jewish, Benji."

We were, in theory. But I didn't know the difference between a kittel and a kippah. If it wasn't for the seldom opened Torah sitting on the coffee table in the living room and eating gefilte fish every year at Passover, we could have been agnostics.

"I know that. I'm not planning to convert," I said. "But it's as close as I'm gonna get to trick or treating this year."

Realization spread across my dad's face. Realization and something like disappointment. "We talked about this, Chief. You're too old." He wasn't able to meet my pleading eyes.

I audibly humphed. "I could go trick or treating, real trick or treating if you lied for me. Can't you just tell everyone I'm younger? You do it at China Buffet all the time. They think I've been twelve for the last two years!"

Dad's eyes widened, and he pointed at me. "What they don't know won't hurt them!"

"If I ever get my growth spurt, we're screwed. I think that skinny waitress who never talks is already suspicious. I swear she was counting my shrimp tails last week."

Dad leaned into his desk and tented his fingers. He took a

deep breath before going on. "Listen, I know you like Halloween—"

I opened his mouth, ready to declare that my feelings for Halloween went far beyond *like*, but dad stopped me with a stern look.

"You're fourteen years old now. You should be lusting over girls and looking forward to driving. Maybe even thinking about getting a job after school and making yourself some cold hard cash. Normal teenager things. All this Halloween stuff..." He twirled a finger in the air. "It's immature. You should have outgrown it by now."

Those well-meaning words hit like a dagger plunged straight into my heart. While my friends, all two of them, longed to grow up and become adults, I was perfectly content being young and, yes, immature.

I couldn't fathom why immaturity was considered a bad character trait. Being mature meant having *responsibilities*. It meant doing a job you hated to buy things you needed but didn't want. It meant having to take fiber to poop. It meant trading in fun and freedom for a world I wanted no part of.

I had no desire to grow up or be mature or leave my childhood behind - the best days of my life quickly forgotten, only to be replaced with meetings and business trips and failed marriages. I wanted to stay a kid forever.

Despite my obvious pouting, Dad didn't back down. "Sorry to be the bearer of bad news, but you have to grow up sooner or later. Even if you don't want to."

I refused to accept my dad's advice, vowing to outwit Father Time. I promised myself I'd be young and immature for the rest of my life.

And I was right, in a way. Because life, as I knew it, came to an end seven days later.

CHAPTER FIVE

"What you need is one of those fake IDs," Stooge said through a mouthful of partially-chewed hot dog, his words booming over the rowdy din of the crowd watching the Sallow Creek Swallows partake in their first playoff game in more than a decade.

"My brother has one. It's got a picture of some Puerto Rican broad with a mustache, but the bartenders serve him anyway. He says they just want you to make an effort."

On the field, Dwayne Carson, my only other teenage friend in the entire world, crouched like a tiger on the prowl as he manned first base. I tried to make eye contact with him, so he'd be aware of my presence and support. After all, I'd dedicated my day to watching him play even though I found sitting through an entire baseball game only slightly more tolerable than having my fingernails yanked off with pliers. But Dwayne's focus was on the batter, and the rest of the universe didn't exist.

With friend number two unavailable, I turned back to Stooge, who took the opportunity to open his mouth wide, wag his tongue, and reveal a sickening amount of masticated meat and soggy bun.

"You're so gross," I said, drawing a triumphant grin from Stooge. "How much does an ID like that cost?"

Stooge shrugged his broad shoulders as he swallowed. "No idea. Probably not cheap, though." He shoved the remainder of the hot dog into his mouth. "I can ask my bro to hook you up if you want."

Even if I could afford a fake ID, I had a feeling such a coveted object wouldn't be ready in time for Halloween. I needed a better plan. I needed Dwayne.

While Stooge was loud and proud, Dwayne was more of a thinker. At least, he had been until he shot up several inches in height between the seventh and eighth grades.

After his growth spurt, the shy kid, who'd once been eye-level with me and an even bigger dork, joined the school baseball team, traded his glasses for contacts, sucked down protein shakes, and lifted weights as he transformed not only his body but his social circle. In the Venn diagram of junior high cliques, our circles now came nowhere close to overlapping.

The changes alarmed me because Dwayne had been my friend since we rode the bus home together on the first day of kindergarten. The driver passed by my house, and, thinking I was never going home again, the five-year-old version of me bawled like the baby I was. I'm talking full-on foot stomping, snot streaming, face turning purple tantrum.

The driver, a tub of lard with more chins than IQ points, must have been used to such shenanigans. Either that or he didn't give a shit. He only threw me the occasional grinning glance via the super wide rearview mirror and never once had the courtesy to tell me the bus would circle a few blocks then drop me off at the end of the line.

It was Dwayne who'd consoled me and convinced me not to climb out a window and leap to almost certain death. He pulled me into his seat, extracted three rubber dinosaurs from his backpack, and asked if I wanted to play. Even then, Dwayne had a good head on his shoulders.

Dwayne was, no slight to Stooge, my *best* friend.

But our connection, which had been pure superglue from ages five to thirteen, was fading at breakneck speed. For the last eight months, Dwayne had been little more than a tangential part of my life. The boys who had done everything together now rarely saw each other outside of school. And the more I felt like I was losing Dwayne, the more desperate I was to hold on.

"You gonna eat that or let it grow hair?" Stooge asked.

He eyed an uneaten funnel cake sitting on a paper plate in my lap. "Take it," I said. Stooge obeyed and went to work.

Bored with the game and stymied when it came to possible ways of salvaging what remained of the Halloween season, my attention drifted across the crowd as I sought a distraction to pass the time. While there were several classmates in attendance, most of the onlookers were parents. A few seemed genuinely invested in the game, but the majority appeared to be there out of obligation.

Looking past them, my eyes settled on an eclectic group of kids who ranged from five to seventeen. There were more than a dozen of them, each one looking like they'd gone on a shopping spree in the Salvation Army's reject bin.

One adult, a stern-looking woman with her gray hair in a no-nonsense bun, sat with them, observing the goings-on with zero cheer. She carried the aura of a teacher, but I'd never seen her at Sallow Creek Middle School.

"Who's that?" I pointed to the self-contained group and the woman who seemed to be supervising.

"Them? They're the losers from the Aid Home," Stooge said. He wasn't the type to make fun, not in a mean-spirited way, but when you were near the bottom of the social ladder, it was a relief to realize there were still a couple rungs beneath you.

"The... orphans?" I shuddered, thinking I was one more missing parent away from joining their ranks.

"Some might be. But most are just from shitty homes. Dads in prison, moms on drugs, that kinda thing." He pointed toward the nearby lot where an elongated, white van was parked. "My uncle Mervin used to drive their bus. Took 'em to the amusement park, the fair, the movies. He even got free admission. It was a sweet gig."

"Why'd he quit?"

"There was an... incident." Stooge didn't volunteer any more info, and I didn't ask. His uncle Mervin had always creeped me out, and I had no desire to hear the scandalous details.

With Stooge's focus back on the game, I continued to check out kids from the Aid Home and noticed a bespectacled girl who looked about my age. She seemed more interested in reading than anything baseball related. Her red hair was pulled back in dueling braids and a snowstorm of freckles covered her fair skin.

I was staring unabashedly at her when she looked up from the book in her lap and straight at me. I snapped my head, embarrassed to have been caught gawking, and focused on spilled popcorn and discarded wads of gum littering the floor of the bleachers.

When I deemed it safe to glance up, she was still looking my way. But instead of shooting me daggers with her eyes, or maybe even chucking me the finger - what most girls would have done - she waved.

It was an airy, gentle motion, just a wiggling of the fingers. Yet it was the most attention I'd received from a female near my own age in, well, my whole life.

I gave a quick wave back, careful not to come across as too enthusiastic. She responded with a gentle smile, then returned her attention to her book. I watched her for a few more moments, hoping she might look my way again, but she didn't. Oh well, it was nice while it lasted.

On the field, a batter for the opposing team struck out, and the overhead speakers crackled to life as a voice announced, "Fans and friends, that brings us to the seventh-inning stretch. So, take these next fifteen minutes to visit the snack bar and drain your bladder. We'll be back shortly."

As the players headed to their respective dugouts, Dwayne separated from his teammates and made a beeline to the nearest Porta Potty. Apparently, he'd taken the announcer's advice to heart.

Needing to talk to him, I jumped up from my seat in the bleachers and moved that way, hearing Stooge lumber after me. Dwayne beat us to the toilet, leaving us standing outside until the door reopened.

The gangly boy's torso hadn't yet caught up to his arms and legs. He would have become handsome someday, but he was going through what adults called *the awkward stage,* and his features appeared distorted and out of proportion. Like you'd asked a blind person to draw a teenage boy and brought the drawing to life. Everything was close to normal but slightly *off*.

Dwayne's face was covered with zits, including one on his forehead that looked like Vesuvius preparing to bury Pompei. His curly, shoulder-length hair had led to some of our peers calling him *Lionel* as in Lionel Ritchie.

Well, the hair and his bi-racial heritage in a town where the population was ninety-nine percent Caucasian. His father being white as ivory snow didn't make it any easier on the son, especially when we were younger and the only place our classmates had seen anyone with skin darker than an Italian was on television.

Dwayne was busy brushing his locks out of his face when he saw us and recoiled. "What do you want?" He threw a panicked look at the dugout to see if any of his teammates were watching, but they were too busy downing Gatorade, stretching, and scratching their balls to notice.

"I, uh..." In the wake of his harsh tone and attitude, I'd forgotten what I'd planned to say. "You're playing really good."

Dwayne gave a blank stare. "I've got one hit so far. Whoopty shit."

"It was a nice one, though!" I said, hating myself.

"Thanks, I guess." He turned away, obviously eager to return to the dugout. Or to get away from us. Or both.

"Wait." I snagged my fingers in his belt, stopping his exit. "Stooge and I were talking about Halloween and trick or treating, and I wanted to see if you--"

Dwayne groaned and gave a theatrical roll of his eyes. "Oh, hell no. Don't start with that crap. Last year was awful enough. I'm never doing that shit again."

It felt like I'd been kicked in the gut, and I had to swallow back a knot in my throat before responding. "What do you mean?"

"What do I mean?" Dwayne parroted. "We were out there, carrying those stupid plastic pumpkins and begging for candy next to five and six-year-old babies. People were giving me the stink eye all night long. Mrs. Gess told me, right to my face, that I was too old to be asking for handouts." He clenched his fists at the memory. "Not again. No way."

"Hey, Kit!" a voice called, and Dwayne craned his neck in that direction.

I followed his gaze and saw one of the other Swallows' players – one of the Raley Twins, Ron or Jon, I wasn't sure which – gesticulating our way. It took me a second to realize the jock was talking to Dwayne.

"I'm coming," Dwayne said to his teammate. Then, to me, "Was this Halloween bullshit all you wanted?"

I had no words and only nodded.

Stooge, however, was never at a loss for words. "Who the fuck is Kit?"

Dwayne sneered. "I am. It's my nickname."

Stooge narrowed one eye down to a slit. "Since when?"

"A while now," Dwayne said. "My dad says it's a good name for a baseball player." His chest puffed. "He says the scouts will pay more attention to *Kit* Carson."

Stooge's pendulous belly jiggled as he guffawed. The explosive sound drew attention from the nearest onlookers, and Dwayne's face blazed crimson.

"Scouts!" Stooge cocked his thumb at Dwayne. "Look at this kid. He hits two home runs all season, and he's the next Reggie Jackson."

Dwayne gave Stooge his best *if looks could kill* glare and stomped away. As he did, Ron or Jon asked, "What did Backdoor and Ed want?"

I should backtrack.

Earlier that year, I'd grown increasingly frustrated as my missing person flyers hadn't brought my mom home. I was certain she'd been abducted or fallen prey to a madman.

My father was quick to correct those worries. "*She took all of her clothes and jewelry,*" Dad had asserted. "*Plus, ten thousand dollars from our joint savings. She left us by choice, not by force.*"

Yet, we hadn't heard a word from her. Not a phone call, not a letter, not a postcard of a beach reading, *Aloha from Hawaii!*

More often than I cared to admit, I would spot women on the street or in the grocery store or at the mall and be convinced my mother was back, but when I circled around to get a good look, I'd realize I was wrong.

Despite those frequent failures, I still believed she was out there, and I wasn't shy about sharing my worries. In my young naivety, I'd once asked Mrs. Lasure in civics class how to get my mother's story featured on 20/20.

My innocent query drew a round of laughter from my classmates, who then started submitting tips directly to me. According to them, they'd seen my mother at a variety of locations. Disney World, Ocean City, a cruise ship in the Bahamas. They thought it was the most amusing prank known to mankind. I was less impressed.

Those gags had been bad enough, but my social life took a dramatic downturn when Drayton Haddix, the class bully, came up with something even worse. During lunch, Haddix strode up to me and announced, loud enough for anyone within a hundred yards to hear, that he'd seen my mother starring in a porno his dad had rented.

According to Haddix, my mother wasn't simply having regular sex in that porno. According to Haddix, she was *Taking it up the back door!* Then he asked me if I liked to take it up the backdoor too.

With that, my new nickname was etched in stone. I'd been *Backdoor Benji* or simply *Backdoor* ever since, and I had a good feeling it was a name I'd wear until I graduated.

So, when Ron or Jon asked what *Backdoor* wanted, I didn't want to hear Dwayne's answer. I tried to block out the coming response in some prescient attempt at self-preservation, but I heard it anyway.

"Nothin'. They're just some losers I went to elementary school with."

Ron or Jon gave Dwayne a playful but hard jab in the shoulder, and they shared a caustic laugh as they moved into the dugout, where a coach launched into his best pep talk.

I chewed on my lower lip, biting hard in hopes the physical pain would trump the emotional hurt that threatened to break me. I'd known this time was coming, had tried to prepare myself, but I'd failed miserably. I was sick and tired of losing people I cared about, especially when there were so few of them.

"Dude," Stooge said. "Don't let that poser get ya down."

I forced myself to peel my eyes away from Dwayne and his new friends. "He hates us, Stooge."

"Naw. It's not personal. It's just the way life goes." Stooge leaned into the plastic door of the temporary toilet, blocking anyone else from gaining access. "Think of us like a band. It was all fine and dandy when we were three nobodies playing in a garage for shits and giggles. But Dwayne ended up being the one with talent. And talent, it goes to a guy's head. Now he wants to go solo. It's the way the world works."

That analogy made sense, but I didn't want to accept the truth of it. "But I liked our band."

Stooge reached out and used his oven-mitt-sized hand to give my forearm a shockingly gentle and reassuring squeeze. "I did too, man. I did too."

Then, he opened the door to the Porta Potty. The combined stench of a hundred bowel movements and emptied bladders whooshed out like a freight train. "Now I've got to shit." With that, Stooge was inside the john, and I was alone.

CHAPTER SIX

"I GOT AN IDEA," STOOGE SAID AS HE EMERGED FROM THE Porta Potty holding half a roll of toilet paper in his unwashed hand. "A real good one."

Stooge's ideas were rarely good, let alone real good. In the second grade, I'd ended up with my left arm in a cast for a couple months because Stooge had the brainstorm to see who could cross the monkey bars quickest.

While that sounds like normal enough elementary school hijinks, Stooge's version didn't involve swinging from bar to bar by hand with our feet dangling a few inches above the ground. His version had us climb on top of the monkey bars and race across on foot, high stepping from rung to rung.

Since the game was his creation, I had to go first. Those were the rules. He hoisted me into the air, and I got my balance, but as soon as I looked at the ground, which seemed a dizzying fifteen feet below but was probably more like six or seven, I realized I was afraid of heights. Or maybe I was afraid of falling from heights, which was exactly what happened after stepping onto the second rung.

I pinwheeled to the ground, landed on the hard dirt, and heard a crack so loud my ears rang. The pain took a moment to set in, probably because I was in shock. When I went to stand, my arm swung freely, no longer connected by whole bones but instead by a bleeding sack of skin. That's when I began to sob.

Stooge never did take his turn.

After bailing early on the ball game, we pedaled our bikes to a more private setting where we could discuss his new, sure to be brilliant, idea. And after listening to it, I had to admit, it wasn't half bad.

I wouldn't go so far as to call it *real good* - that seems an improper label for rolling a friend's house with toilet paper, but it offered a fitting amount of harmless vengeance.

I was in.

We both returned to our houses and confiscated enough bathroom tissue to have fun, but not enough to make our parents suspicious. That meant three rolls for me and eighteen for Stooge. The Deckers had something akin to a bunker in their basement, filled with enough canned goods and personal hygiene products to survive a nuclear winter.

We reunited later that evening, playing Nintendo at his place until well after midnight. When his family had turned in for the night, and we deemed the coast sufficiently clear, the mission was on.

We pulled black sweatshirts and sweatpants over our regular clothes. Stooge then showed me a military duffle bag passed down to him from a great uncle (not uncle Mervin) who'd served in the Korean War. I passed over my three rolls of TP and Stooge added them to his copious haul.

"This is gonna be so rad," Stooge said as he zipped the duffle closed and hoisted it over his shoulder.

We chose to forgo our bikes, worried the reflectors would catch someone's eyes in the night, and instead made the half-mile trip to Dwayne Carson's house on foot. I imagine we must have looked like the world's youngest and dumbest cat burglars as we crept down the sidewalks, walking hunched over and so conspicuous we may as well have had blinking neon lights over our heads warning, *Beware! Kids up to no good!*

Somehow, we made it there without getting caught or tripping over our own feet and bloodying our noses in the gutter. God watches out for the young and dumb, as they say.

All of the lights were out at the Carson residence, but as I examined the house, I was overcome with doubt.

What if we got caught? What if Dwayne's dad saw us and came raging out the front door with a shotgun in hand? What if Dwayne saw us and... And what?

I wasn't sure. Would he hate me? He already seemed to. Would he start making fun of me, calling me Backdoor Benji?

I was used to such treatment from others but wasn't sure I could handle that nickname coming out of his lips. The entire fiasco felt like a point of no return, and I no longer wanted to take such drastic vengeance.

But I heard the duffle unzip, then watched as the first roll went soaring through the air. It arced over a wooden pergola near the Carsons' front door, then cascaded downward, trailing a white streamer of TP that looked like the ghost of a tapeworm.

"If Mr. Carson catches us, we're dead meat!" I hissed to Stooge, knowing my words were hollow and pointless.

It was on. No going back now.

We spent the next three minutes tossing the rolls of toilet paper over the Carsons' property. Nothing was off-limits. Trees, shrubbery, Mrs. Carson's little Ford hatchback, a decorative wishing well, a pair of kissing lawn gnomes.

I wrapped the mailbox and post in TP, circling it around and around until it looked like a skinny mummy. Stooge made wild, abstract patterns and crosshatches on the lawn. We both landed a few good shots through the basketball hoop mounted in the garage.

Plus, of course, the Carsons' house. We saved that for last, worried the sound of toilet paper thudding against the roof would wake someone from a sound sleep. Several of the rolls went all the way over the house, disappearing into the backyard but leaving white ribbons in their wake.

When we finished, it looked like a blizzard had descended upon the neighborhood, but the storm only touched down on a single house. The crisp whiteness of the toilet paper stood out in stark contrast in the night. A beacon of shame. And victory.

Call us *losers*, I thought.

Our mission was complete. Vengeance was ours.

Or so I thought.

I was hurrying toward the sidewalk, ready to flee, when Stooge mounted the three steps to the Carsons' front porch. Confused, I froze.

"Stooge!" I whispered, my thin, hushed voice having no chance of reaching him.

He reached into the duffle, retrieved a brown paper grocery bag, crouched, then set the bag by the front door. Only then did I realize what was coming. It was also the moment I realized why Stooge had smelled like dog crap all evening.

"No, Stooge. Don't do it." I said the words to myself and for my own benefit, believing they would somehow exculpate me from what came next.

Fire spurted from my friend's hand as he flicked a lighter and held it to the sack. It caught slowly at first, then in an instant took off in an orange explosion.

Stooge jumped back, startled by how fast it went ablaze. He reached for the doorbell and tried to hit it but missed. He tried again and missed again like all the hand-eye coordination he'd honed playing video games had vanished.

Seeming to accept that pressing the glowing, round button to ring the bell wasn't going to happen, Stooge took the old-fashioned route and hammered the door with his fist. Four hard raps.

Like four rings of the bell to signify his presence below the treehouse. I wondered if he did that on purpose or if it was his subconscious ratting him out. I never did get around to asking him.

With that, Stooge was sprinting, or his version of sprinting anyway, toward me. We both ran for cover and had just made it across the street, hiding behind a utility van when--

The Carsons' porch light flickered on, and the front door opened inward.

Dwayne stood in the doorway. His tired eyes grew comically wide as the ball of fire on the doorstep stole his attention. He was barefoot, and my heart jumped into my throat and stayed there, threatening to choke me. All the while, Stooge guffawed silently, his big, sweaty body heaving against my own.

Dwayne did what any person would do in that situation. He ignored the potential danger and stomped on the bag. His arms flailed wildly to the sides as both feet pummeled the sack. He looked like a boy who'd suddenly taken up Irish step dancing and the porch was his stage.

Hot shit, liquified by the heat of the fire, splashed up in geyser-like eruptions. It collided with Dwayne's calves, his thighs. He stomped harder, more frantically. The feces hit his shorts, making him look like he'd somehow shit his pants from the outside in.

Finally, the flames were extinguished. Dwayne's crazed,

spastic dancing ceased. He stood there, the lower half of his body covered in excrement.

I could smell the shit twenty yards away.

It was horrible and hilarious in equal parts.

"I'm gonna kick your ass!" Dwayne screamed, his voice cracked mid threat and went boyishly high. Then, I joined Stooge in silent, uncontrollable laughter, the kind where you think you might suffocate because you can't even breathe.

Dwayne glared into the night, eyes scanning back and forth, left and right, trying to find the culprits. But he was standing in the light of the porch, pupils constricted, no way to see us in the darkness. At least, I hoped.

A few moments later, I heard Mrs. Caron's voice from inside the house. "Why's the porch light on?"

Dwayne turned, looking into the house, and Stooge and I took that opportunity to run for our lives. We skipped the sidewalk, sprinting through a lawn and behind a cape cod, dashing through open back yards, dodging sandboxes and grills and big wheels cars, until we were a few blocks away and in the clear.

We made it back to Stooge's undiscovered, so tired from the exertion and from laughing that we collapsed almost as soon as we entered his house.

"Told you it would be rad," Stooge gasped.

I nodded, yanking off the sweats and using them to wick perspiration from my face and body. "What have you been feeding Lowboy? That reeked!"

He stared at me quizzically. "Huh?"

"The dog crap," I said.

Stooge broke into a broad, awful grin. "That wasn't dog shit, dude."

"You mean..."

He dropped into a squatting position. A cherry bomb

version of a fart exploded from his ass. "I saved up all day," he said.

The realization hit me like a tidal wave. Dwayne having stomped out not just a fiery bag of molten crap, but a fiery bag of *Stooge's* molten crap made the whole thing both worse and infinitely better, and we both again dissolved back into that helpless, painful laughter.

I've gotta give it to Stooge. Not all his ideas were terrible.

CHAPTER SEVEN

School on the final Monday before Halloween was uneventful. I passed Dwayne once in the hallway but had decided I wasn't going to make the first move. If our detente was to end, I wanted him to come to me.

When we passed, I half-expected him to grab me by the shirt, slam me into the lockers, and scream at me about the prank. Instead, he strutted past without even a nod of acknowledgment.

He didn't know I was responsible, and that was a relief. But he also didn't care to apologize to me for his cruel dismissiveness at the baseball game.

His silence left me with no choice but to begin the long journey toward accepting the reality of the situation. The friendship I'd so cherished had burned to ashes. The band was not going to reunite.

It hurt, but I'd endured worse. If I could survive without my mom and her smiling face, her laughter, her presence, I could sure as hell survive without Dwayne Carson. Or *Kit* as he now seemed to prefer. The asshole.

Between the time middle school classes dismissed its students and the dinner crowd rolled in around five, Luigi's Pizzeria was a deserted island. I liked it that way and had come to think of the dirty, unkempt restaurant, where it wasn't uncommon to find roaches in the bathroom sink and, even worse, on the bathroom floor, as a home away from home.

The owner was also cool enough to let me put flyers in the big plate glass window looking onto Main Street. Sure, I had to hang them next to papers advertising gun raffles, free kittens, and lawn mowing services, but it was a high traffic area, and I was hopeful they'd bring in a lead someday.

After skipping lunch in school, I'd managed to work up a small appetite and was in the process of splitting a medium meat-zilla with Stooge. We'd eaten mostly in silence until Stooge spoke up.

"Benj, this sad panda act of yours is bumming me out. Are you still in the dumps about this Halloween stuff?" he asked.

I nodded, using my mouthful of food to avoid a verbal response.

"Then I got to know something. Don't get me wrong, I love Halloween too, but you're on a whole other level. And no matter how hard I try to figure it out, I can't get a grip on it. Why's it so important to you?"

I remained mute for a long while. It wasn't because I lacked an answer - it was because I had too many answers.

I loved Halloween because of the way the leaves transformed from boring green to fire in the sky. The crisp, cool air without a hint of humidity. The long nights, full of unknown mystery. The nonstop horror movies on TV. The creepy, yet absurdly fun, decorations in people's lawns. The unmistakable smell of latex masks and the way they made my face sweat. The slimy feeling of sticking my hand inside a pumpkin to pull out its guts.

I loved becoming an entirely different person, someone who wasn't *Backdoor Benji* with the porn star mom, when I put on a costume. Even if that anonymity lasted just one night. I loved every single aspect of October, but how was I supposed to verbalize my feelings without sounding like a fool?

Instead of saying any of those things, when I spoke, I surprised even myself. "Because of my mom." I sucked pop through a straw because my mouth had gone bone dry, swishing it around to lubricate my tongue. I didn't want to empty my whole heart to Stooge, but I owed my lone remaining friend some insight into what I was dealing with.

"She loved Halloween as much as I do. Well, not quite, but almost. It was in early September when she went missing." I never had and would never say *she left* because I refused to believe it.

"Leading up to Halloween that year, she kept talking about how we were gonna to go trick or treating together. We even went to Spencer's and bought costumes. She was going to be Dorothy from *The Wizard of Oz,* and I was gonna be Toto." I smiled, wistful over the bittersweet memory.

"She kept telling me to prepare myself because she was going to steal all my peanut butter cups and give me all her candy corn." I set the uneaten pizza crust aside. "I feel like I owe it to her to try and have as much fun as possible. That way, when she comes back, it'll be like she never left. She won't have to feel guilty or think she ruined Halloween. We can just go back to how life used to be."

The two of us sat there in silence for a long while, and I worried that I'd come off sounding like a fool after all. Then, Stooge unleashed a cacophonous belch that echoed through the eatery, but the only other person around to hear was Luigi himself, and he was too busy smoking a cigar beside the pizza oven to pay attention to our antics.

"I'm not gonna lie, dude," Stooge said. "That's heavy shit for three thirty in the afternoon."

His dead-serious tone got me laughing, a welcome change from the gravity of the discussion.

"I totally expected you to say it was because of the free candy," Stooge added.

I took another drink of pop, careful to hold the chortling at bay so it wouldn't squirt out my nose. "That too."

In our shared revelry, neither of us noticed the girl step past the screen door, which was propped open with a broken cinder block. She slid by the counter and Luigi, not stopping until she was beside our table. Only when she spoke did we realize we had company.

"Um, hello."

Both of us turned toward the voice. She was the girl from the baseball game. The redhead. Her glasses were absent, giving me an unobstructed view of her face.

From afar, I'd thought she was cute. Up close, I found her so beautiful it took my breath away. In reality, she was average or slightly above, but for a boy gearing up for his first hardcore crush, beauty was indeed in the eye of the beholder.

Both Stooge and I stared at the interloper with blank, confused curiosity. The way a farmer might look at an alien which had crash-landed in his cornfield and stumbled into the barn asking for a bandage and some aspirin.

"I hope you don't mind me interrupting, but I recognized you from around school," she said. "I'm Nora Mullan. I'm new, and I don't really know anyone here yet."

Her comment garnered nothing but more silence.

"I can leave you alone if you want. I just thought—"

Stooge stood up so abruptly he knocked over his chair. It clattered against the tile floor, making me jump in my seat, and a startled *Yip* escaped from my mouth. Talk about great first impressions.

"No, don't go," Stooge said as he fumbled to pull out the unused chair at the front of our table. "Sit down. Eat some pizza."

She flashed a shy, tentative smile which caused a fluttering sensation in my stomach. "Okay. If you're sure you don't mind."

"I don't," Stooge said.

"We don't," I added and slid the pizza box nearer to her.

She sat and extracted a skinny slice, pulling off a glob of sausage and popping it into her mouth. "I don't know your names. If you have names, that is. Maybe I should just call you Boy One and Boy Two," she said with another smile, one more sly than shy.

"Benji," Stooge blurted. Then he pointed at me. "I mean, that's Benji. And I'm Stooge. But you can call me Stooge. Everyone does."

"He means he's Stewart," I said.

"Yeah." Stooge nodded. "What he said."

Nora giggled, a sound lighter than air to my ears. Her hair was still in braids, but now, they hung in front of her shoulders, creating leading lines down her pale yellow cardigan and drawing attention to the gentle swell of her bosom. I was careful not to sneak more than a peek.

A crescent-shaped scar lined her chin, and another was carved into her upper lip. But it was her eyes, so intense and emerald green, where I got lost.

"Nice to meet you both," Nora said, then took a bite of pizza.

"Totally," Stooge said, his mouth agape as he stared unabashedly.

The three of us sat in awkward silence for a good half-minute before Nora spoke again. "It seemed like you two were in the midst of a deep conversation before I walked up. Anything juicy? School gossip maybe?"

My eyes darted to Stooge, flashing a warning not to speak the truth and share my thoughts about Halloween and my mom. "Nothing much," I said to Nora. "Halloween, mostly."

Her eyes widened. "Oh, I love Halloween!"

"Well then," Stooge said. "You found the right guys. With us, it's Halloween twenty-four seven."

Nora threw him a quick glance but, to my surprise, her attention seemed focused on me. "I hope I don't hurt your feelings or anything, but this town is really lame. I can't believe they have an age limit on trick or treating."

"I know. I even had a costume ready to go," I told her.

"Me too!" Nora said.

"I was undecided," Stooge said, reminding us he was still seated at the table.

"So, what are you going to do instead?" Nora asked.

I still hadn't come to terms and had formulated no backup plan. "No idea."

Some of the girl's shimmer dulled, and I was desperate to bring back that vibrance. To make her think I was someone interesting and worthy of her attention.

"I've been carving pumpkins. Five so far." Yeah, that made me sound like a badass. A real rebel. Look out, James Dean.

But my bragging didn't work.

"Oh. That's neat. I guess," Nora said, her voice flat. Then she did something even more alarming. She looked around the restaurant as if seeking out better people to associate with. Luckily, the three of us were the only diners, and Luigi was pushing seventy.

Nora Mullan was like some exotic creature, often whispered about but seldom seen, and realizing I might have already bored her was a sickening feeling. If I went to school the next day and saw her hanging out with the popular kids, maybe with Dwayne and his new, better friends, I might lose my will to live.

I had to do something, anything, to keep her interested. "We have a clubhouse. In the tree. A treehouse," I blathered. "It's got a TV and everything. We might rent some scary movies from A&H and watch them. You could come."

Had I just invited this girl, this gorgeous (yes, she was gorgeous by this point) girl whom I'd just met on a date? My throat seized, and I looked at Stooge wide-eyed. *What have I done?* Stooge only stared back, equally alarmed. *What did you do?*

I was certain Nora was going to jump out of her seat and sprint for the door, eager to get away from us creeps. But she didn't. She giggled and shook her head.

"That sounds like fun, but I doubt I'd be allowed."

"Your folks are prudes, huh?" Stooge asked.

He hadn't noticed her sitting amongst the group of kids from the Children's Aid Home at the ball game. I kicked him in the shin, but it was too late. Nora's luster dulled even more.

She stared down at the partially eaten piece of pizza in her hand. "I don't have any parents. I live at the orphanage."

I knew the pain on her face all too well. Without hesitation, without thinking, I reached over and put my hand atop hers.

Her skin felt like warm velvet. I'd never touched anything so soft and delicate. "I'm sorry. My mom went missing two years ago, so I kind of get it."

The girl looked up, her piercing eyes locking onto mine. At first, she was disbelieving, like she was being pranked with one of the world's cruelest jokes, but then she saw the familiarity of loss.

"I actually never knew my parents. They were killed in a wreck when I was a few months old. My grandparents took me in, but my Nanna died last year, and my Granda is pretty sick so..." She shrugged.

"That blows," Stooge said.

Nora nodded. "Yeah. It really does."

Maybe it was the discomfort over the course of the conversation, or maybe she'd confirmed that she didn't enjoy our company and no longer wanted to be around us, but Nora checked the yellow Swatch watch on her wrist, then scooted her chair back and stood. "I have to be back by four thirty. If I'm late, they'll only give me half a serving of gruel."

Then she smiled, so bright it was like staring into the sun, before spinning away and skipping toward the exit, out of our lives. After stepping into the daylight, she stopped and looked back. "I'll see you at school tomorrow," she said, then left before we could respond.

Both of us continued to stare in disbelief long after she was gone.

CHAPTER EIGHT

I had no interest in Tuesday's cafeteria offering - a poor excuse for beef stroganoff - which meant I could skip the regular cattle call and instead head to the a la carte kiosk. There, I got my usual snack-size bag of barbecue chips and a half-pint of chocolate milk, handing the cashier seventy-five cents and receiving a nickel back.

I noticed Dwayne holding court at an overflowing table in the back, the place where all the cool kids ate with boisterous cheer. With no desire to go near that area, I headed to an empty table at the front of the cafeteria and took a seat. Then, I pulled a pristine paperback copy of *Salem's Lot* from my backpack and read in silence as I ate.

I'd finished all of the chips and most of the milk by the time Stooge joined me. The big boy dropped his tray onto the table and straddled two of the circular seats ('*One for each cheek,*' he'd once explained) as he plopped down.

"That shit'll make you go cross-eyed," Stooge said, referring to my book, then grabbed his spork and began shoveling noodles drowned in greasy gravy into his mouth.

Dog-earing a page of one of my prized books was a mortal sin, so I stuck a scrap of construction paper between the pages to mark my place, then set it aside. "It's super scary. You should give it a chance, Stooge."

Stooge wrinkled his nose, giving his round face a piggish appearance. "That's why they make movies, little dude."

We'd had this discussion before. I would explain how books were so much better, how movies left out some of the best parts, how your imagination was scarier than anything they could make out of latex and slap on the screen. Stooge would retort with something sarcastic and dismissive and say he had better ways to spend his time than sticking his nose in a book.

I wasn't certain, but I suspected Stooge's aversion to books, even good ones, stemmed from his almost non-existent reading skills. The boy wasn't stupid, but he'd failed kindergarten twice for a reason, and he'd been stuck in remedial courses ever since.

I'd never seen Stooge read anything longer than a candy wrapper. Even when we rented movies, he would usually hand over the boxes to me and ask what various titles were about rather than skimming the summaries himself.

Oftentimes, I wondered if I should offer to help him out, to tutor him if that's what it took. But fears over possibly hurting my older friend's feelings and making him feel judged kept me from bringing it up. I still regret that. But then, I regret a lot of things.

Stooge experienced enough hurt via the mouths of our classmates. While I was *Backdoor Benji*, Stooge's burden to bear was *Ed*. That didn't seem bad until you realized what *Ed* was short for. *Special-Ed* and *Retard-Ed*.

His near gargantuan size kept him from receiving the sort of physical bullying which I sometimes found myself subjected to, but the insults and comments directed at Stooge were even more personal and mean-spirited.

The big guy always laughed them off and acted like he was in on the joke. He had a shocking amount of confidence for a kid in his situation. But on a few occasions, I'd seen my friend's ears burning bright red after a particularly cruel comment had been lobbed his way like a hand grenade.

If ignoring Stooge's possible illiteracy helped him feel better about himself, I was content to carry on with the lie. Even if it meant we couldn't discuss books.

Throughout the morning, my mind kept going to Nora Mullan, and I wondered if she'd really meant it when she said she'd see us at school. It was a welcome distraction to the other two subjects - my missing mom and Halloween - which usually occupied my mind.

Thus far, I hadn't caught so much of a glimpse of her and was beginning to wonder if the whole thing had been a hallucination. But, with less than ten minutes left in lunch, she breezed up to our table and its ten empty seats.

"Got any room for me?" She didn't wait for an answer before setting her tray down and claiming the stool to my right.

We were so close our shoulders touched. It was the closest I had been to a girl since an awkward health class in which we had to learn how to perform the Heimlich maneuver on a partner of the opposite sex. When I stood behind Shannon Walker and put my arms around her midsection, I was shaking so bad that old Mrs. Phillipi thought I was having a seizure.

"No stroganoff for you?" Nora asked as she checked out my empty chip bag and milk carton.

"I'm not a fan of most of the cafeteria food."

"I'd eat anything," Stooge piped in, stating the obvious.

"It's better than what we get at the orphanage," Nora said, using a plastic knife to saw away at a chunk of rubbery, beyond well-done beef.

"That's tragic," I said, careful to keep my tone upbeat and avoid the maudlin talk of the day prior.

"Tell me about it. After what we've been through, you'd think they'd supply us with all the ice cream and cake we could eat."

"Do they feed you gruel every night, or do they break it up? Like porridge on Wednesdays and half a roll on Sundays for a treat?" My comment made her giggle.

I was surprised I could speak at all. Surprised and relieved. I usually turned mute in the presence of girls within three years of my own age and sometimes even struggled to get out words around Stooge's baby sister.

It was different with Nora, though. She seemed so normal. Like an old friend, even though we'd barely spent ten minutes in each other's presence. She seemed to use a word I hated, *mature*.

"If we behave ourselves, we get an onion twice a week," she added.

"Oh, so that's why your breath smells like that. It explains so much."

That zinger garnered not only a chuckle but a full-on laugh. Stooge and I joined in, and the rare good cheer from our table made some of the other kids in the cafeteria look our way. Kids including Dwayne Carson.

I caught him craning his neck to see what was going on but purposely paid no attention to my one-time best friend. As far as I was concerned, we were auditioning a new bandmate. Dwayne was no longer needed.

WHEN LUNCH ENDED, we agreed to meet up in the courtyard after school. Despite how well we'd connected, I was still a little shocked to find her there. She had her nose in a book as I approached, and I cocked my head to get a look at the title.

"*A Separate Peace*," I said, drawing her attention. "I hope you're not reading that for fun."

She looked up. Her brow had been furrowed in deep thought, but it softened as she smiled.

"Have you read it?"

"I had to read it over the summer for honor's English." *My, don't I sound pretentious*, I thought.

"Does it get better?" she asked, folding over the page and closing the book.

That act almost made me hate her, but since the book was so bad, I decided to give her a pass. Just that once, though.

"Do you want me to be honest?"

She wrinkled her nose. "Say no more."

Nora chucked the book into her backpack and stood. We were the same height, and I was able to look her in the eyes. That rarely happened with my peers. Even ninety percent of the girls had gone at least an inch past me.

Those emerald eyes, though. Looking into them made me feel like the stammering, tongue-tied version of myself from the pizza parlor rather than relaxed Benji from today's lunch. Fortunately, Stooge came to the rescue.

"Look at you two assholes, standing here like you own the place." He ran a super-sized hand over my head, turning my shaggy, black hair into a bird's nest. "So, what's the plan? Pizza part two?"

I looked to Nora with a raised, questioning eyebrow, letting her make the call.

"We just had pizza yesterday," she said.

"And?" Stooge asked.

I got her point, even if I didn't agree. I could eat pizza every day of the week and twice on Sundays, but I didn't care to reveal my gluttonous side.

"What about the creek?" I asked.

The real-life Sallow Creek, where our town got its name, wasn't nearly as unpleasant as the moniker made it sound. As my dad told it, way back in the fifties when he was a kid, it ran yellow with pollution from the mines, but the mines went belly up in the seventies, and the creek kept going, eventually cleansing itself of the sulfuric acid and dissolved iron.

These days, it ran clear, but I wouldn't have drunk the water, not even on a triple dog dare. It was infested with crayfish and tadpole larva and bugs I called water skeeters, but Stooge called Jesus jumpers because they walked on top of the water. Either way, they were ugly little bastards.

The creek wasn't deep enough for fish. Most of it didn't top your calves, but there were a few deep spots where, if you stepped wrong, you'd plunge past your waist, maybe even four feet if it had rained hard the night before.

Before heading to the water, we swung by Stooge's house, where he grabbed a boombox and Lowboy, and then we were on the road again. The ride wasn't far, two and a half, maybe three miles, but the transition from *town* to *country* was abrupt. We passed by Farmer Spivey's fruit stand, and I gave him a wave.

Since Sallow Creek wasn't a fishing spot and wasn't deep enough for swimming or cliff diving, it didn't get much in the way of foot traffic. When the three of us pushed through the jagger bushes and grapevines, emerging into a beaten-down clearing where large, flat rocks baked in the mid-afternoon sun, it was empty of people.

The way I liked it.

We navigated a series of rocks and roots that formed something like steps down to the water, then hopped onto one of the larger stones, worn smooth as glass by centuries of current.

"It's so pretty," Nora remarked.

To Stooge and me, it was a hangout we visited dozens of times each year between May and October and, as inevitably happens with beautiful things you see day in and day out, it had lost its uniqueness. I tried to look at it with fresh eyes, eyes unspoiled by repetition, and I supposed she was right.

Dappled sunlight cascaded through the branches of pines and spruces lining the creek, painting random patterns on the rocks and making the water glisten and sparkle. The steady gurgle of the stream as water passed through gullies and over fallen tree trunks provided a soothing serenade, and we were far enough from town to avoid the din of traffic and voices or other people.

It was serene in its unremarkable placidity, but I think you only appreciate that type of serenity when you're young.

"Pizza would have been better," Stooge said, dropping a shopping bag onto a rock and flopping down beside it. On the way to the creek, we'd swung by Larry Robert's gas station and grabbed a mixture of candy bars, beef jerky, peanuts, bubble gum, and chips, plus three glass bottles of orange Crush pop. Even though the day wasn't hot - the air temperature barely hit sixty - we'd worked up a thirst on the ride and the walk-in.

"You're gonna turn into a pizza," Nora said to Stooge. She walked to the edge of the rock and stared into the shallow water before her, maybe checking for leeches or making sure it was really there and not some mirage. Then she kicked off her shoes and dipped in a bare toe exploratively.

She flinched and giggled. "It's cold."

"You get used to it," I said, also in the process of freeing my feet. I set my tennis shoes to the side, then peeled off my socks and shoved them inside the shoes. I reached out to Nora, and she took my hand.

I went into the water first, stepping gingerly on the downslope as slimy moss tended to grow on the stones below the waterline, and it was slicker than grease. I'd lost count of the number of times I'd lost my footing and cracked my elbow as my feet flew out from under me.

A few summers back, Dwayne had taken a bad fall and landed face first, smashing open a wide gash above his eye and another on his chin. He looked like *Carrie* at the prom, blood pouring down his face, eyes wide and panicked, crying in shock and pain and embarrassment.

Stooge went woozy and almost passed out, but somehow, we got Dwayne to the hospital. An ER doc who smelled like rum put in a few clumsy stitches and told us to be more careful before sending us on our way. He never bothered testing for a concussion or anything more serious than the cut. Sometimes, I wonder how we ever survived.

But on this autumn day, I didn't fall. Neither did Nora. We made it safely into the creek, water rushing over our feet as they sunk into murky silt. We both rolled up our jeans past our knees and went a little further out.

Nora moved away from me, exploring on her own. I knew she was heading toward a spot we uncreatively called *the dip* and almost opened my mouth to warn her but decided against it. Not because I was being mean, but because I already considered her my friend. And friends got to learn things the hard way sometimes, just as had happened to me and to Stooge and to Dwayne years earlier.

"Aren't you coming?" she asked.

I had a second thought and pushed it aside. "Yeah," I said, then took a couple steps her way, but not too far.

She continued on, eventually turning her back to me, lost in the discovery of the place. I stole a glance at Stooge, who wore a grin that could only be described as shit-eating. He, too, knew what was coming.

After traversing another yard, Nora found the dip. The firm ground under her feet suddenly disappeared, dropping a good thirty inches without a hint of the coming transition. One moment she was standing in calf-deep water, the next, she was submerged to her belly button.

She somehow managed to gasp and scream at the same time as the water, which was several degrees below air temperature thanks to the long, cold nights, saturated her jeans and the bottom half of the floral print blouse she was wearing.

Then Nora spun back to me, her porcelain skin even more pale than usual. The freckles on her cheeks and nose stood in even starker contrast, like someone had splattered melted chocolate across a white sheet.

"You jerk!" she screamed, but I didn't have even a second to consider the possibility that she was truly angry before she began baling water at me by the handfuls.

I shivered as a large splash caught me in the neck and drained down my chest, feeling goosebumps erupt across my entire body. Then I was kicking water back at her.

Front the dry rocks, Stooge scratched Lowboy's back and muttered, "Kids."

CHAPTER NINE

After the water fight, Nora and I were both drenched. I peeled off my shirt to let it dry in the sun, but she didn't have that option. Instead, she pulled up her blouse, tying it just below the slight bump of her bosom, baring her midriff.

The sight made the butterfly that lived in my stomach flutter about. Funny how that worked. I sure never got that feeling when Stooge or Dwayne revealed their bellies.

We lounged on the rocks, eating junk and guzzling pop. Unlike the day prior, conversation came easy and fast. We talked about school, about our lives, about a myriad of nonsense that didn't matter a lick to anyone a day past their early teenage years.

Nora shared some stories about her childhood and promised to show us photos sometime. Stooge regaled us with a long, far too detailed tale of the time he'd consumed so many enchiladas at an all-you-can-eat Mexican buffet that he shit his pants on the way out of the exit and diarrhea got over the *Buenos Nachos* welcome mat. And I talked about some of the good times with my mom.

Almost a full hour passed in what felt like seconds. The food was gone, and the three of us laid there like fat rats. Even Stooge, who had the appetite of a bear nearing hibernation, seemed satiated.

The crackly speakers of Stooge's radio had been playing a variety of pop songs. *Money for Nothing, Wake Me Up Before You Go Go, The Power of Love, Papa Don't Preach.* It was background music to our chatter, but that changed when a different song came on.

"This is Two Can Sam, and you're listening to WVSC. To get you kids in the Halloween spirit, here's an oldie but a goodie," the DJ said. "Let's head back in time and do the *Monster Mash* with Boris Pickett." The music began to play.

I'd once loved the cheesy tune, but now, it conjured thoughts of making caramel apples and dancing with my mother in our kitchen. God, I missed her so much there was a physical ache inside me. Like someone had carved out an organ and sewn me back up, the emptiness never to be filled again.

Nora noticed my mood shift, but she didn't know the deeper reason. "I guess you haven't come up with anything fun to do on Friday yet, huh?"

I shook my head, trying to clear it. Trying to push away thoughts of my mom.

I'd been racking my brain for a Halloween adventure but kept coming up empty. The failure to find something fun to do on the best day or the entire year was wearing on me.

"My hometown always had the best Halloween parties," Nora said.

"Really?" I asked.

She nodded, then took a sip of orange drink before going on. "The whole community comes out to celebrate."

"They have trick or treating?"

"Of course! And everyone gives out candy too. There aren't any jerks who hide inside with their lights off."

With that, the subject zagged, changing to school and whether we thought Miss Frampton, the fifty-something-year-old girls' gym teacher, was a lesbian. Both Nora and Stooge were certain she was, while I was convinced she simply preferred really short hair and exercised a lot.

AFTER LEAVING the creek and returning to town, Nora hopped on her pink Huffy bicycle and pedaled toward the Aid Home, but not before assuring us she'd had fun.

Both Stooge and I talked about nothing but the girl for the next ten minutes. We agreed she was *cool* and *funny* and *not like most girls*. Stooge even said, *She's really grown up for her age,* which I guess was a compliment.

Then Stooge said something that surprised me so much I almost crashed my bike into the telephone booth on the corner of Fairview and Franklin. "She's into you, dude."

After steadying myself, I took a glance at Stooge, trying to decide if my friend was being sarcastic. There wasn't a hint of a smirk on his broad face, though, leaving me trying to decide exactly when the kid had lost his mind.

"You're insane," I said.

"Probably. But I'm also right. She even laughs at your lame-ass jokes. Girls don't do that unless they're into you."

We rounded the corner to Colby Avenue, beginning the most arduous part of the ride home. It was uphill for the next half mile and so steep even most cars avoided it.

"You really think she likes me?" I asked, still baffled by this information.

"Totally. If you play your cards right, you might come out of this with your first girlfriend."

I considered his words as we strained to make it up the hill. I liked Nora. *Like* was an understatement. But I didn't want a girlfriend. Not yet, anyway. I hoped we could remain just friends, at least for a few more years.

If she even stuck around that long.

I also had Stooge's feelings to consider and didn't want him to feel excluded. I'd hate myself if Stooge ended up thinking of himself as a third wheel when we were all together.

It annoyed me that life had to be so complex. These were the sort of problems that came with growing up, and the situation did nothing but remind me how much I loathed the inevitability of time.

Two-thirds of the way up the hill, I heard Stooge's heavy feet hit the pavement and glanced back. The boy was off his bike and pushing it instead. I elected to do the same. Lowboy trotted along at our feet.

"I don't *like her* like her," I said as we trudged along side by side.

"Sure you do," Stooge said. "And why wouldn't ya? She's short. And pretty. You two make a good pair."

Stooge sounded content, even encouraging, but I struggled to buy it. "Wouldn't it bother you?"

He threw back his head and barked a laugh. "Hell no! She's too young for me, dude. Besides, I've been seeing a chick from Boswell. She's a junior, and she's all about what the Stoogemeister is packing." In case I didn't get the innuendo, Stooge grabbed his crotch and gave it an enthusiastic shake.

"You never mentioned any girl from Boswell," I said, shocked (and skeptical) to learn there was a secret side of his life, one unknown to me.

"With all the Dwayne drama, I didn't want you to freak out about it."

"Really?"

"Yeah, really. Uncle Stoogie wouldn't lie to you."

"Okay," I said, unconvinced. "But I only want to be friends with Nora."

"Give it time. Give it time."

I didn't think time would change anything. Part of the reason I so enjoyed Nora's company was because she was the first female I'd been able to talk to since my mom. And while the relationship was in no way similar, just being around a feminine presence brought with it a feeling of comfort and compassion life had been lacking. I wasn't about to muck that up with feelings.

We were both out of breath by the time we hit the top of the hill. Since Stooge's house was only a few hundred yards away, we didn't bother reboarding our bicycles.

"What's the name of this Boswell girl you're seeing?" I asked, testing my friend's veracity.

"Nikki," Stooge responded without missing a beat.

That put my mind at rest. Stooge had many assets, but quick wits would never make the list.

"She's got big, fat titties," Stooge added. "I like to bury my face in them."

That was too much information, and I regretted asking. I regretted the mental image of Stooge's face lost in some strange girl's breasts even more.

I wanted to change the subject, and I had a question, one I'd been putting off. "Hey, I've been meaning to ask you for a favor."

"Hit me with it," Stooge said.

I unzipped my backpack and pulled out a couple of the

missing person flyers. "Do you think your dad could put one up in his store?"

Stooge and Dwayne knew all about my obsession with my missing mom. They never razzed me about it like some of our classmates, but I had a feeling they were tired of the never-ending saga.

Decker Beverages, owned by Stooge's dad, sold various brands of beer along with cigarettes, tobacco, snuff, and similar things that would kill you sooner or later. The business sat in a strip mall in between Hess's and Cinema 219, a one-screen movie theater that never played anything good, just cartoons and sappy comedies. Even though the Deckers treated me like a son, I wasn't comfortable going into the business on my own since it was an adult's only establishment.

Stooge looked at the flyers in my hand. "I can ask him."

He didn't take any, though, and I had the feeling he wanted me to say, *Never mind,* or *Don't worry about it.* I said neither and pushed the small stack toward him. "Maybe your mom could hang one in the salon too."

Mrs. Decker, Mary, ran Hairy Mary, a salon where the smell of burnt eggs and ammonia intermixed with perfumes and cigarette smoke to create a noxious concoction. She cut my hair because I was Stooge's friend, but her clientele was ninety percent female. My mom had gone there too, and I'd spent many afternoons sitting in a dryer chair while Mrs. Decker gave her a perm.

The look on Stooge's face told me I was pushing my luck. I don't think he personally had a problem with my request, but he didn't want to burden his parents with the issue. The Deckers were good, albeit perpetually frazzled, people who'd taken me along on a family ski trip to the Pocono's the winter after my mom went missing and who always welcomed me into their home for meals and sleepovers.

But the Deckers, like my own father, my teachers, Mrs. Briner the town librarian, Sheriff Moland, and every other adult I pestered with questions and concerns about my mother, were running out of patience with me. No one had specifically told me to screw off, probably because I was still a kid, but they no longer humored my delusions.

I pressed the flyers against Stooge's closed hand, making it obvious declining wasn't an option. And like the true friend he was, Stooge accepted them.

Before I could share my thanks, a screechy voice reminiscent of a small animal being killed bombarded the street.

"I can smell your stinky butt all the way up here!"

A chubby, nine-year-old girl clad in a denim jumper stood in a hopscotch square on the sidewalk. She pointed a finger, stained red with popsicle juice, at Stooge. The girl was his sister, Janey, and the biggest brat I'd ever had the displeasure of knowing.

"You shut your mouth, Janey!" Stooge bellowed.

She threw the remnants of the popsicle into the street and made a mad dash toward the rambling ranch house that served as the Decker's abode. As she ran, she chanted, "Stewart has a stinky butt! Stewart has a stinky butt!" on an endless loop.

"That little whore," Stooge grunted as Janey disappeared into the house with a slam of the door.

I couldn't hold off a grin. The never-ending battle between Stooge and his baby sister never failed to entertain. It also made me eternally grateful I was an only child.

PART TWO

"Demons are like obedient dogs; they come when they are called."

CHAPTER TEN

Feeling spry and a fraction of his years, Conal strolled through the village on his way to the keeping house. Every morning, he awoke expecting misery, expecting all the pain and weakness he'd endured early the past summer to have returned, only multiplied exponentially.

So far, knock wood, he'd been lucky. But he knew luck would run out sooner rather than later. He wasn't up for another round of Brighid's nostrum to put him feeling right again, but if his fortune held out a few more days, he could avoid the noxious cure.

He came to the apple orchard, where Brothers Seamus and Ewan picked the last of the fruit. Ewan was perched precariously on the wooden ladder with Seamus holding it steady.

"Afternoon, boys," Conal said.

The brothers looked his way, smiled, and nodded. They weren't known for their conversational skills, but they made up for it with their work ethic. Strapping, round-faced men in their thirties, the O'Brien twins were always the first to lend their muscles for whatever tasks needed to be done, never bothering to ask what was in it for them. They put the village first, and Conal admired them for it.

"Glorious day, ain't it?" he asked.

The brothers gave another smile and nod, then returned to their work without a word. Conal reached into a basket full of ruby red fruit, grabbed an apple, and tipped his head.

"Much obliged." He chomped a bite as he continued on. It was sweet as candy, and he reminded himself to grab another on the way back.

But there was business he needed to attend to first.

He continued past the orchard, beyond the McAndrews' pumpkin patch, and toward a squat, stone building. Once there, he pushed aside the slab of wood that served as a door and stepped into the gloom.

The acrid aroma of urine filled the small cavity, the stench hanging in the air so thick Conal could taste it. He pulled a handkerchief from his back pocket and used it to cover his nose and mouth. That helped, but not much. The visit would need to be brief.

Just as well as dawdling would serve no purpose aside from putting him in a melancholy mood. The day was too nice, and he was feeling too good for that.

The only light in the windowless room came via the door through which Conal had entered. He stood in the precipice, letting his eyes adjust. It took a while, but gradually, the space came into focus.

In the center stood a stone table, and upon it laid a woman swaddled in white cloth. Well, it had been white once. But that was weeks ago. Now, the fabric had taken on a fleshy, tan color, almost the same shade as the woman whose body was wrapped in it.

The woman on the table was asleep. Seemed that was all

she did these days, not that Conal could blame her. This wasn't much of a life, but she wouldn't have to endure much longer.

She was in her seventies with a bald head covered in lumpy purple and red scars. In her heyday, that head had been covered in hair as bright and blonde as the sun. In her heyday, her skin had been fair and freckled. Now, her complexion had gone anemic as she faded away. The woman was equally bereft of eyebrows and eyelashes, giving her skull a vaguely alien appearance.

Conal grabbed a pail of milk and carried it deeper into the room. As it sloshed, the smell made it clear the milk had gone over. He'd fetch a new batch in a day or two, but until then, this would suffice.

It was hard to find the woman he'd loved for a great many years lurking somewhere within the decaying husk before him, but he tried anyway. Sentimentality had always been his weakness. He knew why things had to be the way they were, but he struggled to accept the harsher realities of their lives in the village, even after all these years.

A carrion beetle, its back striped black and orange, scurried free from her ear canal and scrabbled across her cheek. Conal lashed out, swatting it away. A small trickle of blood oozed from her ear, and he carefully wiped away the stain.

At his touch, the woman stirred. Her eyelids fluttered, opened briefly, fell shut, opened again. They stayed open. Her gaze drifted aimlessly, eyes full of dull confusion.

"I'm here," Conal said. He wanted to add *love* but bit the word back just in time. This dying creature sprawled before him was no longer his *love*. She was but a vessel with only one purpose left to serve.

Her eyes locked on him, and there was nothing for a long moment, then they grew wide with recognition. Recognition and horror.

She struggled within her cocoon, squirming, rocking, but she was helpless to do anything but shift a few millimeters from side to side. Conal pressed down more firmly on her head, keeping her in place.

"Easy now, dearie," he said. With his free hand, he patted her midsection, which was full, corpulent even, despite the wretched condition of her body. He nodded, satisfied.

He grabbed the bucket and set it on the table, taking a ladle and filling it with clumpy, spoiled milk. As he brought it nearer to the woman's face, her eyes came alive with a feral hunger. She squirmed and stretched, trying to reach the ladle and its soured contents. She still had spunk. He had to give her that much.

"You always did have a fine appetite." Conal brought the ladle to her mouth, then tilted it. The liquid parts drained off first, some spilling down her cheeks, running the maze created by her deeply etched wrinkles, but most made its way into her mouth.

The curds came next. The first plopped onto her chin. Her tongue, a gray, gnarled hunk of meat, poked from her toothless mouth, desperately trying to corral the white clot like a lizard catching flies. But the curd was too far away and her tongue too short.

Conal grimaced as he used his fingers to guide the chunk of coagulated milk up her chin and into her greedy mouth. As he pushed it in, her jaws clamped down, pinching two of his fingers inside her mouth.

The feeling of the hard bones of her jaw, barely covered with tissue, chewing away at his fingers reminded him of a puppy he'd had ages ago, back when he was a boy. Brindle was its name. How he'd loved that dog.

The woman gnawed harmlessly and seemed to lose interest

as she swallowed down the milk curd. He fed her another. And another. And another.

Her voracious appetite horrified him, and he suddenly wanted to be far away from this room, away from her. Her snake-like tongue slithered across her lips, making sure not a single drop went to waste. The smacking, slurping sounds she made had Conal near retching.

He patted her head, but her eyes made it clear she wanted - needed - more.

"There'll be another feeding later," he said, dropping the ladle back into the bucket. Then he stood. His work was done, and it was time to move on, but he lingered, staring at her.

He used his shirt sleeve to wipe away a dribble of drool. She really had been a good woman. A good wife. Pity it had to come to this.

"A few more days, dearie," Conal said, then added another pat on her head. The motion reminded him again of the puppy. The list of things he'd loved and lost throughout his life seemed never-ending.

What was one more?

CHAPTER ELEVEN

On Wednesdays, Stooge had marching band practice after school. He invited Nora and me to come watch him play the trombone, but we weren't that hard up for entertainment. Not even in a place as boring as Sallow Creek.

It was even colder than the day before, maybe fifty in the sun, so the creek lacked its usual appeal. Nora was also still pizza'd out, so another afternoon at Luigi's wasn't a priority. Rather than go our separate ways, I invited her to hang out at my house and was more than a little surprised when she agreed.

As we rode up the drive, Nora's eyes grew wide at the sight of my Halloween decorations. I'd moved the surviving jack o'lanterns onto the porch, but they were just the beginning. Cornstalks and lanterns decorated the picket fence that lined the front of the property. A half dozen plastic skeletons were posed in various tasks, like climbing a tree or lounging in a chair. I'd even mounted one on the roof.

In addition to the jack o'lanterns, I'd added another dozen whole pumpkins of varying sizes, plus gourds and hay bales. The shrubbery at the front of the house was shrouded with beef netting that doubled for spiderwebs. And the coup de grace (at least, as far as I was concerned) was a life-sized scarecrow I'd made from scratch. It hung on a decorative lamp post near the front door and looked pretty damn scary, even in the daylight.

"You weren't kidding when you said you loved Halloween!" Nora exclaimed. "It's amazing!

I felt as proud as a new father showing off his firstborn. "Thanks. I try to add a couple new things every year." I said, hoping it didn't come across as boastful.

"All we have at the Aid Home are a few plastic pumpkins and some orange and black crepe paper streamers."

Even though she didn't mean it in a pitying way, her comment made me feel bad for her. As much of a disappointment as the season had been, my life could be a lot worse.

"Want to come inside?" I asked.

"I want to see your treehouse," Nora said, peering upward and searching for it.

I froze. The treehouse was still littered with rotting pumpkin remnants. It didn't bother me all that much, but this was a girl, and I imagined she had higher standards for cleanliness.

"One of the rungs on the ladder is broken," I lied. "My dad's supposed to fix it any day now, but we can't go up until he does. Safety first and all that. Right?" I was rambling and knew it, so I bit down on my tongue to stop myself.

"Alright," Nora said. "Then show me your room instead."

That was only moderately less distressing, but I couldn't come up with any reason to decline. As we headed inside and through the house, I tried to remember if I'd left any underwear lying on the floor. I kept myself in the lead, blocking her view as I gave the room a quick once over.

No underwear, but there was a pair of jeans and some dirty socks. All things considered, though, I figured it was acceptable and cleared the doorway so she could step inside.

Movie posters filled three of the walls, mostly obscuring the cowboys and Indians wallpaper that had covered them since I was a toddler. I didn't have enough room for all of my favorites, but I had space to display *Friday the 13th Part II*, *Sleepaway Camp*, and *The Burning*.

The fourth wall was covered by a floor-to-ceiling bookcase/dresser combination. Books occupied ninety percent of the shelf space, with the other ten being various knickknacks and action figures I'd collected through the years. A television sat on another dresser, along with a VCR, a Nintendo, and a pile of game cartridges.

I couldn't help but feel guilty as I looked at all of my *things*. I was certain Nora's room at the Aid Home (if she even had a room all to herself) was far less stocked with material possessions.

If she thought my upper-middle-class lifestyle to be gluttonous, she didn't let on. Instead, she grabbed a copy of Christopher Pike's *Slumber Party* off the bookcase and sat on the edge of my waterbed, giggling as it rocked underneath her.

"What happens if this thing leaks?" she asked.

"Then I suppose I have a pool."

She paged through the book. "I haven't read this one."

"It's much better than *A Separate Peace*."

She laughed again, and I was beginning to think I might have a career in stand-up. "Low bar," she said.

"Very." I nodded toward the book. "You can have it if you want it. I already read it."

I didn't add that it wasn't one of my favorites, so there was no personal attachment. It wasn't a bad book, but I'd zoomed past young adult literature when I was still in elementary school and started reading Stephen King in the fifth grade. After that, it was hard to go back.

"Really?" she asked, already depositing the book into her backpack.

"Sure." I rocked on my feet, unsure whether I was expected to give a tour or what came next.

"You can sit," she said, then tapped the bed beside her. "It's your room, after all."

I sat at the corner of the frame, leaving at least two body widths between us. That made her smirk and shake her head. "Dork." She scooted down the bed, the mattress roiling underneath, and stopped when she was at my side.

She was so close I could feel her body heat. Too close for comfort. This distance had been fine in the cafeteria or at Luigi's - in public places - but in my bedroom, it felt awkward and inappropriate. The lavender aroma of her perfume or soap filled my nostrils, and I fought back a sneeze.

"What's your favorite video game?" I suddenly asked, standing and moving to the television.

Nora shrugged. "I've never played one."

"Really?!" It came out as both a question and a shocked declaration.

"Yes, really. Does that make me too boring to hang out with or something?" It was her turn to stand, and she slid in next to me. Again, too close.

"No, I didn't mean it like that," I said, shuffling through the game cartridges. "*Wrecking Crew*'s fun. And you can't go wrong with *Super Mario*."

Nora put her hand on my shoulder, one finger brushing against my neck. I thought my heart might jump out of my chest and splatter all over my prized collections.

"*Hogan's Alley* is one of my favorites too..."

She kept leaning into me. Our faces were a foot and a half apart.

It seemed like she wanted me to kiss her and was waiting for me to make the first move. I didn't want to come off like a loser or hurt her feelings by rejecting her, but this was all happening too fast. I liked Nora more than I'd ever liked any girl, but my mind spun with panicked worry.

A foot and a half became inches. I was looking directly into her hypnotizing green eyes, thinking I should just man up and do it when--

"Hey, you promised me a photo album, remember?" I blurted, backing away, too ashamed to look at her. I felt like the world's biggest loser and wouldn't have been shocked if she kicked me in the sweetmeats. But she didn't.

Nora returned to my bed and rummaged through her backpack, which was sitting on the floor. "I brought it." I thought I heard disappointment in her voice, but it might have been my imagination.

She pulled out a small, cheap photo book, the kind you could pick up for a couple bucks at any department store. It was not the family heirloom I'd been expecting. She passed it to me, and I rejoined her on the bed and flipped it open.

I was first struck by the people in the images. They all wore simple, plain clothes, the kind worn in pioneer days. The women in long, white dresses. The men in trousers, white shirts, and suspenders.

If they'd been black and white photographs, I would have assumed they'd been taken around the time cameras were invented, but they were Polaroids with the signature cool tint and slightly desaturated color scape.

My confusion must have shown because Nora said, "We're kind of old-fashioned."

Her comment about never having played a video game

came back to me, and I realized she must have lived a more sheltered life than I'd realized. "I think it looks quaint," I said, hoping it didn't sound as condescending as it felt.

"Gee, thanks," she laughed, then pointed to various photos and identified the people in them. She pointed out her granda and her nanna. Both looked even older than Farmer Spivey. There were a few photos of kids around our age, friends only though, no cousins, which made sense as she had no family capable or willing to take her in.

We were near the end of the album, which only contained a dozen or so snapshots, and Nora was telling me all about her favorite cow. The animal munched on a knee-high stack of cut grass, but my eyes went to the background.

The camera had captured the image of a woman hanging laundry on a wash line to dry. Only a fourth of her face was visible, but when I saw her, my breath caught in my throat.

Nora went to turn the page, but I stopped her. She flashed me a curious look, her brows knitted. "You like my cow that much?" she asked.

My mouth had turned to the Sahara Desert, and I willed my salivary glands to force some spit so I could get my tongue working again. "Who is that?"

I had my thumb pressed on the woman. The woman I recognized. My mother.

Nora took a good look, like she'd never even noticed the human being occupying the frame with her best bovine.

"Oh. That's Mrs. McAndrews," she said.

Her answer - the *Mrs.* part - made me take another look. But I was certain I was right. I chewed my lip, nervous, anxious. I'd been through false leads like this hundreds of times over the years and always ended up disappointed and hurt, but I was willing to risk it again if there was even the smallest possibility of bringing her home.

"Can I have this picture?" I asked her. "I'll give it back tomorrow, I promise."

I hoped she wouldn't ask the dreaded *why* question because I didn't want to explain any of this to her. I didn't want her to see the desperate, foolish side of me.

Like a good friend, she didn't ask. She slid it free of the plastic holder and handed it to me. "As you wish."

CHAPTER TWELVE

By the time my dad got home, toting a basket of chicken planks and hush puppies from Long John Silvers, I was ready to jump out of my skin. A part of me, an experienced, pessimistic part, understood the coming conversation would not go as hoped, but I plunged forward anyway.

After I showed my dad the Polaroid, he sat in silent contemplation. I kept expecting him to say we'd hop in the Volvo and hit the road. Or, at the very least, call the local police and hand off the lead. Neither happened.

Dad didn't say anything at all. He continued to eat his meal, avoiding eye contact.

Finally, I could wait no longer. "Well? What are we going to do? Are we going there to see if it's her?"

Put on the spot, my dad broke his silence. "No, Benji. We're not going anywhere."

"Why not?"

Dad brought a napkin to his mouth, wiping away grease and batter crumbs. He then folded it and set it beside his plate. "Because the woman in that photo is not your mother. Just as the woman you saw at the Pirate's game last summer, or the background extra that you spotted on *Cheers*, or that woman riding the corkscrew at Cedar Point this past spring weren't your mother either."

He picked up the picture, which had been sitting between us on the table, and held it up for me to see. "The only similarity this woman has to your mother is the color and length of her hair. I, of all people, should know seeing as how I was married to her for sixteen years."

My dad had the courtesy to look me in the eye as he said words that should have been spoken years earlier. "If your mother still wanted to be a part of our lives, there's nothing stopping her. We live in the same house. We have the same phone number. It would take her two seconds to reach out to us if she cared to. Yet, she never has. She doesn't want me in her life, and she doesn't want you either."

I stared back, shocked into silence by his brutal candor.

I'm not going to lie to you. My mom having abandoned us - abandoned me - by choice was a possibility I'd considered. And, when I was being really honest with myself, I understood that to be the most probable scenario.

But my mom loved me. At least, I thought she did. Could a person who loved you simply walk out and never contact you again? That seemed the antithesis of love.

"Wherever she is, I hope she's happy. But for me, and especially for you, it's long past time for us to move on." Dad picked up his plate and went to the sink to clean the dishes.

I headed to my bedroom, shutting the door behind me. A bomb had just been dropped, and I wanted to deal with it alone.

CHAPTER THIRTEEN

THE FOLLOWING DAY, I RETURNED THE PHOTO TO NORA without mentioning why I'd needed to borrow it. Nor did I mention the conversation I'd had with my dad to either her or Stooge. The previous night had left me feeling both dejected and defeated, but after a restless night's sleep, the words began to hit home. Maybe my dad was right, and it was time to move on.

After school Stooge and I were heading home when my heart sank. "Check it out." I pointed up the street to where Dwayne Carson straddled his bike in my driveway looking too cool for his own good in his Calvin's.

Stooge broke into a devilish grin. "I'll be damned. Little pussy has a lot of nerve."

I thought the same and had frozen in place. We were two houses away from Stooge's and walking our bikes. Not because we were tired from traversing Colby Ave (although we were), but because the ache in my groin was far too severe to sit atop my bicycle seat. I needed a restful night and a bag of frozen veggies in the worst kind of way.

"Are you coming with me?" I asked Stooge, my eyes on Dwayne.

"Nah, dude. I'm gonna let you handle this."

I didn't like the sound of that. With no idea what was about to transpire, I wanted back up. I planned to beg Stooge if that's what it took, but he was already halfway up his walkway before I could open my mouth.

"Tell him to..." Stooge made a masturbatory gesture with his hand, then disappeared into his house.

For a fleeting moment, I considered trailing him into the house and leaving Dwayne alone and outcast for a change. Instead, I trudged up the street, approaching the person I'd once believed would be my best friend for life.

When I was about five yards away, Dwayne lowered the kickstand on his bike and pulled a lanky leg over the top tube. "Hey."

"Hey," I responded as I moved past, pushing my bike into the driveway and leaning it against the garage door. When I looked back at Dwayne, I was tempted to tell him to screw off. To go and hang out with his new, better friends. Instead, I said, "Clubhouse?"

Dwayne nodded and followed me into the backyard, through the woods, and up the ladder.

The high, fetid aroma of rotting fruit had been bad enough over the weekend, but now, it was enough to turn my stomach. At least, the recent hard frost had killed the fruit flies. A small relief.

The first three jacks I'd carved were little more than mushy mounds of black decay. The fourth was sagging inward, its flesh wrinkled and reminding me of a toothless grandma. It was a good thing I'd restocked.

After sitting on a plastic crate that served as one of the clubhouse's three chairs, I raised an eyebrow at Dwayne.

"What do you want?" Those were the same words Dwayne had said to me at the baseball game, and I tried to make them equally cutting and accusatory but failed. I wasn't a mean kid, even when I tried. Even when he deserved it.

Dwayne took the crate across from me, his knees almost hitting his chest due to the low seat. "How's it hanging?"

I examined my friend, trying to discern whether there was an ulterior motive at play. Along the way, I realized I didn't care. Dwayne had made his choice, and I felt no obligation to kiss his ass to try to keep our failing friendship afloat. "Do you even care?"

Dwayne sighed. "Don't be like that."

"Like what? A loser you went to elementary school with?"

Dwayne shrugged off the backpack he'd been wearing, set it on the floor, and opened it. He pulled out a bag of Brach's candy corn and tossed it to me. "I hope this is still your favorite."

I held the bag tentatively like it might be a well-camouflaged bomb seconds away from exploding in my hands. "What's this?"

Dwayne smirked. "Candy corn. Duh."

"I'm aware, genius. I mean, why are you giving it to me? Is it supposed to be a bribe? If so, I've gotta say, I'm worth more than ninety-nine cents."

"Just open it," he said.

I did, taking a handful and tilting the bag toward him. He'd always hated the stuff but accepted a few measly kernels and popped one into his mouth.

"I've been a real dick," Dwayne said as he chewed.

It was a half-assed apology. Was I supposed to be the bigger person in this situation and leave him off the hook, or was I allowed to be a dick too? I decided on something in the middle. "Yeah, you have. I never expected that from you."

"None of this has been easy for me." He stuck a second piece of candy into his mouth even though he was still working on the first. "Do you have any idea what I went through when I joined the baseball team?"

"Educate me."

"They hazed me nonstop for the first month. Made fun of me. They even pantsed me in front of Coach's wife. Stripped me bare ass."

To me, that sounded like school, but you were forced to attend school. You weren't forced to join a team and bring that kind of torment upon yourself. "Am I supposed to feel sorry for you?"

He didn't answer.

"Well, I don't. You're the one who decided he wanted to be the next Terry Bradshaw."

He grinned, not the reaction I expected nor wanted to see.

"Terry Bradshaw played football," Dwayne said.

"Screw off. You get what I mean."

"Yeah." Dwayne had swallowed the candy corn and now chewed on his bottom lip. "But you know how my dad is."

I did. I'd always been uncomfortable around Paul Carson and, as a result, rarely visited Dwayne's house. Calling the man high strung was a massive understatement. He was constantly one wrong word or misstep away from smacking whoever had offended him.

Once, I had joined the family for a weekend of camping in Potter County. The first day was fun, filled with fishing and hiking. We roasted wieners over the campfire that night and set marshmallows ablaze, chucking the blacked crust at one another. Then Dwayne threw one at his dad, and the warm gooey mess got stuck in Paul's hair.

I'd never seen a person transition from decent to awful so fast. The man grabbed the stick he'd used to cook his hot dog and whipped Dwayne across the chest and shoulder until Dwayne's mom dove in and used her body as a shield. She took a few licks of her own and would have certainly taken more, but a man at a nearby motorhome stepped into the glow of the fire and asked what was going on.

Paul Carson's savage eyes blazed, and I half expected him to attack the newcomer, but Mrs. Carson got between them and said some roughhousing got out of hand and that it was nothing to be concerned about.

I was so nervous the rest of the weekend I spent half of it in the latrine with the shits. I don't think I'd ever been as happy to go home as when we left early Sunday morning. Dwayne still carried a scar above one nipple where the stick had flayed open his flesh. We never once mentioned it afterward.

"He always gave me crap about not playing sports. Called me a disappointment and said I couldn't be his real son."

Paul Carson had long ago gone to seed, but I'd seen his photos prominently displayed in the trophy case at school. The man had been one of Sallow Creek's all-time greatest athletes, leading several teams to regional and state championships decades earlier.

"When I made the baseball team, he told all his friends about it. He hasn't missed a game either. I think he's really proud of me, Benji. For the first time ever."

I couldn't put myself in Dwayne's shoes. My dad had never treated me like a second-class citizen or tried to force me into any hobbies or sports to live vicariously through me. And he'd most certainly never hit me. Not even a spanking.

But none of this explained why Dwayne had been so dismissive and cruel to his *real* friends. I was on the verge of calling him out when he beat me to the punch.

"I shouldn't have taken it out on you and Stooge, though."

"No, you shouldn't have."

Dwayne looked away, grabbing a comic book and wringing it in his hands, eyes on it instead of me, the friend he'd betrayed. "The guys on the team... It took a while, but they finally accepted me. I'm not *Lionel* anymore. I'm one of them."

"Why do you want to be friends with a bunch of dicks?"

Dwayne didn't answer for a long time. When he did, his answer was brief and unsatisfactory, but it was honest. "Because they're popular. And being their friend makes people think I'm cool."

It was my turn to stay silent. I couldn't understand why someone as smart as Dwayne would care so much about the opinions of other people.

If I'd pressed him to further explain his feelings, the conversation would have gone nowhere because we had two different outlooks on life. Dwayne wanted - needed - people to like him. Maybe it was because his asshole father hadn't liked him all that much. Or maybe the need to fit in was commonplace, and I was the weirdo for not yearning for acceptance. I never did figure out which it was.

"To me, you were always cool," I finally said.

Dwayne's face, which had been contorted with worry and nerves, softened. He met my eyes and smiled at me for the first time in many long months. "Are we okay then?"

"You're on probation." I chucked a piece of candy corn at him. It bounced off the bridge of his nose.

"How long will that last?"

"Undetermined. And you have another fence to mend before we can really move on."

When we arrived at Stooge's house, he had Janey locked in the clothes hamper in the basement bathroom. Her high-pitched shrieks filled the abode, and I was surprised they hadn't shattered every window in the house.

Upon opening the door and seeing Dwayne and me side by side, he rolled his eyes. "If it isn't the goddam doublemint twins." He glowered at me with disappointment. "Why'd you bring this chucklefuck to my doorstep?"

"He wants to apologize," I said.

Winning Stooge over was both more of a challenge and easier than convincing me. Dwayne didn't need to again delve into the deeper, personal issues, but Stooge required considerably more groveling plus a promise to empty the spit valve on his trombone after every practice and football game. Dwayne, perhaps realizing that was his only chance, agreed.

While Janey continued to scream, we resumed our friendship like it had simply gone on pause for a while. Hard feelings were mostly forgotten, and we caught up on lives and gossip while simultaneously playing *Duck Hunt* and tossing Lowboy a rubber hotdog over and over again. It felt like old times. Good times.

Eventually, Dwayne got around to asking us about the new girl at lunch. I filled him in but omitted the part where Stooge said Nora liked me. To my relief, Stooge kept that private too.

While telling Dwayne about Nora, I had an idea, one both devious and perfect.

"Do you really want to get back in my good graces?" I asked.

"I thought I already was," Dwayne said.

"Probation, remember?"

Dwayne nodded knowingly. "Go on then."

"If you want to prove to me, to us, that you still want to be our friend, then you've got to do something you don't want to do."

Dwayne groaned. "I already have to dispose of Stooge's spit. Isn't that punishment enough?"

"That's between you and him. This is between you and me."

"Okay, okay. What do I have to do? Scrape up the rotten pumpkins in the clubhouse? Inspect it every Monday for spiders and kill them?" Dwayne made a beckoning motion with his hand. "Lay it on me."

The spiders thing - I loathed them - wasn't bad at all, but I had something better in mind. I was so damned pleased with my brilliant idea I couldn't hold back a grin. "You have to go trick or treating with us."

The carefree expression Dwayne had been wearing nonstop since the tension had eased vanished. "I can't go trick or treating this year. Even if I wanted to."

I was prepared for his excuse. In fact, it was part of my plan. "We can't go trick or treating in Sallow Creek. But I know of a place where we can go."

Dwayne wore his complete lack of enthusiasm all over his face as I explained the proposition, but he reluctantly agreed. Probably because he didn't think any of it would come to fruition. Even I wasn't convinced my plan would work out, but I was on a mission.

Halloween was Friday night, so there were no worries about school the following days. I would tell my dad that I was spending the weekend at Stooge's. Stooge would tell his parents he was sleeping over at my house, and Dwayne would say the same.

My desire to visit Nora's hometown was twofold. I wanted - needed - to make one hundred percent sure my mother wasn't there, living a new life. A life without me. I was almost certain she wasn't, but I believed going on one final, wild goose chase would allow me to move on once and for all.

If - when - I got there and saw the woman simply had a vague resemblance, then it would be fine because I could still go trick or treating with my friends. Afterward, we could return home, head to the clubhouse, and sleep away the weekend, bellies fat with candy and memories to last a lifetime. Or at least until next Halloween.

It was the perfect opportunity to right immeasurable wrongs, and I wasn't prepared to let it slip through my fingers.

"How are we supposed to get there?" Dwayne asked. His voice sounded hopeful, like he'd pinpointed the fatal flaw which would bring the whole plan crashing down and save him the embarrassment.

"We'll get someone to drive us." Finding a driver would be a challenge, but I wasn't about to let minor details kill my buzz.

"Like who?" Dwayne asked.

It was a good question. One to which I lacked an answer. Then it came to me with triumphant glee.

"Uncle Mervin," I said. If the man had driven the van for the Children's Aid Home all over the county, he could certainly handle a simple trip a few towns away.

"Oh, hell no!" Dwayne said, eyes wide. "I'm going anywhere with him!"

Stooge, who'd been listening in silence as he chewed on a chicken leg like a caveman, said through a mouthful of meat, "What do you have against Uncle Mervin?"

"I don't know. Maybe it's that he masturbates every fifteen minutes no matter who's around to see," Dwayne said.

Stooge set the chicken leg, little more than bone and gristle, to the side. "That's a medical condition. Do you think he enjoys that?"

"He seemed to be enjoying it at your Fourth of July picnic."

"It's a disease," Stooge said.

"You're a disease," Dwayne said.

Their tones were light and playful, but I didn't want to take any chances. The wheels couldn't come off when everything was finally back on track.

"Okay, that's a no on Uncle Mervin," I said.

"He probably had plans anyway," Stooge muttered.

Dwayne opened his mouth for a comeback, but I spoke first and cut him off. "It's okay. I'll think of something. Just give me some time."

The Casio on Dwayne's wrist beeped rapid fire. He pressed a button on the side to silence it and climbed to his feet. "I have to go, or I'll be late for supper."

"You're in, though?" I asked. "You promise?"

Dwayne hesitated too long for comfort but then nodded. "If you find us a ride, I'm in." He moved to the front door, then stole a glance down the stairs to the basement where Janey's screams sounded like an air raid siren. "For God's sake, Stooge, let her out."

"I'm teaching her a lesson."

"That's child abuse. You know that, right?" Dwayne tried to be serious, but a grin broke through.

Stooge threw the chicken bone at him. "Then call CPS, dickweed."

Dwayne was half out the door when he looked back. "I missed you guys."

I nodded but let him leave without a response. I'd missed Dwayne too, more than I want to admit.

CHAPTER FOURTEEN

After telling Nora of my plan to go trick or treating in her hometown, she was thrilled and insisted she would go along to show the way. The news delighted me both because I so enjoyed her company and also because I thought her grandfather might be able to drive us. She dashed those hopes when she revealed her granda didn't have a car. With each passing hour, my expectations, which I'd allowed to soar sky-high, dimmed.

My mood improved, though, when I spotted Dwayne in the small alcove between the water fountains and the girls' restroom. I made a beeline for him but stopped short when I saw he was holding hands with a pretty girl in a cheerleader uniform.

I stood, watching like a perv, and spied on them as they chatted. She giggled and rubbed his arm and tossed her hair while he preened and puffed his chest. It was like watching a mating ritual in a National Geographic documentary.

It was highly amusing until Dwayne, the baseball player, made a mad dash for second base. His arms were around the cheerleader's waist and hers around his neck as they engaged in a heavy-duty make out session.

Because I thought myself funny, or maybe because I was a bit of an asshole, I thought it would be hilarious to mimic these goings on. I embraced my own chest, clasping my hands to my shoulders and kissed the air with fervent glee as I mocked my best friend.

This went on for a short while, and I had almost lost interest in the joke when Dwayne, who was facing in my direction, opened his eyes and spotted me. While I broke into a broad, horsey grin, his eyes first grew wide then narrowed down to slits, and I knew I was in deep shit.

He broke apart from the cheerleader, said something to her while wearing a very fake smile, and gave her a peck on the cheek, then she headed into the restroom. With her out of the way, Dwayne came for me.

I thought his anger might be a ruse until he grabbed me by the shoulders and shoved me into a row of lockers which rattled and clanged upon impact. Wincing in pain, I instinctively raised my hands and made an X to cover my face to fend off coming blows.

He didn't hit me, though. He just glared with disgust, like I was a piece of used chewing gum he had the unfortunate luck to sit on while wearing a new pair of pants.

"You think that's funny?" he asked.

"A little," I said sheepishly.

"Well, you're wrong. That's a real dick thing to do."

"I know. I'm sorry."

"You should be," he said.

We started each other, a short standoff, as a tide of students passed behind us, heading to classes. I'd believed things between us were back to normal, but I'd obviously been wrong.

My mind spun, trying to find a way to climb out the hole I'd dug for myself.

"I didn't know you had a girlfriend," I said. It was the truth. Last I knew, he had never so much as kissed a girl, let alone had a full-on, face-smacking, butt-grabbing, chest-fondling make out session. I was surprised and a little hurt to have been left out of the loop.

"She's not my girlfriend. I just like her."

"Okay," I said. "That's cool. She's really cute."

"She's all right." He glanced up at the big clock showing our next classes would start in less than thirty seconds. "I got to go."

"Want to hang out after school?" I asked, my voice far too eager for my own comfort.

"I have practice," he said, then started to walk away. After a few steps, he stopped and took a half glance over his shoulder. "I'll give you a call later, though." He continued on, disappearing into the sea of our classmates.

I'd dodged a boulder barreling toward me. Scared and relieved and shocked all simultaneously. I hated this walking on eggshells feeling I had in his presence. It seemed so unusual and unfair, considering how tight our bond had been.

I told myself that good things take time. Time heals all wounds. This, too, shall pass. All the cliches people use to make themselves feel better. I didn't believe any of them, but they sounded good.

CHAPTER FIFTEEN

STILL WITH NO DRIVER LINED UP, I WAS RUNNING OUT OF ideas fast. But I had a possibility in mind as I rode to Farmer Spivey's for one last pumpkin for the season. To my shock and dismay, the patch was nearly empty, and I had to settle for a lopsided specimen with no stem and a soft spot on the bottom.

"Pretty picked over, ain't they?" Spivey asked as he set the pumpkin on the scale. It came in at eleven pounds. I handed over a buck and a quarter and told him to keep the change.

"That's good, though," I said. "You won't have many left over. How do you get rid of the ones that don't sell, anyway?"

"Oh, the pigs eat most of 'em. I save a couple for the chickens too. They like to peck and explore, but they're not too impressed most of the time."

Feeding pumpkins to farm animals was a new one for me, but I wasn't there to talk about leftovers. Faking small talk made me feel more than a little guilty.

"You still drive, right?" I asked, getting on with it. I'd heard that elderly people sometimes had their licenses taken away, but I didn't think Farmer Spivey was *that* old.

"Ayuh. You need something delivered? Tomatoes for canning, maybe?"

"No. Not a delivery. But maybe a favor."

Farmer Spivey, his gut telling him to prepare himself, sat in his folding chair. "Go on. Explain yourself."

I took a deep breath, then spat out the story rapid fire. By the time I was finished and got to the most important part, I was winded. "Would you take us?" I was barely able to resist crossing my fingers and toes.

The old farmer lit a Chesterfield before answering, and I could hardly stand the anticipation.

"I'm aware you consider me a friend, Benjamin, and I'm appreciative of that. But--"

"Please, Mister Spivey. Please, help me out with this!"

Spivey went on as if I hadn't spoken, "I'm an old man. And one who's never been accepted into this town." He bit his lips in a pinched mouth grimace. "Me driving four minors around in my pick up, transporting them late at night across county lines, without the permission of their parents..." He took another drag on his cigarette. "You're too young to understand the cynicism the average adult carries in their heart. If anyone saw me doing what you asked, I'd be liable to spend out my remaining years behind bars."

"If we get caught, I'll tell them it was my idea," I promised. "I'd take all the blame."

Spivey wagged a gnarled finger. "It's a no. I'm sorry."

I lingered in case the man changed his mind, but the farmer's stern expression made it obvious a reversal wasn't happening. So, I turned and straddled my bike, putting a foot on the pedal in preparation for a shameful exit when--

"Benjamin?"

I looked back at the farmer but couldn't meet his gaze,

shameful over trying to manipulate a man who'd shown me nothing but kindness.

"I know how much you love this holiday, but it's just a day. Sometimes, the best thing can happen to a man is being denied his desires. I imagine that might be hard for you to accept right about now, but it's the truth."

Spivey set the cigarette on a saucer that served as an ashtray and was overflowing with crushed butts. "If you're open to some advice?" He paused, looking me over, but I kept my eyes on the ground. "I can see you're not. But I'll dole it out nonetheless because that's what old people do. We talk even when no one wants to hear us."

"My advice to you is to spend Halloween here, in Sallow Creek, with your friends. It might not have the spectacle of that other place you told me about, but there are times in life when we're better off *not* getting what we want. I have a feeling this is one of those times."

I accepted the pep talk without protest, not surprised but disappointed.

CHAPTER SIXTEEN

BEFORE HEADING HOME, I STOPPED BY A&H VIDEO, parking my bike beside a somewhat familiar brown Plymouth Duster before heading inside. Skip Haywood sat behind the counter, watching a kung fu movie on a small TV set. He spotted me and flashed a thumbs up.

"Hey, buddy," Skip said. "I got a new tape in, and I'm pretty sure you'll like it." He paused the movie and stepped out from behind the counter. The man was pushing forty and balding but working on a mustache to compensate for what he lacked up top. He made a straight line to the horror section, and I followed, glancing around the store in case the car's driver was lurking about but not finding anyone.

Skip pulled a box off the shelf. "It's called *Re-Animator*. It's supposed to be wicked gross but real funny too," Skip said.

I examined the box art, which showed a doctor in a lab coat holding a syringe filled with green fluid. He appeared ready to jab the needle into a severed head that peered up at him from an exam table. A neon yellow *New Release* sticker clung to the upper right corner.

Skip was correct; it looked right up my alley.

"What do you think? Be a fun watch on Halloween, right?" Skip asked.

"Sure," I said, even though I wasn't there to rent a movie. "Looks awesome."

Skip patted me on the shoulder and headed back to the counter. "I'll knock a buck off for ya. Just have it back before noon Saturday and remember to rewind it."

As I followed Skip, I considered telling him I'd check out the movie some other time, but I needed to keep the man on my good side. "Speaking of Halloween..."

Skip entered the rental info into the massive computer sitting atop the counter. "What about it?"

Before I could answer, a noise in the back of the room caught my attention. I turned and saw a curtain made of red plastic beads sway. The beads clunked together, then the curtain opened.

The man who emerged carried four blank, black plastic VHS cases. His hair, which was glued into a six-inch tall, blue mohawk, became caught in the beads, and he had to pause and use his fingers to extricate himself.

I recognized Milo Woronov from Dwayne's neighborhood. The guy, who was in his early twenties, was punked out in a black leather jacket and matching pants, knee-high black boots, and more chains than you'd find in a dog kennel.

Milo had been heading to the counter to check out but froze upon seeing me, then ducked into the comedy section. I bit back a grin because I knew what was in those black cases, just as I knew what was behind the beaded curtain. Back there was a land unfit for young eyes. The *18+ Only* section.

While Milo feigned interest in *Beverly Hills Cop* and *Top Secret*, I took the opportunity to hit Skip with my request.

"Stooge and Dwayne and I were thinking about going trick or treating."

"Really?" Skip asked, still typing on the keyboard. "I thought they put an age limit on that."

"Just in Sallow Creek. We wanted to check out a place a couple towns over."

"Oh," Skip said distractedly. "Guess you can watch the movie when you get back." He finished typing. "That'll be a buck eighty."

I handed him the cash. "The problem is, none of our parents want to drive us... So..." I gave my most winning and pathetic smile. A smile that said, *Please take mercy on me.* "We need a ride, though."

Skip handed me two dimes and dropped the movie into a paper sack which he also passed over. "Well, I hope you find one. If you don't, enjoy the flick."

I'd been hoping Skip would take the hint and volunteer, but since he hadn't, I took the initiative. "I was wondering if you'd consider driving us." My body tensed like a man preparing to take a hard punch.

"You're talking about tomorrow?" he asked.

Since the man hadn't immediately turned me down, I allowed optimism to again creep into my life. "Yeah."

Then Skip crushed it. "I'm sorry, buddy. Me and my brother are going to the haunted asylum out past Pittsburgh. Supposed to be wicked fun. Maybe next year."

Oblivious to my dismay, Skip turned his attention to Milo Woronov, who had abandoned the safety of the comedy section and was perusing a rack of candy bars. "You ready to check out?" Skip asked him.

I left the store, wallowing in my defeat, and missed Milo observing my exit with avid interest.

I was five blocks away and riding my Schwinn down Church Street when the low rumble of an engine at my left flank caught my attention. I stole a glance and saw the Duster and Milo slouched behind its wheel. But he wasn't simply driving past. He was lurking there, creeping along like some kind of perv.

My legs pumped as I increased my tempo, then made an abrupt right onto Rosina. The Duster followed, its bald tires giving a high screech as it made the sharp turn. For the next two miles, the Duster zagged every time I zigged. Milo even followed when I doubled back and retreated toward the video store.

I pedaled as fast as my short legs would allow, all the while wondering what the guy's deal was or if he was an undercover pedo. My heartbeat thudded in my ears and my lungs burned as I became convinced my face was going to end up on a milk carton.

I whipped my bike into a one-way alley, going the wrong way. If a car came along, I'd be flattened like Wile E. Coyote, but it was a risk I felt necessary to take.

Finally, I'd made a move Milo and his Duster didn't mimic.

With tremendous relief, I began to breathe easier and slowed my pace. I didn't need that kind of excitement on a panicked day when my grand plan was falling apart.

I emerged from the murky alleyway, squinting in the sunlight as I rolled into the parking lot beside the old Sallow Creek Trust bank. I was ready to beeline it home when--

My bike nearly crashed into Milo's car. It was parked diagonally, blocking my path forward. I backpedaled, slamming on the brakes, my tires skidding to a halt.

I was in the process of pivoting and dashing back into the alley when Milo's voice stopped me.

"You hang out with Carson, right?"

I froze.

Milo opened the door of the Duster and stepped out. A black tattoo of a skull with a dagger impaling it was partially visible above the collar of his Ramones t-shirt.

"Dwayne Carson," I said.

Milo smirked, revealing crooked teeth gone yellow with tartar. "Oh, *Dwayne*. And here I was thinking you palled around with Johnny. Thought for sure I'd seen you on the *Tonight Show* yukking it up with him and Ed McMahon."

I'd only been around the guy for a few seconds but already couldn't stand him. "Yeah, Dwayne and I are friends. What of it?"

My attempt at sounding tough failed miserably and drew a chortle from the man. "*What of it?*" Milo parroted, his voice falsetto high.

"Are you being a weirdo for no good reason, or do you want something?" I asked.

Milo strutted to the front of his car, and I backed an equal distance away.

"It's not about what I want, kid. It's about what you want."

"What are you even talking about?" The longer the conversation - if you could even call it a conversation - went on, the more anxious I was to end it. I was fully prepared to ditch my bike and make a run for it if the man got within two yards of me.

"I heard the sob story you gave Mister Clean back there. You need a ride tomorrow, right?"

"Yeah." I swallowed hard.

Milo tapped the hood of his car. "Well, I got wheels."

"You're offering to take us trick or treating?" Unable to believe this was real, I started to think a drunk driver had hopped a curb and run me over, and this was some bizarre version of purgatory.

"Not out of the kindness of my heart. After all, I don't give a shit about any of you," Milo said. "But you live up on Snob Knob and got parents with good-paying jobs."

I didn't bother to correct Milo, didn't clarify it was *parent* singular, not plural.

"That means you've got…" Milo rubbed his thumb and forefinger together in the universal symbol for *money*.

Suddenly, this made more sense and seemed, marginally, less creepy. "You want us to pay you?"

"I sure as hell ain't running a charity cab."

"How much?"

"I'm undecided." Milo returned to the driver's seat of his Duster. "I'll think about it. Stop by my place around seven, and I'll come up with a number we can all live with."

He didn't wait around for a response, shifting the car into reverse and cruising out of the lot. As I watched him drive away, my mind raced. This seemed like the answer to my prayers but selling it to my friends would take an even bigger miracle.

CHAPTER SEVENTEEN

Dwayne, Stooge, and I mulled on the sidewalk, across the street from an aging split level. It needed a refresh to its coat of peach paint and repair to some of the trim, but it wasn't an eyesore, not even in Dwayne's middle-class neighborhood.

Parked in the drive, besides a boxy Volkswagen and Toyota hatchback, sat the Duster. A hand-painted sign above the garage read, "The Woronov's - Enter with love." I never thought of myself as a judgmental person, but I'd expected the house of a shady character like Milo Woronov to look more *Munsters* and less *Brady Bunch*.

"This is insane," Dwayne spat. "Everyone around here, *everyone*, knows Milo's a lowlife. People can't even leave their cats outside anymore because he kills them." He rocked on his feet, his nerves belying the faux toughness in his voice.

"I heard he's an enforcer for the mob over in Uniontown," Stooge added.

The vehemence of their statements had me on edge.

"Come on, you two. Those are just rumors," I said, trying to squelch their apprehension. And maybe some of my own too.

"Not a rumor," Stooge asserted. "When someone doesn't pay up, the mob sends Milo, and he beats 'em up. If they still don't pay, he cuts off their cocks. That's why everyone calls him *Weiner Off*."

Even I wasn't gullible enough to believe that, and I rolled my eyes.

"I swear on my sister's life," Stooge said. *I swear on my sister's life* was one of his favorite phrases, made ironic because of his deep-seated hatred for Janey. A few years earlier, he'd tried to sell the girl on WVSC radio's Friday Flea Market segment. When the Decker's phone started ringing off the hook, it became clear that the *adorable six-year-old, who is friendly, has soft blonde hair, and loves to play,* was a little girl and not a Golden Retriever.

"It wouldn't surprise me," Dwayne said. "The guy's bad news."

"*Bad news*," I mimicked. "You sound like your dad. People call him Weiner Off because it's a play on his last name. It's people being mean."

We all had enough experience with that.

"Then why'd he get kicked out of school?" Dwayne asked.

I knew the real answer to that one. My mom had taught History at the high school when Milo had been expelled, and she couldn't resist sharing the story, which later took on an almost legendary mythos.

"He was kicked out because he put acid in the punch at the Snowball dance. No one realized until Mr. Champlain stripped naked and started running through the gym screaming about ants crawling up his butt hole."

That made Stooge laugh. Dwayne tried to fight it but gave in.

"He's nice enough to help us when no one else will," I said.

"He's probably planning to rob us. Rob us and leave us in the middle of nowhere," Dwayne said. "Maybe even kill us so we can't rat him out."

"Since when are you so scared of people?" I asked. It's amazing the bravado a person can summon when they're out of options. "I'm the smallest of all of us. If anyone should be scared, it's me, but I'm not. Not even a little." I looked at Stooge. "You're not afraid, are you?"

Stooge was, and it was written all over his face, but he wasn't about to let on. He pulled back his shoulders, puffed out his chest, and said, "Hell no. I'm not scared of some punk rock reject."

Now it was two against one. I'd never been a fan of peer pressure, but the circumstances required me to stoop low.

And if encouragement wasn't going to work on Dwayne, I'd try guilt. "If you want to bail on us again, go ahead. We're used to it."

Dwayne looked from the Woronov house to me then back. "Jeeeeesus," he said. "Whatever. Let's go then."

We crossed the street and stepped toward the house. It was five minutes to seven, but Milo's front door opened before we hit the brick pavers leading to the home.

"I see you brought reinforcements," he said as he strolled toward us. He'd lost the all-leather ensemble and now wore flannel pajama pants and a white thermal shirt. He looked shockingly normal, aside from the tattoos and the mohawk that could withstand a category three tornado. "Surprised you showed, kid."

"Why wouldn't we?" I asked. Subconsciously, I'd assumed the lead position among us three friends.

"Because you're a bunch of pussies," Milo said.

"Takes one to know one," Stooge retorted.

Milo raised a pierced eyebrow. "Oh, witty comeback. How long have you been saving that up?"

Stooge, usually quick with retorts, had no response.

"We're here," I said. "Did you come up with a price?"

Milo crossed his arms, ropey with lean muscle, across his chest. He looked from one of us to the next to the next, then returned his gaze to me. "I did," he said.

"Well?"

"Fifty bucks."

That was steeper than I'd hoped, but it was doable if the other guys were willing to chip in.

"Each," Milo added.

"That's horseshit," Stooge grunted.

I thought the same but wasn't ready to give up so fast. "There's no way we can afford that, Milo."

Milo shrugged. "Not my problem. You've got..." He checked a nonexistent watch on his wrist. "About twenty-two hours to find someone who'll drive you on the cheap."

He turned and strode back to the house, calling over his shoulder, "Good luck with that, pussies."

I spun toward my friends, panicked. The plan had seemed so perfect. I could finally put my issues over my mother's disappearance to rest and have a great Halloween with my friends. Yes, the price was steep, but I had to make it happen. "How much do you have?" I asked them.

Stooge's eyes crossed as he considered the predicament. "Maybe thirty bucks if I can find the key to my Abe Lincoln bank."

I looked at Dwayne, pleading.

"I just bought new cleats. I'm broke," Dwayne said.

"Seriously? You don't have anything?"

"I'm lucky if I've got five bucks to my name."

I did the calculations in my head. "Seventy dollars," I proposed to Milo.

The man stopped walking, stood still for a long moment, then turned toward us. "A hundred."

"We don't have it. Wouldn't you rather have seventy dollars versus nothing at all?"

Milo cocked his head in deliberate consideration. "Eighty, and I get half your candy."

I didn't even pause for a breath. "Deal."

CHAPTER EIGHTEEN

The following day, Halloween day, I woke up early. Truth be told, I'd barely slept. I'd forced my eyes closed, but every time I did, visions of pumpkins and costumes and Halloween candy danced in my head. Screw the sugarplums; this was my fantasy. My holiday. And it was going to be perfect.

But if trick or treating had been the only thing on my mind, I would have secured more rest than a cat nap. My nerves were on high alert because my mind couldn't stop playing my fantasy scenarios in which I was reunited with my mother after two long years. I could envision her face, plain as day, when she saw me. Her surprise, her excitement, her joy.

In those fantasies, her glee was surpassed only by my own. Such saccharine sweet, wildly unrealistic delusions would have come off as laughably naive if I'd have written them into one of my stories. No happy endings were so perfect in real life. But I was fourteen, and I was allowed to act the fool.

I found my dad in the kitchen, making a competent bachelor's breakfast of scrambled eggs and bacon fried to a hard crisp. Ordinarily, I fetched my own bowl of cereal while he ate charred toast and drank coffee. So the scene shocked me.

For a moment, I wondered if I'd fallen asleep after all and this was only a dream. I waited for some demon to pop out of the dishwasher or a ghoul to emerge from the garbage disposal, but neither happened.

"Morning, Chief." Dad slid some eggs onto a plate and added three strips of bacon, not bothering to sop away the excess grease. "You want a bagel too?"

I looked at the food, then at my dad, blinking like my eyes were full of sand. It all seemed real enough, and it sure smelled real. Dreams don't have smells, do they?

"No, this is good." I accepted the plate as he passed it off to me. He'd already poured me a glass of orange juice and had it sitting at my usual spot. I claimed the seat and started eating. After filling a plate for himself, Dad joined in.

The previous evening, I'd filled him in on my plans. Not my real plans, of course, but the fabrication where I was sleeping over at Stooge's. He'd granted permission, not that I had any doubts. I had no real rules to follow aside from abstaining from illegal activities, and the *curfew* word had never come out of his mouth.

Sometimes, I realized how lucky I was, despite what happened with my mother. That morning was one of those times.

We ate mostly in silence, with Dad tossing out obligatory statements about the weather or raking up the last of the leaves or needing to get the car in for an oil change to fill the void. Do any sons and fathers talk about important, substantive matters, or is their entire relationship based on chit-chat and shared DNA?

As much as I loved my dad, I can't recall having one single conversation with depth beyond surface level. Sure, there were times when he *told* me things. An awkward lecture about the birds and bees springs to mind straight off and times when he mentioned my mother. But we never talked about our lives and the way they overlapped. And we sure as hell never discussed a topic as verboten as *feelings*.

"Is Stooge taking his little sister trick or treating?" my dad asked out of the blue.

I shook my head. "No. Mrs. Decker's taking her."

"Oh. I thought maybe you boys would tag along. Trick or treat via osmosis, maybe."

That wasn't a bad plan, and I kicked myself for not having thought of it myself. But everything had come together, and I was looking forward to a far better night than putting up with Janey's petulant whining and tantrums.

We went on eating until our plates were so clean they didn't require more than a quick rinse. I moved to gather the dishes and clean up when Dad stopped me.

"I got something for you." He pointed a finger toward one of his drafting tubes leaning against the pantry.

Squinting and curious, I hesitated for a moment before crossing the kitchen and retrieving it. Part of me wondered if it contained plans for an addition to the treehouse, or maybe something even better, like the swimming pool I'd been begging for since I was eight.

"What is it?" I asked.

"Look and see."

I unscrewed the lid, tilted the tube at an angle, and a roll of slick, black paper slid out. I caught it before it hit the floor.

It was a movie poster, and a grin tugged at my lips. Carefully, I held the short end and unfurled it, revealing a pristine *Halloween III: Season of the Witch* one sheet.

"Got it from the guy who manages the Two Nineteen,"

Dad commented. "He said it was still mint because he never displayed it."

Of course he didn't because they never play horror movies, only movies that suck, I thought.

"Well, what do you think?" dad asked.

My friends weren't huge fans. Dwayne, in particular, hated it, lamenting, *'How could they make a Halloween flick and not have Michael Myers? It's like making a sequel to Jaws without a shark.'* I, on the other hand, loved the weird, wild movie.

And it didn't matter what poster my dad had bought me. The man could barely tell the difference between a vampire and a zombie, yet he'd still been thoughtful enough to buy me a horror poster as a Halloween present. How many other fathers gave their sons anything more than a snack-size Snickers on a holiday that held no meaning to adults?

"It's awesome," I said.

"Really? I did good?"

I rolled the poster back up with precision and care, not wanting to add so much as the smallest crinkle. Because the poster wasn't just a poster. It was a gift from my dad on a day when gifts weren't expected, like Christmas or your birthday. He'd done it because he knew I loved the holiday and horror movies and because he loved me.

"You did great!" I meant it too. I placed the poster back into the protective tube and set it aside, then went to my dad and did something I hadn't done in years. I hugged him.

He initially stiffened in surprise, then put his arm around my back and gave me a firm squeeze. "I'm glad you like it. Happy Halloween, Chief."

I think we exchanged a few more words before he headed to work and I to school. But *Happy Halloween, Chief,* is what I remember as the last sentence my dad ever spoke to me.

CHAPTER NINETEEN

After school, Dwayne, Stooge, and I met at the predetermined spot - behind A&H Video. The backside of the store was an empty lot full of nothingness until it hit the turnpike a half-mile away. It gave us the privacy we needed to change into our costumes, something we couldn't do in our homes without tipping others to our plans.

Cold air, fall air, whipped up a dust storm as we undressed and redressed. I pulled on denim biballs, a red and white check shirt, and chunky worker's boots. I'd nabbed an old hatchet from my dad's workshop and slathered red paint onto the blade. It was too bright to pass for real blood, but I thought it added panache nonetheless. Using some black eyeshadow I'd bought at the drugstore, I painted a splotchy beard onto my cheeks and chin.

Once my homicidal lumberjack costume was perfect, I turned to see what my friends had come up with.

"Seriously?" I asked, contempt filling my voice.

"What?" they both said simultaneously.

I motioned to their attire with disgust. "You wore that same shirt and jeans to school last week," I said to Stooge.

"But in school, I didn't have this." Stooge held up the broken electric guitar, the same one he'd toted every recent Halloween. "Besides, no one knows how I usually dress where we're going."

All I could do was sigh. In my heart, I understood this was the last time we'd all go trick or treating together. The least they could have done was put some effort into it.

"Ohhhh! I forgot." Stooge reached into his pocket and pulled out a handkerchief. He folded it into a bandana which he then tied around his forehead.

The bandana helped pull together the Rock Star mystique, but the costume was still lacking. Yet, somehow, Stooge's lame get-up was still far superior to Dwayne's ensemble. Because Dwayne was wearing his baseball uniform and sneakers. He must have seen the disappointment on my face.

"I'm a baseball player," Dwayne stated.

"Yes, you *are* a baseball player. Which means that isn't a costume. A costume is something you're not. What you're wearing is a uniform."

"I thought it was clever," Dwayne said.

"You could have at least brought a bat," I said.

"How was I supposed to get a bat out of the house without my dad noticing?"

"How about a glove then? Or a ball? Or, better yet, some pancake makeup to make yourself into a zombie baseball player?"

His nose twisted into a petulant sneer, and I realized how much he didn't want to be a part of any of this. I almost told him to go home, but I still believed that I could win him over, win him back, and reclaim the friendship that had been so important to me for the majority of my life. "Don't worry about it," I said. "It's fine."

The scowl lingered on his face, and he kept stealing glances in every direction as if the Halloween police were going to burst onto the scene and arrest us. "What time is it?" he asked.

I checked. "Ten till five."

"Milo's not gonna show," Dwayne stated, his voice eager and mocking. "He probably never planned to. He just wanted to screw with you."

The man was supposed to pick us up at five, and I couldn't take a full breath until I actually saw the Duster. Until then, I was worrying myself sick, afraid the rug would be pulled out from under me yet again, and Dwayne's skepticism didn't help matters.

"I need your money," I said to my friends.

Both dug through their bags and handed over cash. Stooge came through with thirty-six dollars. The extra six was a pleasant surprise. A necessary one too as Dwayne passed me a whole three dollars and twenty cents.

"That's all?" I asked.

"I told you I was broke."

I didn't press him. I wanted to keep the mood light and jovial, and it didn't matter anyway because I'd managed to scrounge up sixty bucks the night before. We had enough to pay Milo and a few bucks to spare. All was well in the world.

It got even better when Milo showed up minutes later. He looked over us and our costumes with a leering smile. "You are the three dumbest looking pricks I've ever seen. And I've seen some real losers."

Before Dwayne could anger and say something to make Milo change his mind, I grabbed the handle to the passenger door and yanked it open. I was halfway into the back seat when

Milo snatched my wrist hard enough to turn the skin bright white.

"Not so fast," he said.

I tried to pull my hand free but couldn't. The sucker was strong.

"Cash up front," Milo demanded.

I'd expected this and came prepared. "Not all of it. I'll give you half now and half when we're home. Otherwise, there's nothing to stop you from leaving us out there."

Stooge looked at me with something like admiration. My sudden assertiveness surprised me too, but if pressed, I would have backed down in a heartbeat. Milo had the upper hand, and I knew it.

Milo released my wrist. "Fair enough. Although your cynicism is disheartening. What kind of guy do you think I am?"

"The kind of guy who'd screw over some kids for a few bucks," I dropped into the back seat. Dwayne followed. Stooge took shotgun.

"Very perceptive, grasshopper." Milo gunned the engine and peeled out of the gravel lot, creating a storm of dust and debris as he raced onto the main drag. The back end fishtailed a few times before steadying, leaving black streaks of rubber in the car's wake.

Dwayne looked at me, shook his head, and mouthed, *We're gonna die.*

NORA WAS SUPPOSED to be waiting by the service entrance to the Children's Aid Home, but she wasn't there. Five full minutes passed, and the girl still hadn't shown.

Missing out on her company would have been bad

enough, but Nora was also going to serve as our guide. None of us even knew the name of her hometown, let alone how to get there. If she no showed, the night was over before it began.

I rocked back and forth in the seat, craning my neck, checking the view from every window. Hoping, praying, she'd manifest out of thin air.

Ten more minutes passed.

"Looks like your girly-friend ain't coming," Milo said. He didn't sound upset in the slightest at this development. He had half his payment, and it would have been an easily earned forty dollars. I was certain a refund wasn't an option.

"Let me out," I said, climbing over Dwayne. Stooge hopped out of the car to grant me access.

I was prepared to march into the Aid Home, find someone who worked there and demand to see Nora. I needed to know why she bailed on us when she'd been so excited earlier that day.

As I moved toward the building, a nagging voice in my head insisted she had been pranking us all along. I didn't want to believe the voice, but, in a way, it made sense. Nice, pretty girls didn't waltz into your life and want to be your friend. Nice, pretty girls didn't want anything to do with me.

"Benji!" The voice was both whispered and shouted.

I turned, searching for it, then saw movement by the dumpster of a neighboring gas station. I took one step toward it, then another.

Nora, wearing an ankle-length black dress and a pointed witch's hat, stepped out from behind the dumpster. She was smiling, but her eyes were full of anxiety.

"The janitor came out for a smoke break and almost caught me," she said. "I ran over here to hide."

"They know you're going out, though, right?" Images of

Nora's face plastered across the evening news with a *Kidnapped* banner on the screen raced through my mind.

Nora hurried toward me, her dress swaying in the wind. She looked like a goth version of a debutante on her way to a grand ball. "Yeah, but they think my granda is taking me home for the weekend."

The coast was clear as she ducked into the back seat of the Duster. I climbed in too, and she ended up stuck between Dwayne and me in very cramped quarters.

"Let her sit up front, Stooge," I said.

Stooge shot me a look like I was the dumbest boy in the history of the world. "You really think the three of us can fit back there? Because my fat ass is going to take up three-fourths of that bench seat all by itself."

It was a reasonable observation.

"I'm fine," Nora insisted. "But let's go before someone sees!"

We did. As the car sped down Center, I noticed Milo stealing glances at Nora via the rearview mirror and didn't like the hungry look on the man's face.

"Eyes on the road," I said, feeling tougher than I had any right to feel.

"I'm not your chauffeur, kid."

"We're paying you to drive, so I think you are."

Nora giggled and slapped me playfully in the arm. "I like your costume," she said to me.

With our group finally on the road, it seemed like nothing could go wrong, so I was able to relax and check out her attire. The witch's get-up she wore was simple but effective. She'd even added a black mole to her nose. But the most shocking change was her red hair. She'd always worn it in braids, but it was now free, hanging halfway down her back in lazy curls. She was so adorable that it took my breath away.

"I'm Kit," came the voice to our left.

Nora turned and shook Dwayne's outstretched hand. "Nora Mullan. Nice to meet you."

I should have been annoyed that Dwayne insisted on using that stupid, self-imposed nickname, but I was in too good of a mood for it to bother me. My plan had worked out. All of my friends were together and, soon, we'd be trick or treating, even if we were too old.

And maybe, just maybe, I'd even be reunited with my mother.

The odds were against it, so slim I'd be better off betting my college fund on black in Atlantic City, but there was a chance.

CHAPTER TWENTY

Within ten minutes, we were out of Sallow Creek proper, leaving behind our homes, familiar businesses, and the roads we regularly traveled. Following Nora's lead, we drove southeast, passing through a small town I'd been to a couple times. After that, every site was foreign to me.

I wouldn't say I was poorly traveled. I'd been to Pittsburgh more times than I could count. The Atlantic Ocean by way of places like Cape May, Ocean City, Virginia Beach, and Chincoteague. I'd been north, through most of New England. To the west, I'd made it as far as Chicago, tagging along on one of my dad's business trips.

I'd seen my share of the world, or at least, as much of it as most Americans. But now, we were thirty minutes from my backyard, and it was all unknown land.

The windy two-lane roads were lined by trees on both sides. Houses were rare. Businesses even more so. It was all farmland and forest, mountains and hollows. It's funny how the middle of nowhere isn't all that far from *somewhere*.

We passed through a twenty-mile stretch of state game

lands where the pavement gave way to shale, then transitioned to dirt. Milo's demeanor, which had never been anything to brag about, nosedived every time his reflexes were too slow to miss mud puddles, which were more like craters this far from civilization.

"If I bend a rim on one of these goddamn holes, you bastards are buying me a new one."

None of us responded. None of us even cracked a smile. Ordinarily, laughing at the angry man would have come naturally, but I was unnerved at the thought of getting a flat out there in the boonies, and I think my friends were too. I doubted Milo had AAA. Even if he did, the odds of a tow truck venturing this far out seemed slim.

After another few miles, the trees on our sides transitioned from lush pines to skeletal, charred husks. A fire had raged through the area, burning away every ounce of color and leaving a grayscale world in its wake. Blackened spires, some eighty, a hundred feet high, reached into the sky like fingers clawing at the clouds, trying to catch hold of them and drag them down and into this barren, dead place.

If asked, I would have wagered good money that human eyes hadn't set sight on that land in years. Gone was the illusion of bucolic farm country and remote wilderness. This landscape felt not only abandoned but excommunicated.

Our voyage had started with chit-chat and laughter, high, joyous noise. I realized we'd all gone silent, except for Milo's incessant gripes. There were no birds serenading, no insectile buzz. The only sounds were the tires on the dirt road and the occasional clang of the car hitting some upraised rock or exposed tree root.

It stayed that way for another twenty minutes. We'd been on the road for over an hour, and I was beginning to think Nora had forgotten her way home and was too embarrassed to fess up. I didn't want to put her on the spot, but I had to know.

"About how much further do you think it is?" I asked her.

She leaned forward, between the front seats, staring onto the road ahead as if looking for a landmark. To me, it all appeared the same.

"Not too far," she said, then leaned back into the seat. I tried to read her face, to discern whether the words were truthful or not, but she was a blank canvas.

I could feel Dwayne's eyes on me, boring a hole into me, but I refused to give in and meet his glare. Letting him stew in silence was better than catching the death ray he was sending my way. I might have screwed the pooch on this adventure, but I wasn't willing to own my shame just yet.

Eventually, after what felt like ages, life returned to the forest. Even though we were still in the sticks and possibly lost, having living things around us eased the tension. Even Milo seemed more comfortable as the road, which had been little more than a horse trail, evened out and became less cumbersome.

"I would have doubled my rate if I'd have known how far you were taking me," he said, his tone actually sounding cordial for a change.

"I'll throw in some extra candy," I promised. I meant it too; he'd earned it.

While the forest was alive, it was no longer filled with pines and spruce. In their place were birch and beech and ash. And while the leaves had fallen from every tree in Sallow Creek weeks earlier, here they were lush with foliage ablaze in autumn color. The leaves drowned out the sky above, replacing it with a kaleidoscope of reds and oranges and golds.

"It's only a few more miles!" Nora said. The confidence

had returned to her voice. Confidence along with excitement. She was almost home, and we could all feel it.

The road narrowed further, no longer a true road at all, just two ruts carved into the earth. But it was smooth traveling and still far superior to the rugged terrain we'd already conquered.

As we rounded a sharp bend in the road, the trail dead-ended, and the first sign of civilization in nearly forty-five minutes appeared. A rope bridge. It must have been twenty feet across and spanned a burbling, gurgling river.

"It's just across the bridge." Nora, who'd been bouncing in her seat, grabbed my hand. Her palm was slick with sweat. I squeezed back. The excitement was palpable.

"Well, I sure as shit can't drive over that," Milo said from behind the wheel as he let the car coast to a stop in tall, untamed timothy grass.

"Of course not," Nora said. "We'll walk the rest of the way. It's only a mile or less." She pushed me, encouraging me to flee the car.

I gave Stooge a tap, and he climbed out with us on his heels. In a second, everyone had exited the vehicle and stood in an autumnal scene so picturesque it could have been framed and hung in the Louvre.

I strode toward the rope bridge, peering at the water a few yards below. The colored leaves reflected in the current, and a lurid, carnelian river washed along. Hands pressed against my shoulders. I turned and found Nora.

"Beautiful, isn't it?"

I wasn't sure if she was talking about the foliage, the river, or herself, but the answer to all of the above was *yes*. I had the wild urge to kiss her. It seemed the perfect place, the perfect moment. The kind of story you could tell your grandkids about when you were eighty years old and sitting on the porch in a body riddled with arthritis and stooped by age.

The look on her face, the soft smile, the light in her eyes, made me think she was on the same wavelength. I came within a breath of planting a kiss - my first kiss - on her pink Cupid's bow when--

"There's gotta be a road into this place," Milo said.

The moment spoiled, Nora and I spun to him. He stomped about, peering up and down the river.

"No, just the rope bridge," Nora said.

"Bullshit," Milo muttered.

"Yeah, that doesn't make any sense," Dwayne said. "How do the people who live there drive in and out?"

"No one in Carrick Glynn drives." Nora rolled her eyes and giggled like it was the most foolish notion she'd ever considered.

It was the first time I'd heard the name of Nora's hometown - Carrick Glynn. It sounded exotic and foreign and made me even more excited to see it in person.

"Are you Amish or something?" Stooge asked.

"Do I look Amish?"

She didn't, but what groups in modern society didn't drive? Quakers? Shakers? Some ultra-orthodox religion I'd never heard of?

"What about delivery trucks? How do they get in?" Dwayne asked, pragmatic.

"We don't get deliveries. We grow our own food. Raise our own animals. Make our own clothes."

Dwayne stepped toward her, almost aggressive in his inquisition. "What if someone gets hurt? How does the ambulance get to them?"

The smile was gone from her face. She was tired of the grilling. "We take care of our own."

Something about those words.

We take care of our own.

Made the fine hair in the back of my neck rise to attention.

"That's enough," I said, stepping between Dwayne and Nora, ending the round of twenty questions. "We're not here to go joyriding through town anyway. We're here to trick or treat, and we'll do that on foot, just like we always have."

I grabbed my neon orange plastic pumpkin from my bag and left the rest of my belongings behind. Nora had hers too, and, a second later, Stooge pulled a yellowed, stained pillowcase from his backpack. It looked disgusting, like he might have stolen it from a coffin while robbing graves, but hey, it was Halloween. It worked.

Dwayne lingered, his face pinched in doubt or annoyance or both.

"Well?" I said to him, shaking my plastic pumpkin in a *hurry up* gesture. After a pause, he gave in and took a paper grocery bag from his pack. He trudged toward us with the enthusiasm of a condemned prisoner walking to the gallows.

"What the hell am I supposed to do? Sit here and play pocket pool all night?" Milo asked.

Only then did I realize the man had planned on joining our adventures. Maybe not trick or treating specifically, but he'd clearly intended to drive into town and partake in the festivities.

To my surprise, I felt a little bad for him. An adult wanting to hang out with a bunch of teenagers seemed almost endearing in its patheticness. "Do what you want," I told him. "Come along or stay here. It's up to you."

I hoped he'd opt for the latter. I didn't want a fifth wheel hanging around, and I didn't feel bad enough about his plight to make my offer sound like encouragement.

A blink of dismay, or perhaps disappointment, crossed his face, but he recovered fast. "Fine," he said, dropping back into the driver's seat and letting the door hang open. "I got better things to do than babysit you pussies."

He pushed a cassette into the tape deck. *Hatebreeders* by The Misfits blared from crackly speakers. The noise seemed almost obscene in such a natural, unspoiled wonderland.

Nora was the first on the bridge, striding across it with fearless confidence honed by experience. It swayed to and fro as she walked, sagging slightly, but it seemed stable enough. The wooden planks forming the walkway weren't rotten or decayed in any way. There was no sign that a foot would plunge through, or a section would give way and drop us into the cold river below.

But still, I held my breath until I was a third of the way across. The motion underfoot, the lack of solid ground, gave my head a dizzying, floating away feeling.

Nora was already on the far side, and Stooge was coming in behind me. His added weight and heavy footfalls sent the bridge rocking up and down. I gripped the ropes at the side tight enough to turn my knuckles white.

I hoped looking at my feet might steady my nerves, but seeing the water rush by underneath, through the gaps between the planks, only added to my sudden, sickening case of nerves.

"Get to stepping, little dude," Stooge said, his voice close, and I realized he was only a few planks away.

The crazed notion that our combined weight, so close together, would cause the bridge to fail suddenly came to me, and cold sweat erupted on my brow. My engineer dad would have laughed at my foolishness, but he was over an hour away and may as well have been on another planet for as much use as he provided in the moment.

I forced myself to look up, to look ahead. The sight of Nora, a breeze lifting her loose curls, blowing them out in a blizzard of red, got me moving again. She had made it across safe and sound, and so would I. That's what I told myself, anyway.

And I did. My knees almost locked up when I hit the earthen path, but Nora took my hand and pulled me ahead, and then we were running. I heard Stooge behind us, then Dwayne's voice, "Wait up."

"Last one to town eats a shit pickle," Stooge shouted.

Fear was forgotten.

As we all dashed down the tree-lined trail, the half-light of dusk came on quickly. In the span of minutes, it was too dark to see more than a few yards in front of your face. The colors grew muted and blended together, all the foliage and even the grass, shades of feuille morte.

Just as it grew dark enough to become borderline ominous, the path brightened ahead. Candles in glass canning jars glowed and illuminated our course. There were dozens of them, maybe hundreds, leading the way as if they'd been expecting us.

We hadn't been following the trail for more than five or ten minutes when I caught movement in my peripheral vision. My head snapped toward it, and I saw an antler clattering against some low-hanging tree limbs before disappearing into the deeper cover of the woods.

At the time, I assumed it was a deer, a common enough occurrence in Pennsylvania. But as we continued, I couldn't shake the feeling of being watched. As much as I wanted to be in the moment and enjoy this adventure with my friends, my eyes kept drifting back to the dark woods, searching the forest.

A sour, pungent odor drifted in from the trees, the smell of something foul and decayed. No matter how far we ran, the smell hung in the air. Following us.

I tried to look harder, to focus and separate the trees from whatever might be lurking in them, and I caught a fleeting glimpse of blue - a color so foreign in nature. It was there, beside a tree trunk, then vanished behind the massive oak.

I took a step toward it. Then another. And another. I was a few yards off the path, on the precipice of the dense forest. The smell was almost overpowering, so I brought my hand to my face to cover my mouth and nose. A pine bough scratched at my face, so I used my other hand to push it aside, to hunt with my eyes.

I spotted another antler, or maybe it was a horn, intermixed with branches and tree limbs. I followed the antler - or horn - down, trying to identify the animal to which it belonged when--

"Welcome to Carrick Glynn," Nora said.

I looked back to the trail. All my friends had progressed twenty yards or more past me. Beyond them, the path opened up to a wide clearing from which an orange glow shone.

When I turned back to the woods, whatever I'd seen, or thought I saw, was gone. No matter how hard I looked, I couldn't find it again.

And why did I care? I wasn't there to see a whitetail or an elk. I was there to trick or treat, so I spun on my heels and sprinted toward my friends, ready to see what adventures awaited.

CHAPTER TWENTY-ONE

The lone road leading through the town was ablaze in an orange inferno.

By squinting, I was able to see what actually stretched out before me. There was no fiery path after all. What was burning were pumpkins - jack o'lanterns. Hundreds of them. Each jack contained a fat candle that flickered and gyrated in the evening breeze.

The combined lumens thrown by the jacks were far brighter than the illumination of street lights in Sallow Creek. They lit up not just the cobblestone road but the entire village.

And it was a village. Not a town or a hamlet or even a shire. The houses, all in neat rows on each side of the road, were small and squat and built from rough stone. Leaded glass windows opened the homes to the world around, the amber glow of the pumpkins dancing across the oily apertures. Thatch roofs made of straw and sedge topped the houses, not a shingle or scrap of tin to be found.

The more I took it in, the less it seemed like a real place. It had the feel of a recreation. A place built for tourists who wanted to see what life was like back in the day. Whenever *the day* had been.

If pressed, I would have guessed the early 1700s. It reminded me of an elementary school field trip to Colonial Williamsburg in Virginia, where we had learned what life was like before the Revolution. But even that place, try as it might, had anachronistic, modern elements.

What was missing from Carrick Glynn fascinated me. There were no street lamps, no telephone poles, no power wires creating line drawings in the sky. No fire hydrants, no mailboxes, no businesses or banks or bars. And of course, no cars. Instead, wagons and simple carriages were scattered about.

A few animals roamed freely; sheep, a black goat, a few dogs. An ebony cat, a stereotype on Halloween of all days, wound its way between pumpkins, holding a field mouse in its jaws.

Men and women, no more than a few dozen in total, ambled about without a care or even a glance as we arrived. Their ages were indiscernible, timeless, as every person was costumed.

The people didn't wear the kind of costumes you'd buy at the drugstore for a few dollars or the mall if you felt like spending real money on something that looked good and wasn't made of hard plastic. Their costumes were homemade but, in a rustic, almost archaic, style, unlike anything I'd seen before.

Most of their masks appeared to be fabricated from a plaster-like substance. The faces were human-esque, with eyes and mouths. Some had noses, some did not. The proportions were all skewed and distorted. Some looked hydrocephalic. Some had pinheads. Others had low jowls which sagged to their chests. It was like I'd paid a quarter to enter the freak show.

A few villagers donned animal masks, rabbits and pigs and rats. Those seemed to be crafted of real fur and animal hide. All shared vacant, vacuous expressions. It might have been scary if it hadn't been so damned fascinating.

The *clip, clop, clip, clop* of an approaching pony drew my attention. A boy, younger and even smaller than me, rode on its back. His face was painted ghostly white, and he wore a clown costume with a tall, cone-shaped hat, a hand-sewn suit with frilly ruff collar, and tomato red puffs of fabric forming faux buttons down his chest. A pip squeak Pagliacci. As he passed us by, he stuck out his tongue.

"Friend of yours?" Stooge asked Nora.

So lost in that strange, wonderful place, I'd almost forgotten my friends were still there. I turned back to see them grouped together in their own pack.

"That's Ian," Nora said, referring to the boy on horseback. "He's a bit of a brat."

We moved down the path as one solid foursome, coming nearer to the revelry. The air smelled like pumpkin pies baking in the oven. The warmth thrown by the candlelit jack o'lanterns raised the temperature several degrees, and beads of perspiration broke out on my neck. Or maybe I was sweating because I was so damned excited. Or both.

I was ready to ask Nora if there was any special procedure or if we could just start knocking on doors when--

"That's as motley a bunch as I ever did see."

A man wearing a red suit stepped toward the light cast by the jacks. On his head, he wore an oversized, grinning devil mask the same color as his clothing and, for an instant, I thought the logo for Sherwood Deviled Ham had come to life, ready to drag me to the Underworld.

Then he lifted off his mask and approached us, revealing the placid face of a very old man.

"Granda," Nora shouted and dashed to him. She threw her arms around his neck, and the man used his free hand to lift her off the ground and spin her in an awkward circle.

A tall man at six and a half feet, Nora's grandfather reminded me a bit of Lurch from the old *Addam's Family* reruns I sometimes caught on TV. Despite the suit covering his frame, it was clear he was thin, bordering on frail. His face was sunken, cheekbones protruding, gray eyes lurking deep within the sockets. Sags and folds and dewlaps riddled his face. All combined, they made him look near ancient to my fourteen-year-old eyes.

His receding white hair had been flattened by the mask. When he set Nora back on the ground, he used his fingers to comb it into place, or at least make an attempt. His fingers, skin stretched taught across the bone, were skeletal.

"What a lovely surprise," he said, beaming down at the girl. "How ever did you get here?"

Nora glanced in the general direction from which we'd come. "A guy drove us. He's still back at the bridge."

Only then did he look at the rest of us. "Hello, there. Are you some of Nora's friends from the orphanage?"

Nora answered before any of us got a word out. "No. No one there wanted to come along."

Her answer shocked me. She'd never mentioned having any friends at the Aid Home, let alone inviting more people to go trick or treating. Knowing there had been other options, other kids with whom she'd considered spending Halloween, caused me a pang of jealousy.

Before I could get myself too annoyed, she moved on to introductions, pointing to each of us. "This is Benji, Stooge, and Kit. And this is my granda." She squeezed the old man's hand as if claiming him for her own.

"It's nice to meet you, Mr..." I wasn't sure how to finish the sentence as Nora had never mentioned whether her grandparents were paternal or maternal. "Mullan?" I tried.

"No need for formalities. We're all friends in Carrick Glynn. Call me Conal." He looked me up and down, reflections of orange fire flickering in his eyes. A smile, one that came across as almost ghoulish because he was so thin, pulled at his lips. "I like your costume, young Benjamin," he said. "Very scary."

He raised his hands and wagged his slender fingers like a man who'd been told to *stick 'em up* in an old western.

"Thanks," I said, feeling a surge of pride as he'd singled out my costume. It was nice to have my efforts appreciated. "I didn't buy it at the mall either. I made it myself."

"What a talented lad," Conal said. He dropped a hand onto my shoulder. I wasn't sure when he'd gotten close enough to reach out and touch me, and I flinched. At my reaction, he tightened his grip, which was surprisingly strong for his seemingly poor health and advanced age. Then he gave my arm a reassuring rub. "I'm sure everyone will be quite impressed."

He glanced toward the village behind him. "You children go on now. Fill your bags with goodies, but don't eat too much too soon. There's a feast to come, and it would be a shame if your bellies were too stuffed to enjoy it."

He stepped aside, and we moved past him, into the village, ready to trick or treat.

CHAPTER TWENTY-TWO

We traveled from door to door, not missing a single house. The promises Nora had made earlier all held true. Upon knocking, each door opened, and its owners greeted us cheerfully. They asked our names, discussed our costumes, and fawned over Nora like she was their own long-lost daughter.

They welcomed us into their homes, which were shockingly simple and sparsely furnished. But warmth from fires in cookstoves and fireplaces made the domiciles feel inviting as they gave us mugs of hot chocolate and chatted.

No one asked how old we were or told us we looked too big to be out begging for candy. It was better than the best night of trick or treating in Sallow Creek because the adults seemed as excited about Halloween as we were.

At one point in the evening, Dwayne pulled me aside and whispered in my ear, "Don't you think they're all kind of...weird?"

"What are you talking about?"

"These people. They look like they bathe once a week if they're lucky and smell almost as bad. And the houses are all grimy and old." He wrinkled his nose. "Plus, everyone's so touchy-feely." He looked at an elderly woman, her back hunched, fingers splayed with age and arthritis, and his eyes were full of disdain. "They're gross."

It was the exact opposite impression I'd had, and I was surprised to hear such judgmental words come from his mouth. The Dwayne I grew up with never would have acted like this. But then again, I wasn't with Dwayne. I was with *Kit,* and maybe the attitudes of his new clique had rubbed off more than I'd ever realized.

"They're not gross," I assure him. "They're just old and sheltered. They're not used to new people being around."

"I feel like they're going to give me lice." His hand went instinctively to his head, and he scratched his scalp.

He deserved a scolding. Nora looked back at us and didn't want to dawdle. I gave him a gentle poke in the ribs. "Don't be a pussy." With that, I ran on, and he followed.

A few houses later, a burly, bearded man with carrot red hair invited us into his home, which smelled like cinnamon and cloves. Like fall. As he stepped aside to grant us access, I spotted a middle-aged woman sitting at a chunky, wooden table, tying delicate bows around bags of homemade chocolates. My first glimpse of her was from the side, but it was enough to make my heart lurch in my chest.

I knew she was the woman from Nora's photo, the woman I thought could be my mother. As if trying to force my wish to come true, my brain turned her into the spitting image of my mom, right down to the circular, brown birthmark on her forehead.

The man was saying something, maybe to Nora, but my ears only heard white noise. I moved past the husband, closer to the woman, to my mother. She must have heard my approaching footsteps because she turned to me, a familiar smile on her face, eyes sparkling with cheer.

"Hello, Benji," she said, but the sound was muffled and distorted, like hearing when your head was underwater.

"Mom?" I said.

Then all the soft-focus, dreamy sights and sounds I'd been experiencing snapped back to clear reality. The woman had a vague resemblance to my mother but could have been a distant cousin, at best. Her eyes were the wrong color, there was no birthmark, and the smile revealed a mouthful of crooked teeth, not my mom's perfect, pearly whites.

"Pardon?" she asked.

The house had gone silent as a morgue, and I could feel everyone staring at me. I transformed into Uri Gellar and could read their thoughts.

Poor Benji's finally done it. He's up and lost his marbles. Call the guys with the butterfly nets because Benji's headed to the funny farm.

I wanted to spin and run. Run past my friends, run out the door, run away from the village. I'd never stop running if I could help it.

But running wasn't an option. I had to find a way out of the hole I'd dug and used every bit of wit I possessed. Then it came to me in an inspired stroke of genius known only to liars and charlatans.

"Shalom. I said, Shalom. I'm Jewish, and it just slips out sometimes. Sorry." My eyes darted around the cottage to see if anyone was buying the ruse. Maybe they did, or maybe they were all too drunk on good cheer to notice the shame in my eyes. Either way, they went with it.

The woman, who was clearly not my mother, had never been my mother, not even in Nora's Polaroid, patted my forearm. "No reason to apologize," she said. "We all have our beliefs."

The sudden dashing of my hopes revealed how high I had allowed them to grow. How much I had believed my own foolish dreams in which I was going to find my mother living in this town. Not only find her but bring her home where life would resume as if nothing had gone awry.

As much as I had trained myself to keep my expectations in check, I'd failed miserably. And in that moment, I struggled to keep my composure and not dissolve into a sobbing, blubbering mess. A sobbing, blubbering mess still without his mother. Forever without his mother.

I don't know why I let myself get so blinded. I'd been through pie-eyed fantasies before, so many times. Wouldn't I ever learn my lesson?

"You gotta ignore Benji," Stooge said. "He's a weirdo, but we love him anyway."

"He's our weirdo," Nora said.

Dwayne was the last holdout. For a moment, I thought he was going to leave me hanging. Or, in the ultimate, final act of betrayal, say something cruel. Instead, he grinned. "Yeah, he is," he added.

Their support made me realize I didn't need to keep looking for my mother in every shadow and nook. I had more love than most people ever experience, and I should be grateful.

OVER THE NEXT HOUR, we visited twelve more cottages. The only low point came when a man with a scarred face and a missing eye was handing out pears. Dwayne kept moving his bag, a mean smirk on his face as he fooled with the man's poor depth perception. I shot Dwayne my best *grow up* look, and he stopped, but the mean smirk lingered.

By the time we finished, our bags and totes were overflowing with treats. But there were no Snickers or Smarties, no M&Ms or Mars's bars, nothing prepackaged and processed to be found.

Every treat we received was either natural (apples, both regular and caramel covered, peaches, plums) or homemade (cookies, brownies, pastries, popcorn). All of it made with care and love.

At least, I thought so. As we took a break under a sprawling maple, sitting on a blanket of crimson leaves, I realized at least some of my friends didn't share my gratitude.

Dwayne peeled back a piece of butcher's paper covering a cream puff, his nose wrinkled. "I don't think we should eat this crap." He glanced at the rest of us, trying to get a read on the room. "It's like the first rule of trick or treating. Never eat homemade candy because you don't know what's in it."

Nora examined one of her own treats, her face contorted in confusion. "What could be in them?"

"Razor blades!" Dwayne blurted. "Or poison."

Stooge, who was halfway through a glazed donut almost as big as his face, ceased chewing and let his mouth gape open. A few chunks of food spilled out.

My patience with Dwayne was nearing its end. "Come on. Do you really think there's some crazy person here just waiting for you to come along so they can feed you an apple dipped in arsenic?" I asked. Then, to prove my point, I chomped into a piece of fruit so ripe that juice squirted all over my face.

I chewed, swallowed, then grinned. "Still alive," I said.

"Arsenic might make apples more edible," Stooge said. He held up his hand for a high five, but we all left him hanging.

When no one reciprocated, he clapped his own hand and went back to eating his donut, willing to take the risk.

Dwayne scowled, still inspecting his eclair, trying to peel back the layers of pâte à choux like an archeologist unearthing an ancient burial ground.

Before he could pick the dessert to bits, Nora reached out and snatched it away, popping it into her mouth. She took two chomps, then her eyes grew wide. The cords in her neck stood out as her hands went to her throat, scratching, clawing. She kicked with her feet, carving channels in the earth.

Then her entire body went into convulsions. She gagged, and partially chewed cream puff oozed out of her mouth.

She froze. Stiffened. Toppled over.

I knew it was a prank by the mischievous glint in her eyes, but Dwayne looked ready to jump out of his baseball uniform. He scrambled to his feet, backing away, leaving his shopping bag full of goodies behind. I swear, he was ready to bolt, to run who knows where, when Nora burst out laughing.

She sat up, wiping the food from her chin, trying to reign in her giggling fit but not succeeding. "Apricot. Yuck," she said.

Dwayne trudged back to us, and I expected him to be pissed. I thought he might even abandon us and head back to Milo, but he surprised me by grinning.

"I hate you," he said to Nora.

"You shoulda seen the look on your face, dude!" Stooge bellowed, also laughing. But I'd seen Stooge's own shocked expression.

"She got you too, Stooge," I told him.

"Nah," he said. "Gotta try harder than that to get one past Uncle Stoogie."

I rolled my eyes. "Sure."

Dwayne flopped back into the leaves, his bag of treats back between his legs, his breathing slowing to a normal speed.

"Well," I said to Dwayne. "Are you going to eat any of your haul or are you giving it all to Milo?"

He reached into the bag and grabbed the first item he came across. An oatmeal raisin cookie.

"Better check, make sure those are really raisins. They might be flies," I said.

"I don't know who ever told you that you were funny, but they lied," he shot back, then threw a fistful of leaves in my direction. They danced through the air before landing in my lap.

We all ate more than reasonable but eating until you felt sick was half the fun of trick or treating. Gorged, I flopped onto my back and stared toward the heavens. The waning crescent was barely visible, a sliver of a fingernail in the sky. But the stars, with no light or pollution to steal their shimmer, burned brighter than I'd ever seen them before.

Everything around me felt more vibrant, more alive. Even the air smelled cleaner. Everything about Carrick Glynn felt purer and closer to nature.

"What time is it anyway?" Stooge asked.

I rolled onto my elbow as Dwayne checked his wristwatch. "Half-past seven," he answered. Then he added, "We better head out soon."

My heart sank. Despite not having found my mother, I was having more fun than I'd had in years. Since her disappearance, if I was being honest with myself. I couldn't imagine leaving so soon, leaving before we'd soaked in every last drop of enjoyment to be had. It would have been like visiting Disney World, touring Epcot, and going home without riding any rides or having your picture taken with Goofy.

"We can't go yet," I said, hoping the anxiety I was feeling didn't come through. "Nora's grandpa said there was going to be a meal or something." I looked at her with pleading eyes.

She nodded. "Yes, it's tradition. To celebrate the harvest."

"See," I said, hoping that was reason enough. The doubt on Dwayne's face was obvious, though, and I knew I was pushing my luck. "Everyone's been so nice to us. It would be rude to take our candy and run."

"Yeah, dude," Stooge added. "Besides, I'm always up for a feast."

It was three to one, and even though the one was very strong-willed, he wasn't in a position to get his way. "Alright. But as soon as that's over, we head back to the car, right?"

"Sure," I offered. Anything to buy more time. Anything to extend Halloween and remain a kid a little while longer.

CHAPTER TWENTY-THREE

On the east end of the village stretched an open pasture where picnic tables had been set up in preparation for the meal. Huge wooden bowls overflowing with food were already in place, and it was a better smorgasbord than you'd find in any restaurant.

First came fresh baked bread and rolls. Then corn, potatoes of several varieties, salads, Brussels sprouts, and carrots. Platters of meat, waves of steam wafting in the cool night air, were next. Then desserts. Cakes and pies and trays of cookies and candies. It was enough food to feed the entirety of Sallow Creek middle school.

Even though I was stuffed, the smell was intoxicating, and I yearned to dive in and eat more. But before the feast came games, Nora told us.

Several wooden barrels, filled with water and apples bobbing on the surface, had drawn most of the children in the village, and Nora dashed toward them.

"A contest," she announced. "First one to get an apple gets..." she paused, thinking.

"More candy," Stooge suggested.

"God, no," Dwayne groaned. "If I eat any more sugar, I'm gonna hurl."

"We don't need a prize. Bragging rights is good enough for me," I said.

We found two unoccupied barrels close together and knelt before them. Stooge and Dwayne took one, Nora and I the other.

She set her witch's hat to the side and gave her hair a shake. "Ready?"

I nodded. She looked at the others, who also assured they were set.

"Okay then. On three. And remember, no hands."

She counted and we plunged our heads into the water. It was barely above freezing, and I yelped out a gurgling whoosh of air. Then I sucked in a mouthful of water, coughing it back up instantaneously.

Across from me, I could see Nora striking at an apple, missing, trying again, knocking it toward me. I made an attempt, but it bounced off my chin.

With that, I came up for a breath, sucking in a gasp of air. She was still under, and I knew I had to try harder if I wanted to impress her. And I did want to impress her.

I shoved my face into the tub, prepared for the frigid water, which didn't seem as bad the second time around. Nora and I both went for the same apple at the same time. In the process, the fruit skidded sideways, and our faces met, noses touching. Then, before I could react, she tilted her head and pressed her mouth against my own.

It was my first kiss. I'd never so much as given a girl a peck on the cheek before, and my stomach turned into a lead ball. Time froze, and I stopped breathing, lost in the experience.

Even though my face was bordering on numb, I could feel

the warmth of her mouth against mine, the silken softness of her lips as they locked on my own. The sweet taste of sugar from too many treats.

I kissed her back or tried. Water flooded my mouth, hers too, I'm sure. Her teeth pinned my bottom lip, biting gently, and her tongue flickered across my lip. I didn't care that I couldn't breathe, might even be drowning. If there were better ways to die, my mind sure couldn't imagine them.

I reached for her, my fingers gliding through her wet hair, pulling her in even closer to me when--

"Cheater!" Stooge yelled.

Nora and I broke apart and emerged from the barrel, drenched to our necks. The cold, evening air suddenly felt sub-zero, and I couldn't stop shivering. At least, I told myself I was shivering due to the temperature.

"Benji used his hands," Stooge announced, like a referee who'd called out a defenseman for high sticking.

Stooge's mullet was plastered to his skull, water dripping from the ring in his nose like it was the aerator in a leaky faucet. Beside him, Dwayne sat on his haunches, red apple pinned in his distended jaws, looking like a roasted pig waiting to be carved.

Neither of them had seen Nora kiss me, nor I kiss her back. I was relieved, not because I was embarrassed or regretful, but because I wanted that moment to stay secret. I wanted it to belong to only Nora and me.

PART THREE

"Hell is empty. All the devils are here."

CHAPTER TWENTY-FOUR

Unlike the brats he'd driven, Milo Woronov thought the evening had been long and damned boring. He'd gone through every good tape in the car, and the radio reception out in the sticks was for shit, further souring his mood. On top of that, it was getting cold. Real cold. Put your nipples on attention cold.

His leather jacket was designed for looks, not warmth, and he'd been forced to sit inside the car and roll up the windows to keep his teeth from chattering.

All this grief for eighty bucks and some candy, he thought as he shuffled through the cassettes yet again, trying to decide whether he wanted to listen to a replay of *Too Tough to Die* or a mixtape that Malorie, his ex, had made for him the previous summer.

He decided on the former (the latter carried too many memories, most of them bad), popping it into the tape deck and turning the volume up so loud it made his eyeballs vibrate.

The windows of the Duster had fogged over on the inside. He'd also recently finished off a fat spliff. Nothing good, just forest green shake with so many stems it looked like oregano, but it got a nice buzz going. On the downside, it filled the car with smoke and, cold as he was, he couldn't so much as crack a window to let it escape.

Adrift in the haze of used up pot, for as much as he could see of the world around him, he could have been in the middle of Sallow Creek, the middle of New York City even. But he wasn't in either. He was in the middle of nowhere and all alone.

Or so he thought.

He shifted in his seat, pinching his thighs together. He needed to piss like a Russian racehorse, but the thought of going into the near-freezing temps kept him inside the car for the duration of *Danger Zone* before he gave in and threw open the door.

The cold hit him like an uppercut, turning his skin to gooseflesh. He hurriedly zipped up the jacket and popped the color. He knew he looked like a douche but didn't care. The need to empty his bladder was all-consuming.

More out of habit than due to any practical purpose, Milo moved to a hedge of mountain laurel to find privacy he didn't need to go about his business. He was halfway through one of the longest pisses of his life when the man's voice called to him.

"Better cover up your willy before it freezes and falls off."

Milo spun, shooting an arc of urine through the air, across his boots, and down the right leg of his jeans. The warmth was oddly comforting as it soaked through the denim and caressed his skin.

A tall, old man in a red suit, a man Milo didn't know to be Nora's granda, Conal, stood at the edge of the rope bridge, watching with amused eyes. Milo tucked away his junk, zipped shut his jeans, and strode toward Conal, hoping he looked half as pissed off (pissed on?) as he felt.

"Shitty thing to do, man," Milo said. "Sneaking up on a guy when he's taking a leak."

"Oh, I didn't intend to startle you none," Conal said, striding toward the younger, fit man without a hint of apprehension. "My Nora told me you drove her here, and I felt it proper to show my appreciation."

Conal extended his right hand. In it was a stein of ale. In his other hand was a sack full of food. Milo blinked, making sure he wasn't hallucinating. He was certain the man had been empty-handed when he first saw him.

"Go on and take it. I don't bite," Conal said.

He swirled the beer in the mug, some of it sloshing over the edge. It looked black in the night.

"Is that stout?"

Conal nodded. "Best you'll find east of Killarney."

Milo had no clue where Killarney was, but he accepted the mug. He'd only drank stout once before, at a dive pub in Pittsburgh. O'Malley's or O'Murphy's or something stereotypically Irish. He'd downed three pints and refunded the entirety of it in the gutter behind the bar a few hours later. One failure didn't mean he was averse to a second try, though. Milo Woronov was not a quitter.

Raising it to his lips, he breathed in the aroma of coffee and hops mixed with cocoa. Then he drank. It was sour and bitter, but it went down just fine. He finished half the stein before coming up for a breath.

"What do you say?" Conal asked.

"Two thumbs up." Milo got back to it, guzzling the remainder in three long swallows. Upon finishing, he belched.

Conal grinned and clapped him on the shoulder. "That's a good lad."

"Good beer, too," Milo added. He then took the sack from Conal and checked the contents. It was full of fruits and candy, wedges of fudge, cookies - the works. The pot had stoked his appetite, and this food would help pass the time until the brats came back.

Conal looked him up and down intently. He seemed especially interested in Milo's tattoos and piercings. "That's quite a costume you've got on."

Milo checked out his own attire. It was his daily wear, nothing more, nothing less. His hand went to his head, fingers gliding across the mohawk. "You think this is a costume?"

Conal raised a wiry, white eyebrow. "Is it not?"

Annoyed, Milo shot back, "This ain't no costume, man. This is a way of life!" Despite the gifts, he was tired of the old man's presence and wanted him gone. Besides, what did some country bumpkin know about punk?

"I assure you, I meant no disrespect."

Milo sneered. "Whatever." He spun back toward his Duster and stomped toward it.

"You're welcome to join us in town. The feast isn't far off."

Milo shot him the bird over his shoulder, the skull ring on his middle finger glinting in the meager light thrown by the stars.

"Such a shame you've gone and marked up your body. Spoiled your canvas," Conal said.

But Milo ignored him. He was at the car, grabbing the door handle.

"You might have been useful otherwise."

Milo turned, ready to tell the old bastard to skidoo before he fed him a fist sandwich. But instead of mouthing off, he went mute as he spotted the most beautiful woman he'd ever seen standing on the bridge.

Long, raven-esque hair hung to her waist. She looked twenty at the oldest, not that he intended to ask her age. Her thin, white gown showed off her curvaceous figure, nipples at attention. She beckoned Milo with a wave of her hand.

"Come join us in the village," she said.

Damn, if this was the type of woman available in town, he needed to kick his own ass for sitting in the car all night. He strode toward her, pausing as he reached the bridge.

At first, he thought the old man was gone, but Milo noticed him on the other side of the river. Not that he cared. There was a once-in-a-generation beauty in his presence, and the rest of the world could screw off.

"You can come over here," he said to her. "Party in my ride. I got better shit than candy."

She flashed a demure smile and gave her head a shake. "I don't even know you."

"There's ways to change that," he said.

She pointed her index finger at him and curled it, coaxing. Then she turned and walked away, the bridge swaying underfoot.

Milo stepped onto the first plank, his asshole puckering as the bridge gave a low creak. But it held, and he continued on.

The beauty had reached the opposite side of the river and stood beside Conal, who held up the stein of ale which was again full.

"Hurry on now," Conal said.

Beer and a babe? Milo quickened his pace.

He made it just over the midway point, keeping his eyes on his feet so that he didn't make a misstep, when the bridge suddenly rocked, the right side dropping a good three feet.

Milo lost his balance, slipped, and went down on his ass. He began to slide, one leg dropping over the edge of the bridge, foot dangling into the abyss. He grabbed onto the side rope and held on for dear life. Only once he had a firm grip did he look to the man and woman across the river.

They stood, unmoving, still smiling. Conal still held up the beer. "Hurry on now," Conal repeated as if nothing was amiss. Milo began to wonder if the old coot was senile, but that didn't explain the girl who wasn't reacting at all to his plight.

"I could use a hand here!" Milo shouted, trying not to sound as scared as he felt.

The bridge lurched again, the planks behind him falling. Then the entire back half was swinging down.

"Hey!" Milo got out before the bridge fell out from under him. It happened so fast he lost his grip on the rope, and he hung in mid-air for a moment, like a man who'd spontaneously learned how to levitate.

Then he joined the wood and rope and planks as they all plummeted toward the rocks below. And Milo's night, which had been damned boring up until that point, became much more eventful.

CHAPTER TWENTY-FIVE

I was still flying high after my kiss with Nora when I spotted a man striding toward the edge of the pasture with a torch in his hand. He passed by the tables of food and into the tall grass which separated the clearing from the fields beyond.

Nothing more than the light of his torch floating through the abyss could be seen. It was like the fire itself was strolling through the countryside, and the sight mesmerized me.

"What's he doing?" I asked Nora.

She'd been wringing water out of her long hair. Stopping, she looked up and followed my gaze. A smile crossed her face. "Just watch. It'll take your breath away."

I did. The fire moved deeper into the darkness, growing dimmer and smaller as it traveled away from us.

Dwayne stepped to my side, the apple he'd snagged from the water gnawed down to the core. "How much longer, Benji? I wanna go home already."

I glanced at him distractedly. "After the meal, remember?"

My eyes went back to the torch, which was now a pinprick of light.

"The drive here took like an hour and a half, and that was in the daylight. It'll be two, maybe three hours back in the dark," he whined.

I turned away from the diminishing light in the field and faced my friend. "So what? It's not like we have a bedtime or a curfew."

"I know that," he said. "But I'm over all this shit, and I don't want to be stuck here all night long with these weirdos." He didn't bother to conceal his contempt.

I'd fooled myself into believing we were all enjoying the festivities. When I realized Dwayne was only putting in time, it brought out an angry side of me that rarely made an appearance. "Why'd you even come if you don't want to be with me?" I bit down, chopping off the sentence. "With us, I mean."

He flinched, and I regretted being harsh, but he was pissing me off, and I had a feeling he didn't care. From the look on his face, I thought he might punch me, so I steeled myself for a blow that didn't come.

"Never mind." He stomped toward one of the tables where the food sat around, waiting for someone to eat it.

"Dude, chill," Stooge said, pulling me aside. "You know this isn't his bag. Be glad he didn't pitch a shit fit earlier."

I looked from Stooge to Dwayne, who had claimed a seat alone and was sulking in it, then back to Stooge. He looked oddly serious, maybe even fatherly, and under that gaze, I felt like an unruly child being scolded.

"I just want things to be like they used to be."

Stooge opened his mouth, but before he could say a word, the speck of fire in the distance grew bright enough to claim our attention. First, it was the size of a small car, then became the size of a bus, then a house.

It kept growing, undulating in the breeze. As the orange blaze brightened the surroundings, I realized the field wasn't burning. An enormous pile of limbs and branches and cornstalks was ablaze.

The flames raced across the dry tinder, and we could hear the resulting pops and crackles and hisses from where we stood, even though it was far off. Within seconds, the pile was a fiery mountain bright enough to turn night into day.

"The lighting of the bonfire is the official beginning of the celebration," Nora said, wrapping her hand around my arm and leaning in close. "It's glorious."

I supposed it was, to an arsonist or a pyromaniac. To me, it was intimidating, threatening. Maybe I'd seen too many newsreels of wildfires burning out of control and the charred remnants left in their wake to see any beauty in the blaze. But I wasn't going to tell her that.

"Yeah," I muttered.

The inferno illuminated a nearby cornfield sitting on a gently sloping hillside to the west. Amongst the golden sea of dried stalks, my eyes landed on the most intricate design I'd ever seen in nature - the head of a bull. Or maybe it was a deer as the horns extending from it were long and intricate with numerous curving offshoots.

"What is that?" I asked Nora, my voice suddenly weak with awe. The design spanned four, maybe five hundred feet...

"The labyrinth," she said but didn't expand further.

When I looked harder, I could make out lines running through it and realized I was looking at the mother of all corn mazes.

"Jesus," I muttered.

"Not here." Conal clapped me on the shoulder. "Not tonight, especially."

I turned away from the fields and fire. Conal had traded out his red suit and Devil's head for a white tunic and tan trousers. A length of rope was tied around his waist like a makeshift belt, drawing attention to his slender waist. Beyond him, the rest of the villagers streamed into the pasture.

Every resident of Carrick Glynn came in a row, all carrying their own jack o'lantern, candlelight flickering from inside, the upward glow sending long, macabre shadows into their faces. Suddenly, they didn't look friendly and jovial.

It's just a trick of the light, I assured myself.

There were forty or so people in total. The men were all dressed similarly to Conal, while the women wore white ankle-length dresses with blue shawls wrapped around their shoulders.

When they reached the pasture, they set their pumpkins on the ground one by one, seemingly at random initially. But when the last was put in place, and I looked at the group as a whole, they seemed to form an upside down letter Y but with an extra line extending through the middle. A peace sign without the circle surrounding it.

I was trying to make sense of it when Conal steered me toward the largest of the tables. "Have a seat, young friend. It's almost time to eat."

CHAPTER TWENTY-SIX

THE FEAST KICKED OFF WITH A SERENADE. A MIDDLE-AGED woman with flowing brunette hair sang in a language I couldn't understand, but I did appreciate the soothing quality of her voice. She danced too, but with no rhythm or plan. Her arms raised and lowered, her feet kicked. She spun in circles, at one point so fast I thought she might pass out.

During the performance, Dwayne made his eyes go wide and lolled his head on his neck in a mean-spirited but accurate mimic of the woman. I knew he was waiting for me to signal my approval, but I didn't approve.

Not a single murmur passed through the seated crowd while she sang. Only once the performance had ended did the boisterous revelry recommence.

Conal sat at the head of our table and Nora to his right. I had the seat beside hers while Stooge and Dwayne were across from us. Eight villagers filled the far end of the table, most of whom I recognized from trick or treating earlier. The conversation was light as everyone filled their plates. The food was delicious and never-ending.

The longer the meal went, the more relaxed my friends and I became. I wouldn't go so far as to say we fit in like part of the family, but the awkwardness borne from being surrounded by strangers faded away. Even Dwayne, to my surprise, seemed to be having fun as he chatted - flirted - with an attractive girl in her late teens or early twenties, and Stooge was downright giddy, making lame, off-color jokes to anyone who'd listen.

My family, even when my mom was around, had never been big on holiday get-togethers, the kind where all the aunts and uncles and cousins who you see once a year are crammed into one room and left to pretend like you're best friends. I wasn't a fan of crowds either but sitting in this throng of people felt like the perfect way to cap off a great night.

I hadn't made it halfway through the meal when my belly began to bulge under my biballs. But the food all tasted so good I kept eating anyway, not caring that I was going to suffer all the ride home.

We were through most of the main courses but still pre-dessert when Conal stood and rapped a mug against the table. All of the villagers looked to him, as did my friends and I.

"Friends, if you'll lend an ear for a moment," he said, and the din of the crowd faded, then ceased. "My addled, old mind ain't what it used to be, and I've lost count of how many of these feasts we've had, but I know it's been a many."

"I remember every last one of them," a man called out. He was in his thirties with an unruly mane of sand-colored hair, robust, and glassy-eyed.

Conal tipped his chin toward the man. "Aye, so you say, Edwin. When you're in your cups, your mind's sharp as a pin. I bet you remember Queen Anne too."

"I do! A comely lass she was. But then, I always did like my women on the big side." The man, Edwin, bellowed with laughter and tipped back a mug, guzzling the contents.

The other villagers laughed too. So did I, even though I didn't know Queen Anne from Anne Margaret. I'd been laughing a lot since the meal began. It seemed like every wry comment or witty remark was the funniest thing I'd ever heard. I couldn't recall the last time I'd been so easily amused and carefree.

When the noise settled, Conal went on. "We toil all spring and summer in the fields. Our hard work carries us through the long winter months, which will be upon us in short order, but tonight..." He beamed, staring out at his friends, his neighbors, his granddaughter. "Tonight, we relax and send our thanks to Cernunnos for keeping our bodies safe and our fields full. Let us praise him!"

The crowd simultaneously tipped back their heads and made a noise somewhere between a bull's bellow and a mewling cry. They did that five times in unison. Everyone joined in, even Nora, except for Stooge, Dwayne, and me.

"Praise be," Conal said.

"Praise him," the villagers responded.

"Aye," Conal said and took a swig of drink. "Let me thank a few of you individually for preparing this feast. Mrs. Murdaugh, who made the pies, Mrs. Baldwin, who..."

As I tried to pay attention to the speech, movement in my peripheral vision stole my attention. I looked and saw Stooge waving his hand at me. When our eyes met, he leaned across the table.

"Is it just me or does that broad have three tits?" he asked, then motioned to the table to our right. There, a plain-looking woman with a narrow face sat among other villagers. It took my eyes a long moment to come into focus, but when they did, I thought she looked normal to me, which meant the standard two breasts.

"It's just you," I said.

Stooge squinted, staring at her, then shook his head as if to clear it from a dense fog. "I swear she's got a triple-header going on." He snatched his mug of cider and took a swallow, then belched.

I'd consumed my share of cider too and, as I noticed the vacant, glazed-over look in Stooge's eyes, I began to wonder if our drinks might be alcoholic. I'd never so much as chugged a beer. The most alcohol I'd ever consumed was during a Memorial Day picnic when my mom let me sip her wine cooler. Afterward, I slept away the afternoon.

I was trying to decide whether or not I was drunk when Conal's booming voice brought me back around.

"We're honored to have three very special guests with us to celebrate the harvest!"

All eyes were on us. I felt like I'd been called on to explain the Pythagorean theorem in geometry class and wanted to melt into my seat.

"I believe all of you, or most of you, have met these fine lads. But let me re-introduce them. We have young masters Stewart, Dwayne, and Benjamin. Give 'em a round of applause and show them how much we appreciate their joining us."

The villagers clapped boisterously. A few came over and shook our hands or patted us on the backs. It was flattering and embarrassing, but all the while, I thought about Conal using our names.

Nora knew Stooge's real name was Stewart, but I was sure she'd introduced him by his nickname earlier in the night. Yes, she might have shared Stooge's given name with Conal later on, during some moment when I was otherwise occupied, but that didn't explain Dwayne.

She'd told Conal his name was Kit. And Dwayne had told her his name was Kit when they met in the back seat of Milo's Duster. Had I ever used Dwayne's given name in any of our chats? I tried to focus, but my head was thick and thoughts came slowly.

There was little time to consider the matter before Conal went on.

"I say these lads are our guests of honor, and you know what that means!"

I didn't know what it meant. But I found out soon.

"Labyrinth! Labyrinth!" the villagers chanted.

I stole a glance at Nora, who wore a Cheshire cat grin. She leaned over and hugged me, then whispered into my ear, "It's tradition."

CHAPTER TWENTY-SEVEN

Conal and two men he'd introduced as Seamus and Ewan led us to the corn maze. The twins may as well have been mute for as much as they talked, which was not a single word during the entire walk.

Overhead, bats soared and fluttered, snatching insects out of mid-air. Dwayne stole glances at them, tucking his shoulders in fear. His mother had always made him come inside at dusk, warning that bats would swoop down and get their feet stuck in his hair. Her admonishments had left him with bat-phobia, or whatever the real name is.

The long journey was all uphill, and poor Stooge was already huffing and puffing by the time we got to our destination. I wasn't tired, but my head felt heavy and loose on my shoulders, like my neck was full of worn-out ball bearings. If the cider was indeed alcoholic, and by that point, I was certain it was, that feeling left me wondering why anyone would get drunk by choice.

The entrance to the maze was wider than it looked from a

distance, but the path narrowed inside, funneling down to just two or three feet across. There wasn't even enough room to stand with your arms outstretched at your sides.

"What do you say, lads?" Conal wheezed.

Perspiration beaded on his forehead, and his white shirt had enormous sweat stains in the armpits. He was in worse shape than even Stooge, and I couldn't fathom why such an old man had chosen to lead us there when the village was full of younger, healthier people.

"Say about what?" Dwayne asked. His brow was kitted in skepticism or trepidation. Both, probably. He hadn't consumed much cider, and I suspected he wasn't feeling the effects of the drink as much as Stooge or myself.

"The race!" Conal's pallid complexion had taken on the color of the bonfire, and in the flickering light, with his deep-set eyes, he looked almost like a jack o'lantern himself. "Are you ready?"

Dwayne took a glance into the maze. His body tightened like all the muscles were flexing at once. I'd seen him look the same way as he strutted to home plate, ready to stare down an opposing pitcher.

Seeing the competitive fire in his eyes brought back memories of all the times we'd played Monopoly or Stratego in the treehouse. I'd been just as happy to lose as I was to come out victorious. My dad oftentimes said I lacked a *killer instinct*, but it was the way I was wired. I played for the fun of it and never understood why Dwayne would get so angry over a loss.

Over the years, I'd lost count of how many times he'd flipped the board or sent it hurling into the wall. We sometimes spent days trying to recover all the pieces, but he never bothered with an apology because the losses still gnawed at him.

It eventually reached the point where I preferred losing and would make dumb moves on purpose, trying to throw the games. Even then, a rare win slipped in, and I had to deal with his angst-ridden aftermath. It became easier to quit playing.

I couldn't remember the last time we'd been involved in any type of head-to-head contest. But now, seeing him stretching and flexing in preparation, finally invested on a night where he'd been the ultimate wet blanket... It lit a fire inside me. I didn't want to win so much as I wanted to beat Dwayne.

He didn't deserve a victory. Not here. Not tonight.

"I'm gonna forfeit, friendo," Stooge said. He had both hands on his massive thighs and was bent at the waist, sucking in whooping breaths.

"Ah, there's no fun in that," Conal said. "Give it a go. You got nothin' to lose but your pride."

Stooge looked up at me, his eyelids heavy. "Lost that a long time ago, right?" He hiccuped, then burped, and a dribble of regurgitated cider leaked from his mouth.

"What are we playing for?" I asked Conal.

"Whatever do you mean, young Benjamin?"

"Well, if it's a race, what does the winner get?"

He eyed me, one brow rising like a hook was attached to it and remained silent a long while before answering. "Immortality," he finally said.

I stared at him, confused, wondering if I'd heard correctly. He must have seen my confusion, so he went on. "No one forgets a winner, correct?"

"Right," Dwayne, the perpetual winner, answered.

Conal stepped closer to us. Stooge was nearest, and the old man put his hands on the boy's broad shoulders. They were within a few inches of eye level.

"May the gods make you fleet of foot and strong of spirit, Stewart," Conal said.

He moved to Dwayne and repeated the saying. Then he came to me.

I stared up at him, craning my neck so far back I heard a light popping sound. He looked monstrously tall close up, so large he could eat me if he chose. Our eyes locked, and the cliche about them being windows to the soul never felt more true.

The light of the bonfire shimmering across his face mesmerized me. Some of it was certainly due to the drink, but the longer he stared at me, the more it seemed like he was some sort of mentalist putting me into a deep trance.

I'd never felt so... *inspected* in my life. He was looking me over like a supremely cautious shopper might inspect a used car for dents and nicks in the paint before signing on the dotted line.

"May the gods make you fleet of foot and strong of spirit, Benjamin."

At the time, my brain corrected gods to God, the way you always heard it in small-town USA. In small-town Sallow Creek. Where there was only *God* singular, and anything to the contrary was the talk or heathens, tantamount to blasphemy.

I sometimes wonder if I'd have focused on the word he'd actually used - *gods* - and all the implications that came from the plural, whether I could have saved my friends and myself from the coming pain and misery. On the long nights when sleep refuses to come, I curse myself for not catching on while there was still time.

But, most days, I know the truth.

It was already too late.

Our fates had been sealed.

"Onward, now," Conal ordered.

Dwayne was first, exploding forward like he'd been shot from a canon. I wanted to chase after, to hurry so he didn't build a lead on me, but I didn't want to leave Stooge behind. I grabbed at his shirt and gave it a tug.

"Come on," I said.

With a weary sigh, he joined me and stepped into the maze.

CHAPTER TWENTY-EIGHT

In under a minute, I'd lost sight of Dwayne. In under five, I could no longer hear his forward motion. My only hope was him getting turned around and lost somewhere before the exit, which seemed possible albeit unlikely. I had to play the tortoise role, which was good because Stooge lumbered along behind me, already gassed out and disinterested.

"Let Dwayne take the win on this one. It might improve his mood," he said. His feet barely left the ground, shuffling along. He shoved his sweat-slicked bangs off his forehead, eyes pinched shut in pain and exhaustion.

I didn't want Dwayne to win, though. "We'll take our time. You know how he gets, all laser-focused. He's probably made half a dozen wrong turns already." I tried to sound encouraging but had a hard time convincing myself.

"If you say so."

His heavy feet plodded on.

A few minutes later, we hit a dead end and had to backtrack for what felt like forever. The night air was full of bugs buzzing into our ears and committing hara-kiri in our eyes.

Their incessant attacks slowed us even further and added an extra layer of annoyance.

"You never said physical labor was going to be involved tonight," Stooge said. "I feel misled."

"Think of all the calories you're burning off."

"Yeah, because I'm so worried about my svelte figure."

"Are you having fun, though?" I asked.

He grunted out a laugh. "I was, until this maze from hell."

"It's not so bad," I lied. The sugar high I'd been riding was wearing off fast.

"Yeah, it is," Stooge said.

Another five minutes passed in silence. All was going well until we hit yet another wall of cornstalks blocking the way. They were the last straw for Stooge. "I'm done-zo, little dude. Let's head back and see what's for dessert."

His tone made it clear there was no changing his mind, but I had to give it a try. "We might be close to the end."

"We're not, and you know we're not." He had already turned around and was retracing our steps to the entrance. "Come with me. We'll go hang out with Nora and eat 'til we puke. Dwayne probably already finished anyway."

He was right. There were better ways to spend Halloween than walking in circles. Besides, Dwayne was clearly stronger and more athletic. His winning was expected. It was the natural order of life. Why was I fighting so hard against the inevitable?

Stooge glanced back at me, his brows upraised in a *what are you waiting for* look.

I knew I should follow him but couldn't force my feet to retreat. I wanted revenge on Dwayne for joining the baseball team, for wanting to be cool, for choosing other friends over me. For becoming Kit. I resented his growing up and changing. And for moving on without me.

"You go ahead," I said to Stooge. "Tell Nora I'll be back soon."

He gave his head a sad shake, then obeyed. "Your choice."

I turned back into the maze and continued on.

ANOTHER HALF-HOUR HAD PASSED AND, without Stooge slowing me down, I'd covered considerable ground. I only hit one dead end and corrected the mistake with a minor detour. The longer it went, the more convinced I became that I might have a chance at passing Dwayne. Maybe even beating him. I'm a little ashamed to admit how sweet the thought of victory tasted.

A breeze carried smoke from the bonfire into the maze and it drifted in like a dense fog. My eyes burned and watered, but on the plus side, the smoke chased off the bugs. It cut visibility by more than half, and I couldn't see more than a few yards in front of my nose. But I refused to slow down.

I guess I was in what athletes call *the zone* as I zigged and zagged. Every time I was faced with choosing between a left or a right, I chose correctly.

"Goddamn it!"

It was Dwayne's voice, somewhere to the east. He was close but not so close that I'd run into him any time soon. From his tone, I could tell he'd made a wrong turn.

If I had a chance at winning, this was it.

I doubled my pace, blindly rushing forward. The path had tapered further, and my slender shoulders brushed brittle leaf blades as I passed by them. Between the fog and the increasingly narrow trail, I began to wonder if I was completely off course. Only then did I slow, trying to regain my bearings and ensure I wasn't hopelessly lost.

I checked behind myself, squinting, then tried to peer ahead. I was on the path, I was certain, and I broke into a slow jog, continuing forward when--

An ear-splitting shriek rang out.

It was nearby, and I froze in place, one foot hanging in mid-air, statuesque.

A fraction of a second later came an inhuman scream, so mournful it made the hair on my arms stand up.

Countless nights spent in the treehouse had educated me on the harsh sounds of the forest. I told myself, assured myself, an owl had snatched a rabbit. I listened, waiting to see if any more noise followed. None did.

I realized I'd been holding my breath and let it out in a long whoosh. Then I shook my head for being so easily spooked. "Stupid," I muttered to myself and continued forward.

I didn't make it ten more yards before I heard footsteps behind me. Dwayne was on my heels, and I sighed with frustration. If I'd had a lead, had a chance at beating him, it was over. I'd never best him in a sprint, and I tried to not let my annoyance show as I turned back to greet him.

"I thought you were--"

No one was there.

I took a few steps in that direction, trying to see through the smoke, certain that Dwayne's smug face would appear like a phantasm in the fog. But there was nothing to see.

Nothing isn't quite right, though. *No one* is more accurate. Because I did see something. Movement. A wide, dark shape drifted around a corner.

"Stooge?"

My voice didn't carry. Maybe it was the smoke that seemed denser than ever before, or maybe it was the heaviness of the night air, but the name came out of my mouth and fell to my feet.

"Stooge?" I tried again, louder.

No response.

The effects of the cider still lingered, and I blinked repeatedly, trying to clear both my vision and my thoughts. It only half worked.

The path behind me was empty, so I turned back and continued on. I made it around three turns, then chose right when I should have picked left and hit a blockade of corn. Maybe it even was the same dead-end that had caused Dwayne's frustrated shout a few minutes earlier.

I backed to the intersection and chose the opposite route, shifting gears into a brisk jog.

Footsteps.

I spun around so fast that whoever was following me would have no chance to hide. I was going to catch the jerk this time.

But I didn't find Dwayne or Stooge. What I found, lurking in the fog like a ghost ship coming to port, was a bull.

Bull is too simplistic, but it was the only way I could think of it at the time. The creature was not like the animals which grazed in farmers' fields back in Sallow Creek. This monstrosity had the features and head of a bull but far too many horns.

A pair of them jutted from the side of its head, then they curved downward in long, swooping arcs. Think of a Texas longhorn steer, but these horns curled inward, below its jaw, framing its garish face.

There were more protrusions from its skull, but they weren't bovine horns. They were antlers, bigger than a buck's. Long and jagged with more points than I could count. The animal, if you could call it that, had shaggy brown fur and opaque, dead eyes. Those eyes seemed both blind and all-seeing and they were directed at me.

Overall, the thing stood as tall as the corn, which must have been seven, maybe eight feet high. Its antlers extended above the tassels, glinting in the night. But, perhaps most strangely of all, was the beast's body. I couldn't make out details in the smoke, but I could see the color.

It was blue.

I was certain this was the creature that had been stalking us - me - on the trail into Carrick Glynn. Even though I hadn't caught more than a few glimpses of it then, I just knew. And here it was again, following me. Hunting me.

When the creature moved forward, its legion of antlers collided with the cornstalks, sending them tumbling sideways and widening the path by force. It came slowly at first, one step, another, another. Gradually increasing its pace. Charging at me.

The steady *chuff, chuff* of its breathing was only overpowered by its footfalls, which I swear shook the ground. It took me a long moment to snap out of my shock.

Run.

At first, I thought someone had said the word to me. Then I realized it was my own voice inside my head, telling me what I needed to do if I wanted to stay alive.

So, I listened to that voice and ran.

CHAPTER TWENTY-NINE

In my frantic, mad dash, I gave little concern to where I was going. In seconds, I was off the path, pushing through tight rows of dead corn. The crisp, hard leaves sliced into my skin, giving me papercuts from hell as stalks battered my body.

The beast charged after me, its feet setting off low-grade earthquakes every time they hit the ground. The faster I ran, the faster it ran.

But it was gaining on me. I sensed it.

I risked a look back, making the cardinal mistake you're always told to never commit, and immediately regretted it. The creature had halved the distance between us and was no more than fifteen feet back. Steam erupted from its nostrils with each chuffing breath, intermixing with the smoke and becoming one with it.

I faked like I was going to make a hard right, hoping to throw the bull off, then dove to the left. A thick cornstalk, rigid as a steel rod, smacked into my nose. The ensuing crunch as my septal cartilage snapped rattled my teeth. Blood burst from both nostrils, raining down my neck and chest. The blood, so hot against the cold night, gave me chills.

The pain had a dizzying effect. Coupled with being drunk for the first time, remaining upright was one hell of a challenge.

Running, even moving, became impossible. I stumbled, dropping to a knee, and watched as crimson rain fell from my face and puddled in the dry earth below. It was fascinatingly ghoulish, the kind of thing I loved to watch unfold on TV while I ate popcorn and laughed at the poor hero's plight.

But I could find no humor now. Between the pain surging in my face and the charging creature growing ever nearer, all I could think about was screaming.

So, I did.

I tried to form the sounds into words. To make the guttural, primal noise emerging from my mouth into something coherent, but I failed at even that simple task.

My high-pitched wails acted like a beacon. Any chance I had of remaining unfound was gone.

The beast was upon me, the heat from its body rolling over me. A rancid, unclean smell rode along, an odor like the dumpster of a seafood restaurant at high noon during the throes of an August heatwave.

I pushed my hands into the ground, muddy with my own blood, and forced myself to my feet. All I could focus on was my deep need to be away from the thing. Away from its stench, its warmth. Grabbing a cornstalk to steady myself, I made my feet move, shuffling at first, then actual steps.

Forcing my weary legs into action, I plunged deeper into the densest part of the maze, using a forearm to shield my face and eyes. I ran blindly but fast, spurred forward by the steady crushing noise of the horned beast chasing after me.

My forward momentum suddenly became unimpeded, and I risked lowering my arm for a good look. I was back on a path, one at least as wide as the entrance. The glow of the bonfire was so bright I had to squint as my eyes adjusted.

I was at the exit, the finish line. I was yards away from freedom.

The creature was still chasing after, but knowing I was almost out sent a surge of adrenaline through me, and I dashed ahead. Using a fourteen-year-old's logic, I believed the monster couldn't get me once I was out of the maze. In my head, it had become the minotaur trapped in the labyrinth for eternity, only permitted to attack those within its domain.

Ten feet.

Five.

I half ran, half fell through the exit, breaking free of the maze and into the wide open field that looked down on the village of Carrick Glynn. Collapsing in a heap, sucking in breath after breath, I tried to collect myself.

In the distance, I could see ant-sized humans gathered in the pasture where the feast had taken place. The urge to laugh - laugh like an insane person - welled up inside me as tears simultaneously welled in my eyes.

I was out. I was safe.

Glancing back into the maze, I expected to see the bull lurking in the passage, glaring at me, snorting in frustration.

But the maze was empty.

I wiped at my eyes with the back of my hand, accidentally brushing my broken nose and sending a flare of misery through my face. Was I so drunk I'd imagined the monster? It seemed the only rational explanation.

With great effort, I again pushed myself to my feet, swaying like a greenhorn fisherman who hadn't yet got his sea legs. I made a loping circle, looking for my friends, for Conal. Even the mute twins would have been a welcome sight.

But I was alone.

"Stooge?" I called but got no answer. "Dwayne?" Again, nothing.

I didn't want to spend another moment on the hillside, so I shuffled toward the village, hoping my friends were already there. I no longer cared about the dessert or any other Halloween-related activities the town had planned.

All I wanted was to go home.

Before I had covered twenty feet, heavy footsteps rushed me from behind. I turned, fully expecting to find the beast had escaped the labyrinth after all and was coming to settle the score.

Too tired to run, all I could do was stand there and accept my fate.

Instead of the bull, I found Seamus sprinting toward me. His face was as blank and expressionless as ever, but his eyes had purpose.

Because I was too tired, too drunk, too stupid - or all three - I didn't even consider I might be in danger. My exhausted eyes fell shut. Then everything went black.

CHAPTER THIRTY

The darkness smelled like old dirt and putrefied potatoes.

Two strong arms carried me through the night, but I had no clue where they were taking me as I couldn't see a thing. My closed eyes were sealed shut by the sticky blood blanketing my face.

I squeezed my eyes closed, then tried to force them open. Squeezed and forced. Squeezed and forced.

On the fourth or fifth try, my lids separated with a slow pop, but I was still locked in the darkness.

It wasn't quite as dark, though. Pinpricks of light shone through the blackness like stars from a distant galaxy. When I turned my head to get a better look, rough fabric brushed against my skin, and I realized my head was covered by a sack.

Whoever was carrying me dropped me hard to the ground, and my body cried in protest. I tried to roll into a sitting position, but all I could do was rock to and fro like a turtle on its back, helpless and at the mercy of whoever was around.

"Easy now." It was Conal's voice.

As I strained to listen, I heard other voices too. Murmurs and whispers drifting in from the distance. Somehow, even though the stench that filled my nostrils, I was able to discern the smell of the feast.

I was back at the pasture.

"Why do you got a bag on the boy's head?" Conal asked.

"Dunno," came the response from an unfamiliar voice.

A hand grabbed the sack covering my head, pulling it off with gentle care. Conal loomed over me, peering down with a bemused expression.

"Bloody hell." He looked away from me. I followed his gaze and saw Seamus standing nearby, digging one booted toe into the ground and not looking back. "What have you done to the poor lad?" Conal asked.

Seamus suddenly possessed the ability to speak. "He passed out."

"I told you to be easy on him. Look at the poor little fellow." Conal grabbed me by the shoulders and sat me upright. He squatted, aligning his face with my own, and he shook his head in annoyance. "I'm sorry, young Benjamin. Wasn't supposed to go like this."

I opened my mouth to respond but couldn't think of anything to say. My eyes darted around the clearing and found Nora. She stood amongst the others, staring at me wide-eyed. I tried to connect with her telepathically, to ask her what was going on and to beg her to stop it from getting worse. But she only stood there and stared back. My attempts to read her expression failed.

Conal put his hands under my arms and raised me to my feet. The sudden rush of blood to my head made me woozy, and I would have fallen if the old man hadn't been holding on. But he was, and he supported me with fatherly care.

He steered me to the wooden barrels where I'd bobbed for

apples earlier that night. With a gentle push on my shoulders, he directed me into a kneeling position, then he leaned me over the water and dipped my face into it.

The cold stole my breath, but it was also a welcome feeling as it comforted my many wounds and bruises. Conal's gnarled fingers swished through the liquid, then caressed my face, washing it clean.

His hands, so rough and calloused, were surprisingly gentle, and although I was still in pain, it felt like I was being tended to by a friend. After he apparently deemed me clean enough, he lifted me again and carried me to a wooden bench that sat beside a large chunk of granite. The stone looked like some type of low monument, the kind you'd see in a park with names engraved, or maybe an uplifting quote.

Conal slicked back my hair and examined me again. He frowned, shook his head, and looked toward Seamus once more. "For the love of Mike, what did you do to his nose?"

Seamus shook his head. "That wasn't me."

Conal looked in a different direction, and my eyes again followed his gaze. There, on the far end of the clearing, I saw the bull.

I gasped and tried to get up, to run, but Conal had his hands on my shoulders, pinning me firmly in place.

"Be still," he said. "You got nothing to be a'feared of."

I started to tell him he was a damned liar but only got out a muffled grunt before the bull spoke.

"I didn't touch him. The boy did that to himself," the bull said.

Squirming in my seat but unable to escape, I watched this all go down with a sort of bewildered, paranoid terror. How was Conal telling me there was nothing to fear when the minotaur was here, free from its prison? And... talking?

My eyes, still adjusting to the light, came more into focus as

I stared at the animal. Then reality arrived in one abrupt, jarring flash.

It wasn't a monster at all. It was a man.

Ewan, the other twin. Atop his head, he wore a gory and very real head of a bull. All that was missing was the lower jaw which had been ripped away, leaving long tendrils of flesh swaying in the wind.

Antlers had been poked through the bull's hide at wanton angles, and the eyes had gone cloudy in death. Below the mask, Ewan's own eyes were mostly hidden by the hanging fur, but the bottom part of his face was visible. His face, like the skin of his neck and bare torso, had been painted blue. Cowhide hung across his back and covered his shoulders. From the waist down, he was all man, still clad in his trousers and boots.

"Don't know what I'm going to do with you," Conal said to Ewan, his voice full of contempt.

Ewan pulled the mask off of his head and held it in the crook of his arm. His hair was drenched with sweat, and he stared at the ground, ashamed.

Conal turned back to me and looked into my eyes. He raised a hand to my face. "I'm afraid this might be uncomfortable, but it needs done."

Before I could react, his thumb and index finger pinched my broken nose. In one quick, practiced motion, he snapped it sideways, sending an electric jolt of pain through my skull.

My field of vision flared white, obscuring everything, everyone.

"There you go. Right as rain." Conal patted my shoulder.

Gradually, my sight returned to normal, and I could see again. Everyone from the village had gathered around, forming a near-perfect circle around the stone slab. To my left was Conal, looking down on me with a wizened smile. I noticed

Nora in the throng, but she wasn't who I needed to find. I kept looking, searching, then I finally saw who I was looking for.

Stooge and Dwayne were both unharmed. I stood, fighting back a moment of dizziness, and moved toward them. I expected someone to stop me, to grab me and tie me up, or maybe throw another sack over my head, but it didn't happen. I was free to move as I pleased.

"Dude, what happened to your face? You look like you caught a piledriver from Hulk Hogan," Stooge said.

I didn't care about answering his question. "I'm fine. I think. What happened to you at the maze?" I asked them both at the same time.

"Nothing," Stooge said. "After I left you, I worked my way back to the beginning."

Dwayne gave a nonchalant but still somehow smug shrug. "I found the exit. Then Nora's gramps brought Stooge and me back here."

"What about the minotaur?" I asked.

"What the hell are you talking about?" Dwayne asked.

I looked for Ewan in the circle, found him, and pointed. "That!"

"Oh," Dwayne said. "He jumped out at me, trying to scare me. But I just laughed and kept going."

Laughed? At the damned monster which was seconds away from killing me? I checked Stooge to see if he was buying the bravado. To my dismay, he was nodding in agreement.

"He almost fooled me for a second, but then I took a good look. When I said, 'Gnarly costume, dude,' he sulked away. Think I hurt his feelings," Stooge said.

I thought they were lying to me. How did they know it was a mask when I, the boy who lived and breathed Halloween, believed it was a Greek legend come to life?

"You didn't think it was real?"

Dwayne broke into a wide grin. "Shit no. I expected something like that. Like on the haunted hayride we went on a few years ago. They had people jumping out from everywhere. Remember the guy with the chainsaw?"

I did. And I remembered the hot, wet stain that had spread across the front of my jeans when he scared me so bad my bladder let loose.

The more I thought about it, the more I realized he was right. I should have expected it too. After all, what's Halloween without a few good scares?

But it looked so much more authentic in the maze. It moved like an animal. Smelled like one too. The man and his mask standing nearby didn't carry that same sense of dread and foreboding. How had I been so fooled? At least, I hadn't pissed myself - again. That was something, I guess.

"Friends," Conal's voice announced.

Every person in attendance looked to him, myself included.

"It's time for the offering."

Hushed murmurs passed between the villagers, but none of their words reached our ears. Despite the inability to hear what was being said, it was impossible to miss the pulse of excitement that practically hummed.

"Offering?" Stooge muttered. "Last time I heard that, the pastor at my mom's church caught me stealing a fiver out of the little silver bowl they were passing around and told me I was gonna burn in Hell."

Dwayne laughed. I wished I could join in, but I couldn't even force a chuckle.

A gritty, grinding sound of metal against rocks screeched through the night. Everyone looked in the direction of the sound. There, emerging from the darkness, were two muscled workhorses hauling a wooden sledge across the pasture.

The hushed murmurs weren't so hushed anymore. They

became high and eager with anticipation. Yet, with all of the villagers talking at once, it was still impossible to decipher their words.

But talk didn't matter because I looked past the horses and their sweat-slicked, black bodies. I ignored the sledge itself, which looked like an oversized version of the radio flyer sled I would ride down Breakneck Hill before I became old enough to know better. All I could focus on were the contents of the sledge itself.

Lying on the wooden base was what, on first glance, looked like a bloated, white worm. It was narrow at one end, fat in the middle, then tapered back down. It wasn't until the horses dragged the sledge closer to us when I realized the worm was a human being.

It was a woman, a quite old woman judging by what I could make out of her scarred face. She was wrapped in cloth, almost like the mummy in all those bad, black and white monster movies. Only, her legs and arms were all wrapped tightly together, making her unable to move anything but her head.

That head lolled from side to side, maybe on purpose, or maybe just because of the uneven terrain. She didn't look scared, which surprised me because I'd have been damned terrified if I were in her position. Her face carried a blank, almost serene expression. The circle of villagers parted and allowed the sledge to be hauled into their midst, then closed again, encapsulating it once it passed.

Confused by the goings-on, I sought out Nora, who was beside her grandfather. She didn't notice me, though. Her gaze was glued on the woman, her mouth contorted in a grimace, tears leaking from her eyes.

Conal wrapped an arm around Nora's shoulders. He leaned down and said something into her ear. She nodded and wiped at her tears with her fingers. Then Conal kissed her on the corner of the mouth. Coming from a family where physical affection was uncommon, the kiss and its placement - so close to her lips - nearly made me recoil.

Before I could waste time wondering if such a kiss was inappropriate between a grandfather and granddaughter, the sledge ground to a halt. A burly, bald man with a beard down to his belly stepped toward it and used his hulking frame to lift the wrapped woman.

He carried her to the slab of granite, which I only then noticed had a large hole in the center and inserted the woman's feet into that hole. After her feet went her calves and hips until she was propped up and only her upper body was visible.

Her distended midsection filled the cavity, keeping her mostly in place, but she swayed lazily to and fro like a cobra being charmed with a pungi. I couldn't take my eyes off her, even when I felt Dwayne's hot breath in my ear.

"What in the hell's going on?" he asked.

I had no answer and stayed silent.

The burly man then grabbed a coil of rope from the nearby ground and tied off a loop, or a lasso.

He looked to Conal as if awaiting instruction. Then Conal held up a thin hand, and the crowd went silent.

"I'm sure you all recognize our dear sister, even though it's been a year since she's been out amongst you," he said. "Few thought she'd last this long, and her survival is both a testament to her will and our bodies which the gods have blessed. And they've so blessed us because we believe! Praise the gods," his voice boomed, a thunderclap in the silent night.

"Praise them!" the villagers responded.

"She lived for us," Conal said. "Proud to make the offering for our village so that the rest of us may carry on and continue our worship for another passing year. Show her your appreciation!" Conal shouted.

The villagers rushed toward the woman, pulling small handfuls of food from their pockets and shoving them into her mouth. For the first time, she looked alert and aware, her jaws working frantically, her throat swelling and swallowing down the sustenance.

The lower half of her face became covered with smears of fruit, stains of vegetables. She couldn't consume some of the offerings quickly enough and they drained down her chin and dripped onto her cloth bounds. All the while, the villagers cheerfully offered their verbal gratitude.

Dwayne had hold of my arm, pulling me backward, away from the circle. "Dude, this is super fucked up," he said.

A few of the nearest villagers glanced our way but made no move to silence us or corral us. It was clear we could do as we pleased, and their ambivalence lulled me into a sense of security. Surely, if something bad were about to happen, we'd be restrained.

"Let's get the hell out of here!" Dwayne kept pulling at me, trying to get me away, but I was frozen in curious awe. I had to see what happened next.

Nora, holding a single piece of chocolate in her hand, was the last to approach. When the woman saw her, the feral hunger she'd displayed transformed into a look of wide-eyed confusion. They stared at one another for a long moment and the crowd fell silent.

"Go on now," Conal instructed.

Nora extended the chocolate to the woman, her hand shaking so badly she almost dropped it as she guided it to the woman's mouth and pushed it between her lips.

She spoke to the woman. I couldn't hear the actual words, but I read her lips.

Thank you for your selflessness.

Then, Nora backed - scurried - away, returning to Conal's side. He pulled her into him, protective, consoling.

"Brother Robert," Conal said, then he made a circle gesture toward the man with the rope.

The man looped the lasso around the woman's neck. She reacted not at all, not even when the man pulled the knot tight, pinning it against her throat. The hard fibers dug into her doughy flesh and contorted the skin. Once he could not tighten it any more, the man stepped away, rejoining the circle.

Over the next half-minute, the woman's face transformed from ghostly gray to blue to plum purple. She rocked back and forth, frantic. Her eyes bulged and looked ready to burst from their sockets. Her mouth fell open and her tongue, littered with partially devoured food, lolled out. Drool and saliva and traces of blood followed.

Dwayne released my arm. His running footsteps moved further and further from me, but still, I couldn't look away. Not even when Conal crouched down, picked something off the ground, and straightened. He held a long scythe, the blade rust red.

"Dude..." Stooge said. "Dude."

I sensed him too moving away from me, and I knew I should go along, but I'd seen too much to stop now. A real-life horror movie was unfolding before me, and I had to see how it would end. I couldn't miss the grand finale.

"Brothers, sisters, I give my thanks to the gods and to every last one of you for another glorious year. For another bountiful harvest. Praise be," Conal said.

With that, he swung the scythe, severing the woman's head with one clean blow. Immediately, a fountain of blood spurted from her neck, pint after pint after pint until she was empty. It shot high into the air then came down like red rain.

The villagers turned their faces up and into it, letting it

wash over them, swallowing what fell into their mouths. My horror-obsessed mind immediately went to the obvious - vampires - and I was about to start searching for a chunk of wood I could fashion into a stake when I realized they weren't drinking the blood after all.

They were bathing in it.

Most had stripped off their tops, using their hands to massage the blood into their flesh like they were lathering up with soap in the shower. The woman who I'd thought might be my mother ripped open her husband's shirt and smeared blood across his chest, her fingers becoming entangled in his wiry chest hair.

Seamus went to the dead woman and straddled her body, pushing into her, not in a sexual manner, but milking her corpse, forcing the remaining ichor from the stump of her neck. With each stream that squirted out, a villager would try to catch it and rub it across themselves or someone else. Lubed-up men and women danced and sang and frolicked like they were background talent in some macabre version of *Singing in the Rain*.

Through all this horror, I tried to find Nora to see how she was reacting to the depravity because I knew she must be as disgusted as I was. She was normal, like me. She wasn't one of these crazed savages basking in someone's blood and death. I wanted to locate her and rescue her, take her away from this madness and back to civilization. Even then, I wanted to be her hero.

But when I found her, she was covered in blood, holding hands with Conal as they sang and laughed and danced, delirious with joy, their faces masks of mad glee. Finally, I had seen enough.

Too much.

I turned and ran.

CHAPTER THIRTY-ONE

My feet flew far faster than I'd ever run in my life. This wasn't trying to earn the presidential fitness award in gym class. This was survival, and I found a deep well of athleticism I never knew I possessed. By the time I reached the village, I could see Dwayne far ahead, and I'd almost caught up to Stooge.

He heard me approaching and glanced back with terror as he must have thought the villagers were coming to collect him. When he saw it was me, a sliver of fear left his face, but most remained behind.

"Holy shitballs, dude. This place is Gonzo!" he shouted even though a normal decibel level would have sufficed.

I didn't respond. He'd summed it up pretty well. Besides, I wanted to save my breath for running.

Dwayne made it to the edge of the forest, where the path would carry him back to the rope bridge. I grabbed Stooge's hand like we were courting teenagers, and we hurried along as fast as he could move. I would have been able to pass him with ease, but there was no way I was leaving my friend behind. Not when I didn't know if the villages were coming for us.

But the further we fled from the village, the deeper we dove into the forest, I realized we weren't being followed at all. The villagers, the heathens, were probably still back at the pasture, licking up that poor woman's essence. Or maybe they were in the throes of some depraved orgy. I didn't want to think about it, couldn't think about it. I wanted to forget what I had seen. I wanted to forget this entire night.

Stooge, too, had found a level of energy I'd never seen in him before, and we managed to actually gain ground on Dwayne. We were only twenty or so yards behind. Finally, I risked using my voice.

"Dwayne," I called out.

He snapped his head back, eyes wide and disbelieving, but he stopped until we'd caught up with him. "What happened back there?" he asked.

"You don't fucking wanna know," Stooge said.

The gurgle of the river came through the woods. It wasn't far off, which meant the bride wasn't far off either. The bridge meant Milo and the car were close, and the car meant escape. That knowledge gave us all renewed vigor, and we sprinted.

This time, I wouldn't be scared of crossing the bridge or falling through. I'd seen real horror, and the made-up paranoia in my mind couldn't come close. I wouldn't even slow down as I raced across it, not caring if it swayed and undulated underneath me. I wouldn't stop moving until I was in the car, and we were speeding back to Sallow Creek. To home.

Far from the light of the lanterns, the forest was pitch black. The stars overhead did little to illuminate the trail, so we followed the sound of the rushing water, which grew louder and louder until--

"What the hell?" Dwayne asked, shouting his question, his voice full of panicked confusion.

He was standing on the edge of the ravine, and Stooge and I joined him. Looking down, the waters ran below, but there was no bridge to cross.

"Where's the bridge?" Stooge said, the obvious question.

I scanned the riverbank, up and down, certain we must have emerged from the forest at a different spot and the bridge was still there, just a few yards away. But no matter how hard I looked, I couldn't see anything.

I changed tactics, straining to see across the chasm and look for Milo's car, but it was too dark. All I could see was black woods, so dense their contents remained hidden.

"Oh shit," Dwayne muttered.

I looked for him and saw he'd moved a twenty feet up river. He was on his hands and knees, head extended over the precipice.

"What?" I asked.

He didn't answer. Didn't even look my way. Stooge and I exchanged a confused, fearful look before going to him, moving much slower now.

"What is it? What's down there."

Noise was coming from Dwayne, but it wasn't words. I'd never heard him sound like this before, and it took me far too long to realize why it seemed so strange and foreign coming from him.

Dwayne was crying. Not full-on sobs, but boyish, sniffling hitches. It didn't come across as sad as much as it sounded defeated.

We'd reached his side and followed his gaze. Sprawled on the rocks below was Milo, or what was left of him. His body was twisted and broken, his head smashed in against a large boulder. His face was a jumble of black blood and white bone, so destroyed and foreign-looking it wasn't even scary, just shocking. It was the kind of carnage left behind by real violence, not the glorified movie version.

Remnants of the bridge were strewn across Milo. More of it, planks and rope, led into the waters before disappearing in their depths.

"We're all gonna die," Dwayne said between sniffles.

I tore my eyes away from Milo's corpse. Dwayne was sitting on the ground, holding his knees as he rocked back and forth. A streamer of snot hung from his nose and connected with his chin. He made no efforts to wipe it away. I'd never seen a person in shock before, but assumed it looked like this.

I dropped my hand onto his shoulder, trying to be strong and consoling. He flinched. "We'll follow the river," I told him. "There has to be another way across somewhere."

"There isn't. You know there isn't. No other bridge. No road. Nora said so, remember?"

"Nora said a lot of things that apparently weren't true," I said. Saying her name made me remember our kiss, which in turn brought the vision of her and Conal dancing in the storm of blood back into my mind. A bitter jet of bile rose up my gullet and into my mouth. I spat it into the dirt. "We'll find a way across," I promised.

I hoped my words would console him, but they had the opposite effect as he jumped to his feet, knocking my arm away. If he'd been in shock, he snapped out of it in an instant.

"This is your fault!" he screamed. The streamer of snot still connected his nostril and chin and it thrummed like a guitar string as his voice passed through it.

I tried to come up with something to say, a way to defuse the tension that was a lit fuse on a powder keg. Before I could, he swung at me. Dwayne's fist connected with my already broken nose, snapping it out of place once more.

I was already somewhat numb to the pain, and his blow barely had an effect. I didn't even bleed.

"Why'd you have to bring us here?" Dwayne shouted, then didn't wait for an answer before continuing his tirade. "Milo's dead because of you! We'll all be dead before the night's over!"

He rushed me in a tackle, slamming his shoulder into my chest. Momentum carried me backward and to the ground and he landed on top of me. There was no time to react before Dwayne began slamming his fists into my face and torso. One connected with my throat and left me choking and wheezing for breath.

Then, Dwayne floated up and off me like he was being raptured. Through my bleary vision, I saw Stooge pulling him away, then dropping him to the ground.

"Knock it off, dude," Stooge said. "This isn't the time."

Dwayne tried to come at me again, but Stooge remained between us, playing referee to two weary pugilists.

I had no will to fight back, though. I deserved a beating. I deserved whatever verbal abuse Dwayne could hurl my way.

He was right, after all. They were only stuck in this nightmare because I'd insisted on going trick or treating. Without my grand plan, we'd be back home, probably watching movies in the treehouse where the only scares were on TV.

"Don't stick up for him!" Dwayne shouted at Stooge. "He dragged us out here, and why? Just so he could keep being an immature, little asshole who's scared to grow up?" He glared at me, so angry his nostrils flared. "I'm sick of your shit, Benji! I hate you!"

He suddenly dove past Stooge and raced toward me, but Stooge scooped him up in a bear hug, raising his feet off the ground and holding tight. Dwayne squirmed and struggled and kicked, but even though he was the athlete in our trio, he was no match for Stooge's heft. After more than a minute, Dwayne tired himself out and stopped struggling.

"Are you done now?" Stooge asked.

Dwayne nodded.

"Use your words," Stooge said. "If I let you go, will you stop being a prick?"

Dwayne nodded again, then added, "Sure."

Stooge held fast a moment longer as if playing a human lie detector, then seemed satisfied. He set Dwayne down, and I was sure he was going to deke past Stooge and renew his attack, but he remained where he'd been planted.

Without taking his eyes off Dwayne, Stooge reached out and extended a hand to me. I grabbed onto it with both of my own, and he hauled me to my feet.

All three of us remained quiet for a long while. By the time we felt like talking, there wasn't much left to say. I moved to the embankment leading to the river below, dropping onto my butt and scooting to the edge.

"What are you doing?" Stooge asked.

"I'll check and see how deep the water is. Maybe we can wade across." I had little hope the brainstorm would work, but it was all I'd come up with.

"No way, dude," Stooge said. "That ain't Sallow Creek down there. It'd wash you away before you made it two steps."

"Let me try. I owe you guys that much."

Stooge looked to Dwayne as if expecting him to toss in some sage wisdom to make me change my mind, but Dwayne kept his mouth shut. From the look in his eyes, I suspected he wouldn't shed a tear if Stooge was right, and I was swept downstream and smashed against boulders.

I hadn't made it more than a few feet down the riverbank when--

"I wouldn't try that if I were you," a man's voice said.

The burly villager who'd put the rope around the woman's neck stood at the end of the path. He held a wooden crossbow. A bolt was already loaded.

"That water's near freezing. If the current don't get ya, the cold will," he said.

"Then what do you suggest?" Stooge asked him.

"I say you come with me before this gets needlessly messy." In case we didn't know what *messy* meant, he shouldered the crossbow and aimed it in our general direction.

"Let us go, and we won't tell anyone what happened or what we saw." I spoke the words knowing they were cliched and pointless. The bad guys never let you go.

Brother Robert smiled, revealing a hole where his two front teeth had once been. His tongue poked through the gap like a ground mole sticking its head out of a tunnel to see if the coast was clear. "Oh, I know you won't say nothin'," he said. "Because you're coming with me. The celebration isn't over yet, and Conal requests your presence."

I held up my hands. "Please. Don't do this."

"You come here right now, and you're right, I don't got to do anything untoward."

None of us moved to join him, so the man aimed the bow at Dwayne, then he pointed it at Stooge, then me. He kept directing it back and forth, pausing for just a moment over each of us.

"Take him," Dwayne said, giving me a hard shove in the back. I stumbled forward, closer to Brother Robert and his crossbow. "Let me and Stooge go and take Benji back with you."

I heard a hard smack, skin against skin. Dwayne held his face, a red welt already rising on his cheek. Stooge's palm was upraised, ready to strike again if Dwayne said another word.

It wasn't a wholly bad idea, though. In fact, from where I

stood, it was the only idea worth considering. "I'll go," I said to the man. "I won't fight. I'll do whatever you want if you let my friends go home."

I took a step toward him, willing to accept my fate, whatever it might be.

The man shook his head. "Can't do that. You three are a package deal. Come along now. No sense drawin' out the inevitable."

It was a stalemate, but he had the upper hand, and he knew it.

"Have it your way then," he said.

He aimed the bow at me. "Eina."

At Stooge. "Mina."

At Dwayne. "Pera."

At me. "Peppera."

He kept the crossbow aimed at my chest. "Last chance," he said.

We held our ground.

He bit his lip and shook his bald head. "Pinn."

I closed my eyes as he squeezed the trigger.

CHAPTER THIRTY-TWO

I stood frozen in place, waiting for the impact of the bolt. When it never came, I thought maybe I'd been hit and didn't realize it. I'd once read that most gunshot victims didn't even realize they'd been shot until they saw the blood.

Needing to know, I opened my eyes and looked down, examining my body. There was no arrow jutting from my chest. No hole oozing blood.

I looked to Robert, assuming he'd been bluffing and hadn't shot after all. He still held the crossbow, now at his side. There was no bolt loaded.

Wheezing groans emanated from behind me. I spun around, first seeing Dwayne, who stared slack jawed. Then I followed his eyes and found Stooge, and what I found made me wish I was dead.

The bolt had plunged deep into his chest, dead center on the Judas Priest logo emblazoned on his t-shirt. The black shirt had somehow gone an even deeper shade of black around the arrow, and the stain kept growing.

Somehow, Stooge was still on his feet, albeit swaying back

and forth. With one of his big hands, he grabbed the exposed shaft of the bolt and closed his fingers around it. He gave it a tug, but it didn't budge.

Stooge looked at me and opened his mouth. Blood spilled through his lips as he said, "I think I'm dyin', Benji."

He dropped in a heap, crashing down onto his side. I dashed to him, using my meager strength to roll him onto his back so he wouldn't fall onto the arrow and sink it in deeper. As I covered his wound with my hands, hot blood pumped out and oozed between my fingers. Within seconds, both my hands were stained red.

I'd started crying - sobbing - without realizing or caring. My tears fell onto Stooge's face, and he somehow managed a grin. "You're making Uncle Stoogie all wet."

The joke only made me cry harder. My chest heaved in hitching sobs, and I tried to distract myself by pushing harder against his wound even though I knew it was pointless. "You'll be fine," I said.

"You always were a shitty liar, little dude." Stooge stared up at me, his eyes already going unfocused. He reached up and cupped my cheek with his bloody hand, streaking warpaint across my face. "Stop cryin'," he ordered.

I tried but only partially succeeded. I gave up on covering his wound and grabbed onto his palm, squeezing so hard the bones in his hand shifted and repositioned. "I'm so sorry, Stooge. I'm so sorry I brought you here. Oh, shit. Oh, fucking shit. I'm so sorry."

His fingers closed around mine. "I like it when you cuss. Makes you sound like a man."

"I'll say whatever the hell you want me to say if you just promise me, you'll be okay."

His head shook side to side. "Nope. It's you who's got to make me a promise."

"Anything," I said.

"You take care of Lowboy for me." He coughed, spitting up a half-pint of blood. It ran down both sides of his face, giving him a Glasgow smile. "Janey pulls his tail because she's a little bitch. He doesn't like that. Promise you won't let her be mean to him."

I nodded. My throat was on fire, and it was too hard to speak.

"Say it," he said, his voice quieter. Fading.

"I promise to watch out for Lowboy."

His eyes fluttered, went shut, then opened again but only a fraction of an inch. "Good."

Stooge then looked to Dwayne, who lurked a few yards away. He was crying too. His arms were crossed over his chest as he embraced himself and tried to keep his shit together.

"And you," Stooge said to him.

Dwayne remained where he stood, but he met Stooge's gaze.

"Stop being an asshole," Stooge ordered him. "Benji di--" He coughed up more blood. His face suddenly looked as white as a catfish's belly. "Benji didn't do anything wrong. He just wanted us to be together on Halloween…"

Dwayne nodded without looking at me, but I wasn't offended. He looked as broken as I felt.

"Because we're friends," Stooge finished. The last word was nothing more than a whisper.

I wanted to say something back to Stooge. To tell him what a great friend he was. To tell him I loved him even though boys our age never said such things. I wanted to tell him so many things.

Before I could, the life went out of his eyes and out of his body. I fell onto him, pulling myself into him, not wanting to ever let go.

"I regret it had to come to that," Brother Robert said from behind me.

I didn't want to look. I wanted to hold onto Stooge until he went cold and stiff. Hell, I wanted to die right there beside him. But I still had one friend left, and it was his voice that drew me out of my grief-stricken fugue.

"Benji," Dwayne said, his voice raspy.

I turned toward him and saw the crossbow had been reloaded, and a new bolt was pressed against Dwayne's neck. A thin red line of blood trickled down, ending against the hemmed neckline of his baseball jersey.

Brother Robert's finger was curled around the trigger of the crossbow. "Time to get going," he said.

CHAPTER THIRTY-THREE

When we retreated to the pasture, the woman's body was gone, as was the sledge which had hauled her in. All of the villagers were seated at the dining tables, feasting on dessert and chatting amongst themselves as if nothing amiss had occurred. Many were still partially nude, and all of them were stained red with blood and gore.

As Dwayne and I trudged in, side by side, they barely glanced our way. Robert was at our backs, crossbow loaded and ready to fire if we tried anything. Only Conal paid attention to our return, rising from his seat beside Nora and tipping the hat he wasn't wearing.

"Well done, Brother Robert. We saved you some essence." Conal motioned to a pail filled with blood so dark it looked black.

The man steered us to Conal's table, where there were three empty seats. He pushed us toward them, and Dwayne and I both sat.

Conal looked at the empty seat, then to Robert, one eyebrow raised high.

"It was necessary to show them I was serious," the man said.

Conal's mouth turned downward in a scowl, and his eyes flared, but he recovered in short order. "I trust your judgment." He left his seat and went to two large men who were in the midst of devouring an entire pumpkin pie between them. After Conal leaned in and spoke to them, the men rose and left the clearing.

I stared at Nora. Her hair was saturated with blood, no longer that lovely shade of orange fire, instead the deep red of dried scabs. She was busy cutting a slice of cake into bite-sized pieces and doing her best to pretend she didn't know I was watching her.

"I trusted you," I said to her.

She flinched, her knife slipping and skittering across the plate, but she didn't look up.

"That asshole killed Stooge!" My voice, hoarse from sobbing, cracked.

Nora poked a chunk of cake with a fork, bringing it to her mouth. Only then did she acknowledge my presence. "You should eat, Benji. You'll need your strength." She shoved the cake in her mouth and chewed.

A grape-sized clot of blood was nestled in her ear. I wanted to grab a knife, reach across the table, and skewer it. Then I'd keep pushing, ramming the blade into her brain.

Instead of striking out in violence, I said, "I thought you were our friend."

Nora swallowed down the cake, then used a cloth napkin to blot at her mouth. As if a few crumbs were a problem when her entire face was painted red. "I was. I am." She shook her head. "You can't understand."

"Then explain it to me!"

She opened her mouth, ready to say something, when

Conal returned and reclaimed his seat. He looked us over, then at the barren dishes before us. "Empty plates are not permitted. Please, eat, my young friends. There's plenty to go around."

Villagers seated at the table began offering dishes to us like this was Thanksgiving dinner, and I'd asked them to pass the potatoes and corn. I didn't accept any of them, and they all sat there, holding the plates and trays mid-air.

"You're being ungrateful," Nora said, eyes cast downward.

"Ungrateful! Are you insane?" I shouted. The revelry which had been boisterous and carefree faded as everyone gawked at me. To get my point across, I slammed my fist into my empty plate, shattering the ceramic into a dozen pieces. One of them cut my palm, but I didn't care. If anything, the pain helped me focus.

"What's wrong with you people?" I asked anyone who would listen. "My friend was just murdered, and he never hurt anyone in his entire life."

"Calm yourself," Conal said. He reached across the table, grabbing at my wrist, but I was quicker and avoided his grasp. I snatched one of the chunks of ceramic, holding it like a dagger, and lunged at him.

My makeshift blade embedded itself in Conal's forearm, deep enough to hit the bone, then snapped off in my hand. Nora lunged in front of her grandfather, protective, eyes blazing as she glared at me.

"Don't you touch him!" she ordered.

I was scrambling for another piece, another weapon, but strong arms grabbed me from behind, holding me at bay. A few of the other bloodstained villagers had risen to their feet during the commotion, ready to beat me to a pulp for the offense I'd committed.

"Easy now, all of you," Conal said, and the villagers backed down, returning to where they'd been seated. Whoever had been holding me let go.

Conal used his slender fingers to dig into the wound I'd given him and pluck out the piece of plate embedded in his arm. Once finished, he set it aside and wiped his fingers clean on his trousers. "Lads, I understand this is all a bit mysterious to you. I'll explain when the time is right, but that time isn't now. Won't you please enjoy the meal for the time being?"

A man, with a mole the size of an acorn clinging to his upper lip, offered Dwayne and me a tray of white candies. Dwayne claimed one and took a bite no bigger than a nibble. I folded my arms, petulant.

Conal examined me, his old, nearly colorless eyes clinical. I almost melted under that gaze but refused to break eye contact and waited until he looked away first.

After he did, I turned to Dwayne, who was still chewing the not even bite-sized piece of candy in his mouth, his jaw shifting side to side like a cow enjoying an afternoon snack of cud. I noticed the watch still on his wrist and was hit with an idea so damned great it bordered on brilliant. "What time is it?"

Dwayne looked at me, confused, like I'd just spoken to him in a foreign language. Then I tapped my wrist, and he understood.

He checked his watch. "Twenty till twelve?" It came out like a question, and I wasn't sure if he had forgotten how to tell time or if he was simply confused by why it mattered.

I went with it, turning to Conal. "It'll be midnight soon. Then you can't hurt us."

"Is that so?" Conal asked.

I nodded.

"And what brings you to that conclusion?"

I gave my best impression of a smile, smug for no good reason. "Because Halloween ends at midnight. And whatever screwed-up rituals you freaks practice to mark the holiday will be over."

It made perfect sense to my fourteen-year-old mind. The mind that had consumed hundreds of scary movies and read almost as many horror novels. Regardless of the situation, no matter what the monster, there were rules to follow and no exceptions.

Conal seemed to consider this and, the longer he stayed silent, the more convinced I became I was right. Then, he broke into a wide, leering grin, and any smile I'd managed to hold vanished.

"Oh, sweet, innocent boy." He reached across the table and put his wounded hand, which was still leaking plasma, on my forearm. His skin was cold and moist. "Perhaps your assumption would hold true if we celebrated Halloween, but we do not." He looked to Nora, a smile tugging at her lips, then to his friends and neighbors, his people.

Their faces, caked with dried blood, were amused and knowing, as if they all had heard the punchline to a joke being told and knew it was a doozy.

I had a feeling that I was the punchline. Defeated, I slumped back into my seat. Any moxie I'd mustered was gone.

"Halloween," Conal spat the word like it was unclean, "is something the Americans use to sell candy bars and mass-produced plastic masks. Halloween is a perversion of the true holiday - holy day." Conal leaned in so close I could smell the stale, metallic aroma of blood wafting off his flesh. "In Carrick Glynn, we celebrate Samhain!" Conal shouted.

The villagers pounded the tables with their fists, rattling the dishes and plates and food. Even the ground seemed to shake, thrumming with frenetic excitement.

Conal leaned across the table, getting in close so I could

hear him over the racket. "Tell me, Benjamin, was tonight everything you hoped it to be?" he asked.

I didn't, couldn't, answer. I'd been right about one thing. I was the butt of the joke.

Conal went on, addressing the villagers. "It seems our guests have lost their appetites. Brother Andrew, Brother Jonathan, please take them to the stables."

As two men came for us, Conal spoke directly to us. "I suggest you get a good night's sleep. The morrow shall be quite eventful."

CHAPTER THIRTY-FOUR

Dwayne and I shared a stall next to corrals holding the huge draught horses which had hauled the sledge. They'd snorted and stomped about upon our arrival, but after a while, they'd grown bored of our presence and comfortable enough to unleash noxious-smelling clumps of manure every half hour or so.

We hadn't spoken, either to one another, ourselves, or even the horses, since the men had locked us in the stall. Dwayne had dozed once. Not for long, just enough to start snoring, and then he woke himself. He'd glanced at me and looked like he was trying to decide whether to be embarrassed or angry. When I didn't acknowledge him, he tucked his head again and closed his eyes.

I don't think he'd slept since, though. No snoring, for one, but his breathing occasionally quickened, the way it does when your nerves take hold of you. After a few minutes, he'd settle back down, but the panic kept coming back.

As the hours passed, I waffled between boredom, fear, and a crushing grief which made my insides hurt. Even my mother's disappearance hadn't caused an actual physical pain like what I was enduring now. When it came to my mom, I could tell myself she was alive and healthy, and I'd see her again someday.

For the first time, I was experiencing genuine, honest to God heartbreak, and I could barely handle it. Knowing Stooge was gone forever caused an ache so severe I couldn't even contemplate sleep, although I longed to. I curled up in the corner and closed my eyes, hoping to go unconscious so I could forget.

Forget about everything.

The cold and the grief kept me awake. I buried my hands in my armpits, trying to make myself into a small, tight ball to conserve what little heat still remained in my body. Every breath left me in a cloud of fog. I longed for my hoodie, but then again, I longed for many things I'd never see again.

"Are you awake?" Dwayne asked.

His voice startled me, and I jumped a good two inches off the floor. What surprised me even more was the ensuing chuckle.

"Guess you are now," he said.

I scooted on my butt, rough hay scratching at my backside, and swiveled toward him. "Can't sleep."

"Me neither," he said, and I didn't bother to correct him. If there was any hope of making peace, I didn't want to blow it.

Dwayne sat up, brushing dirt and mold and dried animal waste from the side on which he'd been laying. He bent his knees at ninety-degree angles and rested his long, gangly arms over them. "What are they going to do to us?"

I shrugged, shocked to learn my opinion meant anything to him. "No clue."

"You never read anything like this in all those books?"

"No. I wish I could say I did, but no."

He sighed, annoyed. "What about that holiday the old bastard said they celebrate? What was it? Sow when?"

His pronunciation wasn't bad. "Samhain's like a precursor to Halloween. The Druids celebrated it. But that's all I know."

"Is that what these people are? Druids?"

Another shrug. My horror encyclopedia brain wasn't of much use when it mattered.

"Do you think they're, like, witches?"

I'd wondered something similar but gave it more serious consideration after his query.

"No. Not the *Double, double, toil, and trouble* kind anyway. I think they're regular people. Vicious, crazy people, and I guess you could call them a cult, but they don't have any magic powers."

He seemed relieved, but the crease in his brow showed he was dubious. "What makes you so sure?"

"Because they use weapons. They killed that woman with a scythe. And they ki--" I chewed my cheek. "Used a crossbow on Stooge. Everything we've seen here tonight is weird but real. Nothing supernatural."

Dwayne nodded wordlessly, and some of the tension that had been living in his shoulders seemed to drain away. I was glad to have allayed some of his trepidation, although we still had plenty to fear.

I pushed myself to a standing position. The stall had a four-pane window with a view of the hillsides. It had iced over since our arrival, and I scratched the glass with my fingernails to clear a section.

The bonfire had burned to embers, but the sky had started to brighten as day lazily approached. I hadn't seen any villagers strolling about or checking in on us all night and saw none now.

The stall door was closed and securely locked. I'd checked, but I had a feeling they didn't consider us flight risks. Maybe because the people of Carrick Glynn knew there was nowhere for us to go.

"Can I ask you something else?" Dwayne said.

"Sure."

"Did you TP my house?"

My cheeks burned as I turned to him, blushing the approximate shade of Mars. I didn't have to answer.

"At first, I thought it was some of the guys from the baseball team," he said. "Just another hazing thing. But the more I thought about it, the more I convinced myself it was you."

"And Stooge. It was his idea," I said, feeling guilty for throwing my dead friend under the bus, even if it was the truth.

"I didn't mind the toilet paper. I actually thought it was kind of funny. But the sack of burning shit..."

I checked his face, expecting to find rage. Instead, he wore a smirk. "That was all Stooge."

Dwayne nodded. "Shoulda known. No one else's shit stink could stink that bad."

"I'm sorry," I muttered, as if it mattered.

It was Dwayne's turn to shrug. "Don't be."

"Do you hate me?" I asked, my throat seizing. I regretted asking the question as soon as it passed through my lips because I didn't want to know the answer.

"Because of the TP?"

"Because of everything."

He stayed silent for a long moment, long enough for my nerves to build to a crescendo, then said, "No, Benji. I don't hate you."

"You should."

He grabbed a leather strap nailed to the wall and used it to haul himself to his feet. His gaze alternated between the view and me.

"If I could take back what I said at the river, I would. I was just hot. And scared. None of this is your fault."

My eyes burned, but I was cried out. It might have been easier if he had been angry because the acceptance, the kindness, he was showing me was unearned and only made me loathe myself even more.

"You didn't want to come, though," I said. "I talked you into it. And Stooge would've been as happy eating Fritos in the treehouse and watching *Swamp Thing* for the fiftieth time."

"He really liked Adrienne Barbeau's tits," Dwayne said, his voice nasally. I knew he was close to crying but spared him the indignity of looking at him and acknowledging it.

I did my best impression of Stooge's gruff voice, *"Best set west of the Mississippi!"*

A startled laugh burst from Dwayne's mouth. Then, in an instant, he was bawling. He slammed his fist against the window, cracking one of the glass panes and sending up an explosion of dust. Warm, predawn illumination shined through, creating a fractured ray of light.

"Damn it, why'd they kill him?" Dwayne asked. His shoulders hitched, and he wrapped his arms around his own chest, trying to keep the misery inside.

Unsure what I should do, what I needed to do at the moment, I put my hand on his shoulder in a weak show of support. Even then, with everything we'd gone through and were still dealing with, I didn't know the proper way to show physical affection.

Dwayne knew, though. He turned into me and leaned against me. He needed my strength, and I wrapped my arms around his waist and held him as he wept.

How long he cried, I'm unsure, but by the time he finished, the gash of yellow on the horizon had given way to a mosaic of purples and reds in the sky. Its beauty would have taken my breath away if I wasn't so damned scared.

CHAPTER THIRTY-FIVE

"We're getting out of here," I said, staring out of the window. The villagers had been awake and celebrating until near dawn and the time to act - if such a thing existed - was now.

Dwayne gawked at me like I'd just spoken some archaic language for which there was no translation.

"We're not going to sit here and accept whatever they have planned for us."

He'd been sitting in the corner, his head lolled back against the wood as he rested, but he rose and shook off the exhaustion. He was ready to dive into whatever half-assed plan I'd come up with feet first.

His unquestioning eagerness made me want to puke. I'd doubted him, doubted our friendship, but even after dragging his ass into this hellscape, he trusted me.

I'd been working at the window Dwayne had earlier punched and extracted the broken pieces of glass. The crosshatches where the muntins and mullions held the other panes in place were soft and rotting and I'd used a discarded nail to scratch away at them until they were little more than sawdust.

"Help me take the glass out," I said to Dwayne, not wanting to risk it falling and shattering against a stone, drawing the attention of anyone who wasn't too hungover to hear the crash.

Together, we palmed the panes, our arms intertwined, his reaching outside, mine inside. We probably made it more complicated than necessary, but I wasn't taking chances.

When we finished, a two-foot by three-foot opening stood between us and freedom. *Freedom* is an exaggeration. We'd still be in Carrick Glynn, but it beat sitting in the stall until they came for us.

Dwayne was out first. After he dropped to the ground, he reached a hand inside for me and helped me through. Then we were both standing in the dew-soaked grass, so wet it seeped through my boots and wetted my feet. The least of my worries, though.

We crept along the edge of the barn until we reached the corner. Then I eased my head out, almost certain that Brother Robert would send an arrow hurtling at my face. But no arrow came, and the only person I saw was a drunk passed out beside the smoldering remains of a jack o'lantern which had burned itself into a pile of mush.

"Let's go," I said.

There was no point in going toward the village. Even if we made it through without getting caught, the only place to go from there was the path through the woods and to the river.

Despite my protestations the night prior, I didn't believe there was a safe way across, and, maybe even more to the heart of it, I didn't want to see Stooge's body laying there, bugs crawling over him, maybe already torn and ripped by animal predation. As much as I hated leaving him behind, I couldn't bear seeing what had become of him.

So, I pointed to the east, and that's where we ran. I had no clue what laid in that direction, but I also didn't care. I'd keep running all the way to Philadelphia if that's what it took. Anything to get away from the place I'd been so desperate to visit.

Talk about being careful what you wish for.

We crested one small knoll, then dashed through an apple orchard before coming to the rotting remains of a pumpkin patch. It made me think of Farmer Spivey and how I'd loved spending afternoons strolling through his sea of pumpkins. Now, I didn't want to see another pumpkin for as long as I lived.

After the field, we came to a copse of brittle and dead pine trees and continued along a lightly beaten path. It looked more like a deer trail than something traversed by human feet and the unforgiving branches of the pines clawed at our bodies as we passed by.

When we broke through the last of the trees, we came on to a large clearing, one which hadn't been plowed and planted recently, if ever. It only took a cursory glance to see why.

The land was barren. Not a blade of grass, not a single weed, no vegetation whatsoever grew in the expanse. There was nothing but dirt. Hard clay, dry and compacted together. Unyielding beneath our feet. It felt like walking on cement.

Behind us, I heard the first of the voices. Although I was unable to make out the words, I knew what voices meant. The villagers knew we'd escaped and were coming for us. Barking dogs joined the conversation, hot on our trail.

We doubled our pace, full out sprinting. Dwayne easily outpaced me, gaining ten, twenty, then fifty yards on me. He was so far away I was afraid I'd never catch up, but I didn't dare call him to ask him to wait or slow down. I was already responsible for one of my friends dying. I wasn't going to risk his life too.

As I prepared to lose him altogether, he glanced back at me and shouted something. "Round log," I thought he said.

I scanned the landscape as I ran, but I didn't see any logs. Even if I did, what did it matter? I'd almost reached the spot Dwayne had occupied when he called back when I spied the real subject.

A groundhog. Startled by our arrival, the fat fellow galloped across the dirt quicker than I'd ever seen a groundhog run. For some reason, it made me smile. I welcomed the distraction from the terror as the sounds of the villagers and hounds echoed in the distance behind me. It gave me something to focus on aside from my own likely demise. As I gained on the animal, it stole a glance back at me and shook its stubby black tail.

"Don't worry, buddy. I won't hurt you."

I ran for another ten seconds or so when my foot suddenly plunged downward. The abrupt halt sent me reeling forward, wrenching the bottom half of my leg at an angle it wasn't supposed to bend.

Too shocked to scream, I could only look down and saw my leg calf-deep in a groundhog hole. Ahead of me, the rodent congratulated itself on taking me down.

By the time I pulled my foot from the hole, my ankle was swollen tight within the boot, which had been a full size too big but now fit perfectly. I tried taking a step, but as soon as I put weight on my injured leg, I felt ready to fall. Partly because of the pain, but more so because it felt disconnected from my body, the way it feels when your foot's asleep and you try to walk on it anyway.

I gritted my teeth and tried to take another step when--

"I got you."

He was at my side, there for me when I needed him the most. He put an arm around my back, having to stoop because he was so much taller, and we started the most important three-legged race of our lives.

The sounds of the oncoming search party grew louder as they gained on us. We tried to move faster, but our height difference made it nearly impossible to build a smooth rhythm, and every few steps, my injured foot would hit the ground and make me want to sob in pain.

In the distance, near the edge of that dead land, a house loomed. Calling it a house is a vast exaggeration, though. It was a hovel. It looked as if it had been constructed centuries ago and abandoned for almost as long.

The structure stood high upon its perch of ground. The only way I can think to describe it is by comparing it to an apple core rising up from the earth, a house perched on top where the stem would usually go. It looked like something had gnawed away at the dirt which had once formed the barrow, leaving behind just a scrap of land and the house which sat on it.

It looked so bizarre and out of place, but we ran toward it nonetheless because there was nowhere else to go. Upon reaching it, I got a better look. Rough stones formed the foundation, but unlike the stone huts in Carrick Glynn, this house seemed much older.

It was assembled haphazardly with hand-hewn wood, so strewn together it looked like something built with Lincoln Logs by a demented toddler. The wood had gone black with mold and grime, and the chinking between the logs had long ago crumbled to dust.

All but one window was boarded over, and that exception was so heavily painted with dirt it provided no view. A wooden roof topped the house and holes dotted the cedar shakes, like it had endured the worst hailstorm in the history of the world. Surrounding the foundation was an eclectic collection of dead things. Rotting pumpkins, sheep skulls, brown vines.

A rickety wood ladder connected the ground upon which we stood and the shack above. Dwayne craned his neck and peered up. "We have to go up there," he said.

I couldn't believe my ears. The home looked straight out of a nightmare. "Are you nuts?"

"There might be something inside we can use to wrap up your ankle. Maybe even some weapons."

I looked to the house, then to the field behind us, expecting the entire village to burst through the trees at any second. "I feel like this has the potential to be a really bad idea."

"Can you think of anything better?" he asked.

I considered the question, then shook my head. "No."

"Then climb."

Although I had my doubts, we were already up the proverbial creek. Maybe, inside this place, there might be a paddle.

I climbed the ladder, expecting every rung to snap as I put weight on it, but they all held. At the top, I had to claw at the ground to gain access because the land sloped up even harder there, a sixty-degree angle leading to the shack.

Dwayne was on my tail, and I grabbed both of his hands as he stepped off the ladder to steady him. He wasn't looking at the house, though. He was looking behind us, and I followed his gaze. From this vantage point, we could see the town and its surrounding farmlands in the distance. It still appeared so near. It felt like we'd been running forever, but Carrick Glynn was still within eyesight, which meant we hadn't run far enough.

Could we ever run far enough?

There was no knob on the door, just a chunk of wood

nailed fast. I grabbed onto it and pulled, but it was unyielding. I tried again, throwing all of my hundred pounds into it. It gave way with an eerie, plaintive creak.

As soon as it came open, dozens of rats scurried from the house, running over our feet. One climbed up Dwayne's pants, making it all the way to his knee. He unleashed a yelp and kicked his foot out, sending the rat soaring through the air, past the ladder, and gliding into the ground below. It bounced twice before regaining its footing.

Beyond the doorway lay a black hole. Even though the day had grown bright, it seemed as if no light could penetrate the interior of the structure. I thought again how insane it was to go inside, but knowing I had nothing left to lose made the decision easier.

The stable had smelled like a bakery compared to the aroma of this dank, musty place. The smell of the air forced me to breathe through my mouth, but whatever caused the odor settled on my taste buds and left its flavor behind for eternity. I pulled my shirt up and over my nose and mouth, using it as a filter, but it didn't help.

Dwayne's footsteps followed me inside, and I again realized how lucky I was to have him as a friend despite everything we had been through. He'd have been smarter to save himself and keep running, leaving me behind to face the consequence of my own actions. But he didn't abandon me. Even when he should have.

Once inside, the smoldering coals from a stone fireplace shed enough light to be able to see where we were going. The cabin was small, only two rooms so far as I could tell. The room we'd entered into seemed to be the primary living quarters but calling them such was being generous.

A rocking chair sat empty beside the fireplace. A rickety end table with a ball of what looked like wool rested beside the chair. A pile of straw and moldy animal pelts were heaped in the corner. It looked like a nest, a place where some wild thing might curl up and sleep.

The floor was covered in animal waste - fat rat turds as big as Tootsie Rolls and tablespoon-sized clumps of chicken crap. If you're wondering how I was able to identify the latter as chicken droppings, it was because a bird pecked clean of all its feathers strutted back and forth, occasionally coming close enough to peck at my feet. It looked like a scrawny, pink rotisserie chicken up and walking.

I tried to tolerate it, but Dwayne was less forgiving. When the bird pecked his ankle hard enough to draw blood, he kicked the bird across the room. It gave a startled *Buck-Aw!* as it flapped its wings to no avail and bounced off the wall.

The room offered nothing of use, so we continued to the only other option, the kitchen. A table sat in the middle, and two rats rode on top of it, scavenging scraps of food left behind. They gave us a wary look as we entered but quickly returned to their snacks.

One wall held shelves, all full of glass canning jars. But, so far as I could see, the jars didn't hold the usual contents like corn, peas, or green beans. They contained much less appetizing fare.

Some were filled with writhing worms, nightcrawlers by the looks of them, long and thick as rope. Several jars were packed full of insects, too many types to count. There were small lizards, salamanders probably, but the old witch's recipe - *Eye of newt* - came to mind, and I couldn't shake it. I'd promised Dwayne no witches. Had I been wrong about that too?

The jars were never-ending. There were maggots, roaches, centipedes, silverfish. Some held chunks of vaguely gray meat. I tried to tell myself it was venison but failed. One perched atop the highest of the floor-to-ceiling shelves contained human hair in a variety of colors. Another held fingernail clippings, hundreds of crescent-shaped hunks of keratin.

What I didn't find was a weapon. Not a knife, not a meat tenderizer, not a fancy corkscrew, not even a fork. The house seemed devoid of anything useful, and I turned to Dwayne, ready to tell him that we should go when--

"Find anything you like?" an old woman's voice crowed.

I jumped, both feet coming off the floor. When I came down, my right foot - my injured foot - landed on the tail of a rat which shrieked and spun at me, attacking my boots with its yellow incisors. Its fat, fleshy tail rolled under my heel, and I lost my balance, careering backward, arms windmilling.

My hand hit a jar. I watched it teeter on the shelf in what felt like slow motion, and I saw its living contents skittering inside the glass. The jaw was filled to the brim with spiders.

It rocked on the edge of the shelf, tipping forward, falling back, tipping forward.

Please God, let it tip back and settle. Don't let it fall. Not spiders, I thought.

Then, it fell, tumbling end over end before shattering against the floor.

Hundreds, maybe thousands, of spiders exploded from the container, and they seemed especially pissed off at me. They didn't care that I'd freed them from their prison. They were hungry, and all they wanted to do was feed.

The spiders, everything from grandaddy long legs (tolerable) to orb weavers and wolf spiders (terrifying), used their alien legs to scrabble up my boots, making proverbial hay and wasting no time as they climbed over the leather and onto my socks.

Those socks were my last defense. From there, the spiders would go under my biballs and onto bare skin, where they would bite and suck blood and masticate my flesh. If I'd had a rational, functioning brain, I might have reminded myself that spiders in Pennsylvania were almost never poisonous and that they rarely bit unless provoked. I would have told myself these spiders were simply crawling around and doing what spiders do, not meaning me any harm.

But my brain was not functioning and wasn't anything close to rational. As their alien appendages prickled against my skin, I screamed bloody murder. Forgetting about my sprained ankle, I stomped my feet, pistoning them up and down, trying to shake off the legions of arachnids that had climbed onto me and smash whatever remained underfoot. At the same time, I beat my fists into my pant legs, trying to crush any spiders which hadn't fallen off and were trapped between the denim and my flesh.

I was breathing so fast and hard I got light-headed, but the last thing I could allow to happen was collapsing into this sea of spiders. They were still coming for me, still on the attack, and all I could focus on was getting away from them.

I spun toward the kitchen table and dragged myself into it. The rats, still busy dining, hissed upon my arrival, but I didn't care about them. When it came to rodents versus spiders, I'd take rodents every time. On the floor below, the chicken had returned and dashed about, devouring the spiders like they were beluga caviar.

"B-B-Benji..." Dwayne stuttered, reminding me he was still there.

I'd never heard him stutter, not once in all the years we'd known each other, and I knew he must be as scared as I was. I turned to him, expecting to find him overrun with spiders, covered head to toe, only his eyes visible. He'd have a hand outstretched, reaching for me, begging for help, would die without my help. Yet I didn't know if I could help him. Was I prepared to sit there and lose another friend?

Thankfully, I didn't have to make that decision because Dwayne wasn't covered with spiders. He seemed unconcerned or unaware of their presence. Instead, he stared into the corner of the room.

There, a woman sat on a wooden stool, perched there like a gargoyle on a parapet. She wore a gray, featureless dress, so weathered it was practically transparent. Draped across her odd body, it held no shape or form. She was thin in the arms and legs, but her belly bulged and sagged low.

It was her face I found the most unnerving. She looked older than anyone I'd ever seen, even the people Willard Scott wished a Happy Birthday on the *Today Show*. Older than time.

Her hair was long enough to touch the floor and the approximate color of fishing line. Her nose looked like a finger had been glued to her face, angling down at the end. Her lips curled inward at her mouth, which I assumed must be toothless. And her eyes... What I could see of them, hidden deep in the sockets, behind skeletal cheekbones, looked like white marbles.

She wasn't there when we came into the room - I was certain. We'd have looked straight at her as we entered, she would have been impossible to miss. Yet there she was, and the room contained no other doors or points of entry, so where had she come from?

I forced myself to look away from her and back to Dwayne to see if he was as baffled by this development as I was. When my eyes found him, the old woman was there, standing in front of him, between Dwayne and me.

I stole a fast glance into the corner to ensure there weren't two of her and found the stool empty. Then I turned to

Dwayne, who was trembling as the hag stood two feet from him.

"We-- we-- we--" Dwayne stammered.

My mind, which I'm pretty sure was cracked at that point, immediately added, in a singsong voice, *All the way home*. It could have, should have, been funny. Stooge, especially, would have laughed. But humor had been extinguished from our world over the last twelve hours.

"We need help," Dwayne got out, then he pointed at me. "Benji hurt his ankle."

The woman turned to me, her head not moving in a fluid movement atop her neck but seeming to tick its way around. "Did you now?"

I nodded. "In the field. I stepped in a hole."

She raised an eyebrow that had no hair, just wrinkled skin which arced upward. "That's the trouble with boys. They don't look where they goin'."

"We can leave," I said. "I'm sorry we didn't knock before coming inside, but we thought the house was abandoned."

"Abandoned?" she repeated. "Whatever gave you that idea?"

I couldn't tell her the truth, couldn't tell her the house looked ready to fall over if you breathed on it too hard, but neither could I come up with a lie. I checked Dwayne to see if he had any ideas.

To my surprise, he'd snapped out of his stuttering, stammering fear and grabbed a ceramic bowl off the table. He was in the process of swinging it at her head when--

Her arm flew up and collided with Dwayne's hand, deflecting the coming blow. I couldn't fathom how something so ancient could move so fast. Dwayne's hand and the bowl collided with the nearby wall, the dish crumbling.

I searched the table for something I could use to attack, but all that remained were me and the rats. Two rats, which became one after the woman snatched a rodent in her claw-like hand.

The rat squealed in protest as she closed her fist around it, its beady eyes bulging. But its pain was cut short when the woman used a fingernail, one which looked barbed like a fishing hook, to slice open the animal's throat.

Blood burst from the rat's body, saturating the woman's hand. She squeezed it harder, and I could hear its bones breaking and the squishy sounds of its insides imploding. Once it was wrung dry, she dropped it and turned back to Dwayne.

All this unfolded in five seconds tops, and Dwayne was still staring at the small shard of ceramic clutched in his hand when the woman reached out with her blood-covered fingers and touched his forehead.

She drew an upside-down Y, then added a third fork in the middle. The design looked familiar, and it only took me a second to connect the dots. It was the same shape in which the villagers had laid out their jack o'lanterns before the feast.

"Calm," the woman said to Dwayne, and his eyes went glassy.

I grabbed two handfuls of her hair, jerking it hard, trying to pull her away from him. But when I pulled, her hair tore free from her scalp, along with small chunks of oozing flesh.

She smiled at me, an awful, wretched smile. She wasn't toothless after all. When she grinned, her lips pulled back to reveal small nubs of teeth protruding from gray gums. In one deft movement, she raised her bloody hand to her mouth, then blew.

The rat's blood, still hot, spattered my face, my eyes. Some went into my mouth, and it tasted like I'd sucked on an old penny.

"Stay," she said to me.

I couldn't move. Not because I was terrified - I was - but because I was physically incapable of movement. No matter how hard I tried, how strong my will, I couldn't so much as bend a finger. All the while, I could still feel the spiders crawling on my legs and the fiery burn as they bit me with impunity.

The old woman went to the house's lone window and pushed it open. Then she reached to the floor and grabbed a ram's horn. She brought the pointed end to her mouth and blew into it.

A hollow, mournful sound came from the makeshift instrument. A shofar, I thought, not sure how I remembered anything from my barely Jewish upbringing. The sound carried into the air, into the fields, and drifted toward the village.

After a long pause, a nearly identical note blew back.

The old woman returned the horn to its previous resting place, and then she returned to me. She brought a withered hand to my face and dragged her thick nails across my cheek. It felt like running through a thorn bush in the forest and my skin sizzled where she scratched me.

Next, she pushed my hair out of my eyes, away from my forehead, and leaned in so close her obscenity of a nose touched mine. It was cold and dense, like a hunk of raw pot roast fresh from the fridge. I wanted to shiver but couldn't.

"Now what you gone and done to your leg, boy?" She crouched before me, skeletal fingers untying my shoelaces. Once the knot was undone, she pulled the boot loose at the top. Seemingly satisfied the boot was now capable of being removed from my swollen foot, she put one hand on the heel and the other on the toe and gave it a hard yank.

Pain surged as it felt like my foot might come off with the boot, but I couldn't cry out, couldn't draw back, couldn't so much as flinch. I had to stand there and take it.

The boot had not come off, and the hag's hairless brows furrowed. "You did a number on it, that's for certain," she said, then worked her long fingers into the boot, prying it off slowly and with great effort. The pain was nearly unbearable and made my broken nose feel like a bee sting in comparison.

Once free, my foot dangled uselessly. The woman peeled off my sock, then rubbed her hands across the swollen skin, which had already gone aubergine.

"Sure did a number on it," she repeated as she moved to her shelves. She studied them carefully, then took down three jars and carried them to a slab of wood that served as the kitchen counter. There, she took another ceramic bowl and a pestle and displayed them to me.

"Gonna make ya some nostrum," she said.

I had no idea what nostrum was, but I hadn't seen anything in those jars that I wanted near me. But all I could do was watch apprehensive as she went to work.

She cracked the lids of the jars, then used her fingers to extract the contents. From the first, she took two fat slugs, so covered with slime they left a string of it behind, and the woman had to sever it with her fingers. Next, she grabbed what looked like a rotten pear. Finally, she dipped her fingers into a dark jar, one full of liquid. After fishing around inside, she came up with a single but fully engorged tick.

Once all had been added to the mixing bowl, she took another look at me, her familiar wretched, leering smile pulling at her colorless lips. "Mustn't forget the nectar," she said.

With that, the woman reached down and grabbed the hem of her sack dress. Slowly, she pulled it up, first revealing her knees, then her thighs, then -- God, no.

I didn't want to see. I tried closing my eyes, but my frozen body failed to cooperate. I couldn't even move my eyeballs to stare at the floor or the ceiling. I was helpless and prayed I'd go blind before I saw more of her nakedness.

To my tremendous relief, her low-hanging gut covered most of her crotch. All that was visible were some wiry, white pubes dangling below her pallid belly. But she continued raising the dress and, soon, my young eyes witnessed their first set of real-life, in-person breasts.

I'd never seen a naked woman or girl outside of the movies or the *Playboy* magazines Stooge sometimes filched from his dad and snuck into the treehouse. But the bodies I'd seen on display on screen or print hadn't prepared me for this. Real life was awful.

Her breasts hung long and low. They looked like white tube socks dangling from her chest, tube socks with billiard balls hidden in the feet. On the round ends of each were puffy, gray areolas, as big around as oranges. I could see all the veins, all the bumps and lumps in hideous detail. And, capping them off, were grotesque nipples which must have been two inches long and pointed at the floor like accusatory fingers.

My field of vision was wide enough that I could see both her and Dwayne simultaneously, and I tried to focus on him. He looked ready to shit his pants, and I imagined I came across the same to him. I wished we could communicate telepathically and give running commentary to what was unfolding before us, but all we could do was stare in silence, statue-still.

The hag grabbed onto one of her long, deformed breasts, taking hold where it connected to her chest wall. Then she used both hands to squeeze it. The already alabaster skin somehow went even more white as her hands worked their way down, squeezing, undulating, stretching the already elongated skin.

Eventually, after what seemed like hours, her hands had closed in on the areola which she had directed over the ceramic bowl. With a perversely pleasured moan, she gave one final squeeze, and a long squirt of milk the color of custard and the consistency of cottage cheese surged from her nipple and fell into the bowl with a viscid *glop*.

She released her breast and allowed the dress to fall and cover her body. Then she grabbed the pestle and ground the ingredients together. All the while, she hummed tunelessly, like a chef preparing a fine roux. With a nod, she finished, removing the pestle and setting it aside.

I could see the chunky, coagulated contents of the bowl as she brought it to me. If she expected me to eat it, I'd projectile vomit the mixture back into her face. But even the thought of eating made me realize my tongue was as frozen as the rest of me. I couldn't chew nor swallow.

Did she plan to pry my mouth ajar and pour it down my throat? Surely, I'd choke. But would a person frozen stiff even be capable of choking? Or would it drain down my gullet and into my stomach with even my internal organs incapable of protesting?

In a glorious reprieve, the old woman didn't force the contents of the bowl into my mouth. Instead, she rubbed them on my swollen ankle. Her hands became slick with it as she caressed and fondled my foot, still humming along. She didn't stop until the bowl was empty, and my leg was coated from calf to toes.

As disgusted as I was, the pain which had been throbbing in my ankle had retreated to a dull ache, no worse than a stubbed toe. After a few seconds, even that was gone. Of course, I couldn't move my ankle to try it out, but I was pain-free.

The woman looked at me and gave a quick nod, then patted me on the thigh. "You're welcome."

It was only then, my head cleared of the horror of watching

her make the salve when I realized the barking hounds and voices of the villagers were right outside. She'd called them, and they came.

She went to the window, leaned through it, and said, "Send up some strong bodies. I've got the boys locked, so you'll need to carry 'em."

CHAPTER THIRTY-SIX

Conal wasn't amongst the group of villagers who collected us and carried us back to Carrick Glynn, but he was the first face to greet us upon our return. I'd expected him to be furious, maybe lay into us with some sort of weapon, but the man was every bit as cheerful as when we'd first met the evening before.

"Good to have you back, lads!" he said as the men who'd hauled our rigid bodies stood us on the ground like a group of landscapers trying to find the perfect spot for a new pair of statues.

Conal came to me first, ruffling my hair with a fatherly grin. "Sorry about Brighid," he said. "She can be rather peculiar."

As if that wasn't the understatement of all understatements.

Brother Robert had been one of the search party. He handed Conal a bag tied off with a strand of hair. "She said this will unlock them, whatever the hell that means."

Conal accepted it and untied the knot, bringing the sack to his face so he could examine the contents. His nostrils furled as he got a whiff, and he snapped his head back and away. He looked at me, shaking his head. "A pungent concoction, that's for certain."

The old man moved away from us, conferring with some of the others, and I tried to take in my surroundings or as much of them as I could see with my limited viewpoint. We were in the same clearing where the feast had been held, but the tables were gone, as was the food.

The pumpkins, arranged in their sigil or rune or hieroglyph - whatever the shape was - remained, and the candles inside somehow still burned, but they were less impressive in the daylight. Spread across the ground were several white quilts, each large enough to cover a king-size bed with plenty to spare.

In the distance, the bonfire had completely died off, leaving behind a mound of black ash. Occasionally, a puff of smoke emanated up from the remnants and got lost in the breeze. Perhaps the most shocking change was the corn maze. Sometime through the night or early morning, it had been completely razed, the corn and stalks gathered and removed.

I'd noticed the same on the fleeting glimpses I caught while being carried back into the village. All of the crops had been collected, and all the remnants cleaned so the ground was clear and fresh for the coming winter.

The harvest was complete.

But what did that leave for us?

Conal circled around, back into my line of vision. He still held the bag, but now, his hand was plunged into it. He nodded to two of the men who took hold of my arms, which seemed pointless as I couldn't try to escape even if I wanted.

"I'd tell you to open wide, but I suppose I must do that on your behalf." Conal used his free hand to grab hold of my chin and dragged down my lower jaw.

I stood there, mouth propped open, and for a long moment

became obsessed with the sudden, crazed worry that a wasp might fly in and sting my tongue. Like that was my biggest worry in life.

Before a wasp, or something similarly dangerous, could come along, Conal pulled his other hand out of the sack. It was full of oozing amber-colored goo, which seeped between his fingers and dripped as he brought his hand and its contents to my mouth.

It's honey, I told myself. *Only honey. You eat it at least twice a week on English muffins, so this is no big deal.*

It didn't smell like honey, though. It smelled like infection. Infection crossed with ground beef lost in the back of the refrigerator for a few weeks before you remembered it was there.

As the fistful of goo neared my mouth, my eyes began to water. I guess I wasn't dry after all. And when Conal pushed it into my mouth, I wanted - needed - to revolt, but I couldn't.

The man used his fingers to push it deeper into my maw, sliding it across my tongue, shoving it into the back of my throat. Then he pulled his hand free and slammed shut my mouth so hard my teeth ached.

I've tried to block out the memory of the taste. It was indescribable in its awfulness, and that's coming from someone who once ate pickled cow tongue on a dare. Even worse than the flavor was the way it slithered down my throat, slow and warm, almost like it was crawling into my awaiting stomach.

Then, within seconds, my entire body went limp. Only the men who'd been holding onto me kept me from collapsing to the ground, but they held me aloft, even as my legs let go.

Able to move, able to work my body again, I tilted my head forward and retched. The puke which came had the consistency of snot, and it somehow managed to taste and feel even worse coming up than it had been going down.

I'd closed my eyes while I vomited and didn't know Nora had joined the party until I heard her voice.

"Drink this, Benji."

My eyes, streaming tears, popped open, and I found her before me. She held a goblet. I should have been wary about accepting food or drink from anyone, but I needed to cleanse my palate. When she tilted it into my mouth, I swallowed greedily.

It was milk, and I'd never tasted anything finer. I swished it around in my mouth, gargled it like mouthwash, then drank some more. The taste of whatever Conal had fed me lingered, but it was mostly just a bad memory.

I glanced toward Dwayne and saw he'd already taken his cure and was now accepting a mug of milk from one of the females in the village, the same girl he'd been flirting with the night before. He looked as terrible as I felt, and I could only imagine the blow his ego had taken.

The men who'd been holding my arms released me, and I stayed on my feet. My ankle, so badly sprained less than an hour before, was perfect and bearing weight wasn't a problem at all. Yet the thought of running - again - never occurred to me. We'd tried that twice, only to endure something awful and then be dragged back. Why put myself through it yet again?

Nora grabbed my hand and tried to lead me, but I pulled away. Her touch, which had felt so delicate before, disgusted me.

"Don't act that way," she said, anger in her eyes.

I couldn't believe her audacity. How dare she be upset with me after she'd lied to us, betrayed us? I spun toward her and opened my mouth to snap at her, but then I saw Stooge.

Or what had once been Stooge.

My friend was propped on a large, wooden bench, secured to it by a multitude of ropes, each staked into the ground like a tent being held down in high winds. A second bench, an empty bench, sat beside him.

Stooge's Judas Priest t-shirt had been torn away and the arrow that killed him had been removed. A black hole marred the center of his torso, and flies crawled in and around the wound, eating, defecating, laying eggs, which would turn to maggots in the coming hours. Only the bitterly cold weather of the night before had kept him from bloating, but even the cold could only delay that humiliation for so long.

Stooge's mouth hung open, and his tongue, which had gone the color of pencil lead, hung out like he was gearing up to blow an epic raspberry. His eyelids had been propped open by small slivers of wood, and he stared at me with dull, lifeless eyes, eyes that seemed to scold, *This is your fault, little dude. All your fault.*

"Let me go!" Dwayne said.

Two men had grabbed onto him while a third approached with a long coil of rope. I had visions of the woman who'd had a lasso looped around her neck before being decapitated. Was that the plan for Dwayne? For me too?

I started toward him, but Nora grabbed the straps on my biballs, slowing me down enough to say, "Let it be."

I pivoted my gaze between her and Dwayne, who'd had his arms tied tight to his sides. The man working the rope was moving on to his legs.

"Are they going to cut his head off? So you freaks can dance in his blood?" I asked Nora.

She gave her head a shake, making her orange curls dance. "No. Nothing like that for him."

I didn't believe her, but what purpose was there in lying? They didn't need to mislead me, to coddle me. There were twenty or more grown men in the clearing, and any one of them could break me in two if he so chose.

"Then what?" I asked her.

"His fate isn't up to us," she said.

If her statement was supposed to be reassuring, it didn't work. Dwayne's legs were tied together, multiple loops and knots, impossible to escape. Then he was carried to the benches and placed on the empty seat.

With him locked down, I expected the men to come for me. Instead, they moved to a heaping mound of brown cornstalks and began to strip the leaves from the rest of the plant. They piled the leaves together, then tossed the other parts aside.

As the men worked the corn, I noticed the women of the village were using the barrels in which we'd bobbed for apples to clean the previous night's bloody clothes. The water had turned red, but they scrubbed, using washboards and heavy washing paddles, then ran them through a ringer to dry.

Both chores looked tedious and as if they'd go on for hours. The sun had gone high in the sky, and I assumed it to be around noon. How much longer would this last? And what did they have planned for us?

"Come with us," Nora said, reaching for my hand, but I pulled it away. Conal stood a few yards from us.

"Why should I?"

She looked me in the eyes, and I saw the girl I'd met back in Sallow Creek. The girl I'd considered a friend and maybe even more. I wanted to hate her but couldn't bring myself.

"We need to talk," she said.

I looked past her to Conal and addressed him because I knew he was the one truly in charge. "Can I talk to Dwayne first?"

"But of course. You are free to do whatever you choose, young Benjamin," he said.

I had my doubts, but when I went to Dwayne, no one moved to stop me. With him sitting on the bench, we were about at eye level. I leaned in close to him, speaking directly into his ear so no one could overhear. "I'll come back. I promise."

He shook his head frantically. "Don't leave me, Benji."

I looked at Conal and called out, "If I go with you, nothing will happen to him while I'm away? He won't be hurt?"

Conal gave a genial wave of his hand. "He'll be unharmed and right where you left him. You have my word."

His word didn't mean much to me, but this was a risk I had to take. We couldn't get out of Carrick Glynn via our physical efforts, that much was clear. Maybe I would have better luck using my brain and trying to talk our way out of this.

CHAPTER THIRTY-SEVEN

I followed Conal and Nora to an ordinary, unassuming cottage. It was no larger than any other in the village and had nothing identifying it as the home of their leader. No signs, no plaques, no banners saying, 'Hail Conal.' Nevertheless, he pushed the door open and walked in as if he owned the place.

Before entering, I glanced around the empty village, wary, almost expecting a throng of men with pitchforks and torches to burst out from their hiding spot and attack. But the streets and alcoves were empty. Even the animals had moved on.

"Please, come in," Conal beckoned.

After taking one more look around, I entered the cottage.

A cook pot simmered over an open flame in the fireplace, and I'd be lying if I said it didn't smell delicious. I hadn't eaten - well, eaten by choice - anything since the feast the night before, and I was starving. My salivary glands erupted, and, despite my misgivings, I knew I would be helpless to resist whatever food they offered me.

The home was sparsely furnished and decorated similarly

to the others I'd been inside while trick or treating. A dining table stood in the center of the main quarters, and Conal directed me toward it. He pulled out a chair and motioned for me to sit. Nora went to the pot, took a ladle from a hook, and gave whatever was inside a good stir.

I looked down at the chair in which Conal had motioned for me to sit as if checking to see it was booby-trapped. But it was just a chair, and I sat.

"I'm so glad you decided to join us," Conal said.

It seemed rude to not thank him for the invitation. I guess it was being a kid in the presence of an adult, but it seemed like I should still have good manners. He didn't seem to mind, though, and carried on. "I hope you will fill your belly. Nora is an excellent cook."

"Did your grandmother teach you?" I asked her.

She averted her eyes and gave a quick nod. "Yes." Then she grabbed three bowls and began filling them.

When she finished, she came to the table and set one before me, one before Conal, then one in front of the empty chair for herself. Finally, with the meal served, she joined us in sitting.

The food she had prepared was vegetable soup, almost overflowing with bounty from the harvest and, from the smell, seasoned to perfection. I didn't dally, grabbing a spoon and taking a bite. Aside from being near scalding hot, it was perfect.

Conal sawed away at a loaf of bread and handed me a piece. "Would you like some butter?"

I shook my head, dipping the bread into the soup and letting it soak up the rich broth. I took a bite and found it to be heavenly.

Conal reached over and patted my shoulder. "Ah, good boy. Eat up now."

For a horrible, sickening moment, I realized they hadn't eaten yet and thought I had been poisoned. I almost forced myself to regurgitate the food, but then Conal dove in, and Nora followed suit.

We ate in silence for the next few minutes. I felt beyond guilty for filling my stomach in this cozy cottage while Dwayne was out there, tied up in the cold beside our dead friend. I couldn't imagine what must be going through his head.

So often in the last few months, I'd felt like *he* was the bad friend. *He* was one who had abandoned us. Now the shoe was on the other foot. I was the one hanging out with other people and excluding him. I was the one being an ass.

The guilt was nearly enough to make me lose my appetite. Nearly. I kept eating until the bowl was empty and the bread was gone. Conal offered me another slice of bread, which I accepted, but with less enthusiasm.

I looked up at him, took a glance at Nora, and went back to the man. "What are you going to do to Dwayne? Why is he tied up?"

"It's part of the sacrament," he said.

"That doesn't answer my question."

A wry grin pulled at his lips. "My, you are a bright boy. Nora chose well." He ate a spoonful of soup and went on. "I don't intend to be cryptic, but it's something that must be seen, not explained."

"Are you going to murder him?"

Conal belched a laugh and wiped his mouth with a napkin. "Good gods, of course not."

"Why should I believe you?"

The old man, who looked much older indoors where the shadows filled in his wrinkles, set his spoon in the bowl and tented his fingers. "Have I caused you any physical harm since you've been here?"

I considered the question, replaying the events of the last sixteen hours in my head. Neither Conal himself nor any of the others had injured me. All of my wounds were self-inflicted, but I was loath to admit it.

He took my silence as confirmation. "You have the wrong impression of us," he said.

"My impression is that you're a bunch of murderers," I said

The smile he'd been wearing constantly fell off his face. He gave his head a sober shake. "Balderdash," he said. "There hasn't been a murder committed on the village property in centuries."

It was my turn to want to laugh, but I couldn't not even fake one. "You murdered Stooge."

"His death was unfortunate and unplanned," Conal said. "A rash decision and one Brother Robert sincerely regrets. But there was no malice involved. It was done to protect the village. It was not murder."

I thought that was a poor excuse and had a counterargument at the ready. "What about that old woman last night? You chopped off her head. Are you going to sit there and lie to my face and tell me that wasn't murder?"

"She was suffering. Her end was nigh with or without me. What I did was show her compassion and put an end to her suffering." He examined me, eyes intense and genuine. "You saw her. Do you believe she was a healthy woman?"

I didn't answer because he was right. She'd been on death's doorstep even before the rope was put around her neck.

"Then tell me, if you come upon a bird in the street with two broken wings, is it murder to give it a quick end rather than letting it linger? Or do you show mercy by giving it a dignified death?"

"Being decapitated is dignified?"

"How do you think chickens are slaughtered?" he asked.

I checked Nora to see if I could get a read on her and was

surprised to see a few tears slipping down her cheeks. Her emotion gave me hope, hope that I was getting through.

"Can I talk to Nora? Alone?" I asked Conal.

He didn't even pause to consider the question. "Of course. My old bones need stretching anyway." He rose from his seat, left the table, then left the cottage.

Nora sipped her soup, not looking at me.

"You've been out in the real world," I said to her. "Even if you grew up here, you've seen how the rest of the world exists. You can't believe what goes on here is acceptable."

She didn't answer.

"Maybe people living like heathens was normal a few hundred years ago, but the world doesn't work like this anymore. People don't behave this way."

She threw down her spoon. It splashed in the soup, creating a tidal wave which ended with a quarter of the meal spilling onto the table.

"Yes, I've seen how life goes out in what you call the real world, Benji. I've seen how selfish everyone is. How cruel they are to others. I've seen rich people take advantage of the poor solely because they can. I've seen homeless people sleeping on sidewalks while men in fine suits step over them like they're litter. I've seen parents choose drugs over their own children. I've seen babies near starving because your society has no use for them. Nothing like that happens here. Here we take care of our own."

Her words were filled with fire and vitriol. Any hope I'd had of convincing her to join my side, to set Dwayne and me free, seemed foolish. But I wasn't ready to quit yet.

"You were abandoned," I counted. "When your grandmother died, they sent you out because no one here wanted to take care of you. That's what you told me."

Even though the cottage was warm, there was an abrupt

change in the temperature of the room. Nora rose and began gathering the dishes. Whatever I'd said had certainly hit a nerve, and her cordiality was gone.

"How could you do this to us?" My voice cracked when asking the question, and her back stiffened.

She turned back to me, drying her hands on a rag. "You're angry with me?"

I only nodded in response.

"I didn't bring you here to hurt you, Benji. I'm giving you a great gift. You have no idea how fortunate you are."

"I'm lucky? You've ruined everything. Ruined my life. I thought you were my friend!"

She came to me and cupped my face in her hands. "The first time I saw you, I knew you were special. I didn't trick you. I'm saving you."

I couldn't take any more of her nonsense and shoved myself back from the table, striding to the door. When I opened it, I found Conal standing outside, chewing on an apple.

I tried to slip past him, but he grabbed hold of my wrist. "Why don't you change out of that costume?" he asked. "This afternoon is going to be very special, and I believe you would find it more comfortable if you were dressed properly."

CHAPTER THIRTY-EIGHT

The clothing Conal gave me was basic but comfortable and a welcome change from my psycho lumberjack costume, which, considering everything we'd been through, had lost its appeal. He also supplied me with a basin filled with warm water and a bar of handmade soap.

I washed up and got dressed in the privacy of Conal's cramped bedroom, which contained nothing more than the bed and a lone dresser for furniture. On the wall hung a few needlepoint designs, all framed in barnwood. I glanced over them, reading the quaint saying, which seemed insincere considering everything I'd seen of the village.

May all who come unto my door sweet welcome find and peace of mind.

You are as welcome as flowers in May.

Kind words can never die.

I wanted to tear them from the wall, crumple them into balls, and toss them in the fire. Instead, I finished buttoning up the white cotton shirt I'd been given and tucked it into the wool pants, which I thought itchy, but the warmth they provided made up for it. I took a few seconds to scratch some of the spider bites, which had turned to angry welts, then decided I'd put off the inevitable long enough and left the room.

The cottage was empty. Conal and Nora were both gone, but I spotted a plate of cookies on the table and a slip of paper beneath it.

The fine, feminine handwriting belonged to Nora.

Benji,

Help yourself to the cookies. They're peanut butter, and I remembered they're your favorites. You can bring some for Dwayne too. We'll be in the meadow.

- N

She had the audacity to add a heart after her name.

I grabbed a cookie and chomped off a mouthful. It was so good that I gobbled down the rest in short order, then downed a second. I went to the door, opened it, and stared into the village. It was still empty of people, but I could hear singing in the distance, coming from the direction of the clearing.

They knew I wouldn't leave Dwayne and trusted me to follow at my leisure. As much as I wanted to run - again - they were correct. But before I left the cottage, I searched the kitchen and found a small paring knife. It was the perfect size to fit in my pocket, and that's where I put it.

The walk to the meadow was only half a mile or so, and I didn't pass another person. They were all in the clearing, prepared for whatever was to come. I moved with the dread of a man marching toward his own funeral, fully convinced I wouldn't survive the day. But I had promised Dwayne I'd come back for him and, after what we'd been through, my word held more value than my life.

Whereas the night prior, the villagers had been clad in

simple, peasant clothing, now everyone wore what I assumed to be their finest outfits. All of the men wore simple suits. Not Brooks Brothers, of course, but they all had jackets and ties. Some bow, some regular.

The women wore boldly colored dresses. I found Nora in the crowd. She sported an emerald, velvet dress which made her look older than her fourteen years. As much as I'd grown to resent the girl, my heartbeat still quickened at the sight of her. She saw me and flashed a radiant smile.

I wouldn't allow myself to be enamored with her, to get lost in her again. I moved on, skirting the crowd. The men and women had formed two separate groups. It reminded me of an orthodox wedding my parents had dragged me to when I was about five years old. The men had sat on one side of a partition and the women on the other. There wasn't a partition here, but it carried the same vibe.

To my relief, promises had been kept, and I found Dwayne unharmed, still bound and sitting on the bench, still clad in his baseball uniform. His chin was glued to his chest as I approached. It stayed that way even when I was directly in front of him. He had never looked so defeated.

"Are you okay?" I asked.

At my voice, he looked up. His eyes were narrowed, skeptical at first as he took in my new clothes, but when he saw my face, he relaxed, at least marginally.

"I thought maybe they killed you," he said.

Him worrying about me made me feel even worse. I suddenly wished I'd left the cookies behind rather than have him know that, while he was fretting over me, I was eating a meal and dessert. But the tray was in my hand, and I had no way of hiding it.

"They just talked to me," I said. "Talked without saying anything important. I still don't know what's going on."

He noticed the cookies, and his brows went up. "Give me one."

I held out a cookie, and he took a bite, chewing fast and swallowing it down, then going in for seconds.

A swarm of flies had descended on Stooge's body, the air thick with them. A few caught wind of the sweets I held and came over to explore. I had to keep swatting them away before they could land on the food. The thought of the same insects which had just been crawling over my deceased friend's skin landing on the food made me nauseous.

"Gimme another," Dwayne said. He didn't seem to share my aversion to the flies. I suppose he'd gotten used to them.

I broke a cookie in two and fed him the first half. I was ready to offer the second when--

From the tree line at the north end of the clearing came a cacophony of crashes and snaps. All eyes and heads turned toward the sounds, mine included. It sounded like a slow-motion freight train rolling through the woods, and I half expected to see something in that vein. Maybe a Mack truck or a Panzer tank.

Instead, I saw the bull.

I blinked once, twice, a third time, certain my eyes were betraying me. But every time my lids parted, and the world reappeared, the bull was still present. And closer.

I searched through the men's side of the crowd for Ewan to ensure this wasn't still some humorless gag. I found him, entwined with his neighbors, staring, enraptured at the coming beast.

Somehow, seeing the monster in the daylight was even worse than seeing it under the starlit skies in the labyrinth. At night, I could pretend it was a ghost or specter or even a trick of my imagination. But with the sun shining down, revealing its abominable existence, it was impossible to deny.

As I had thought the night before, the creature had the head of a bull. Horns and antlers and something like tusks jutted from its head, from its jaws, from its ears. They curved in wild, violent angles, made for goring and ripping. For killing.

Its head tapered into a thick, muscular neck, and then came the chest and abdomen of a man. A human torso, not painted cerulean blue but that color by nature, connected to legs that were some bizarre meld of a man and a beast. Its feet and hands were cloven hoofs.

It had closed half the distance between the forest and the meadow, and all the villagers stared in rapt awe. All save for Conal.

The old man had broken away from the men and strode toward the creature, which walked upright as it came toward us. When they were within a few yards of one another, the beast stopped, and Conal stopped. Then the man who I thought to be a leader of this godforsaken place bent on one knee and bowed his head.

The bull came to him, stopping just inches away. It tilted its head toward Conal's in some animalistic impression of a bow, then gave a deep snort.

Conal stood and put his hands on each side of the creature's face. "I've been waiting for you, old friend," he said, then he gave it a kiss on the cheek.

When Conal turned and returned to the clearing, the beast dropped on all fours and followed. Its barrel chest heaved and sighed with each labored breath. As imposing as it seemed, it also looked tired, like it had finally completed a long, exhausting journey.

In the bright afternoon sunlight, its fur glistened with sweat, its coloring was more gray than brown. It approached an enormous barrel of food that had been left for it. After sniffing and grunting, it seemed satisfied and ate gluttonously but slowly as there were only a few teeth remaining and its mouth with which to chew.

It's old, I realized. *Very, very old.*

The villagers crowded around it, stroking its back, caressing it, loving on it the way normal people handle their favorite dog. None of them seemed scared in the slightest, and I had a foolish notion that this creature wasn't meant to be feared.

As it ate, Conal addressed the villagers. "Friends and neighbors, we're blessed by Cernunnos' appearance. Let us give praise."

"Praise be," they chanted.

Their excited chatter and murmurs continued until the beast finished eating. Then it raised its big head, wobbling from side to side under the weight of its plethora of horns. It looked almost unable to endure the burden of them.

"It's been a good, long run, my friend. But our time is nigh." Conal put a hand on the bull's muzzle, caressing it affectionately. "We offer delightful alms for you to choose from."

Then he looked to the benches where I stood with Dwayne and Stooge's corpse, and my blood ran cold.

I don't know when it happened, but I had my arm around Dwayne's shoulders, and I could feel him trembling. His body shook so hard I thought he might be having an epileptic fit until I looked at his face and saw the bewildered terror in his eyes. I imagine he saw the same look in mine.

"I'm so fucking scared, Benji," he said.

I understood because I felt the exact same way.

Conal walked side by side with the beast as they came toward us. Meanwhile, the villages had intermixed, men and women together, and taken seats on the quilts. Front row seats.

"Untie these ropes!" Dwayne hissed to me, pleading.

My fingers worked at the knots, desperate and frantic, but these weren't double slips or bowlines. Every time I pulled on a rope, it tightened somewhere else. Every time I thought I had one knot coming free, it cinched tighter as if mocking my futile efforts.

Dwayne's chest heaved in retching sobs. I was letting him down, failing him. I tried harder, but nothing I was doing worked. If anything, I was only making the jumble ropes and knots even more impossible to escape.

I suddenly remembered the knife I had stolen and pulled it from my pocket. I began sawing away at the ropes and cut one. Cut another.

I was halfway through the third, the third of a dozen or more, when Conal was beside me. He reached out and grabbed my wrist, but I pulled it free and held the knife toward him like a would-be assassin ready to plunge the blade into his chest.

I should have.

"This ain't the time to play the fool. You are in the presence of greatness. Show some respect." Conal grabbed the knife by the blade, the metal sinking deep into the skin of his hand. Blood followed, but he was entirely unconcerned. He closed his fist around the blade and was able to pull it from my grip with ease.

Conal tossed the knife to the side and shook his hand, sending a spray of blood cascading downward. Some of it fell over my shirt, which had been so pristine and white until that moment, painting abstract patterns on the cotton.

Maybe it was the smell of the blood, or maybe it was just destiny, but the beast, which had seemed so exhausted and almost disinterested up until that point, raised its head, sniffing the air. It made an excited, guttural sound, and then it rose onto its hind legs, towering over all of us.

"Help me, Benji!" Dwayne begged.

With no tool at my disposal, I pulled at the ropes until the skin on my hands was raw and bleeding. I couldn't let Dwayne down. No one moved to stop me, as if everyone in attendance, even the beast, knew I was bound to fail.

Conal gazed up at the creature, waving toward Stooge, then Dwayne, as if he were hosting a game show and displaying the prizes. "We have fine, young specimens. I trust you will choose wisely. You always do," Conal said to the bull.

He stepped back, rejoining his people, leaving me and Dwayne alone with the beast.

My bloodied fingers still strained at the ropes, but my eyes were on the monster as it stepped up to Stooge's body. When it got close, all of the flies zoomed away, not a single one lingering behind. The beast stared down on my friend with black, cloudy eyes. Then it leaned in, sniffing.

The first sniff was shallow, exploratory. The next was deeper, the animal's nostrils flaring. Its head snapped to the villagers, to Conal, who wore a sheepish, shamed expression on his face.

"Aye, that one is starting to spoil, but he can still serve as a fine vessel," Conal said. "Look at his girth!"

The bull returned its attention to the lifeless body. It crouched down, aligning its face with Stooge's. It took a few more quick sniffs, then nudged Stooge's face with its snout. Stooge's head lolled back and to the side, his face now directed at Dwayne and me.

His eyes came open, and I jumped back a step instinctively. Then I got a better look at his milky irises, which had no spark and saw nothing. It was gravity, nothing more.

The beast straddled Stooge, looking down onto his dead face. Long strands of mucus-filled saliva dripped from its jaws, some of it spilling into Stooge's open, gaping mouth. My stomach seized, and the soup I'd recently eaten tried to fight its way back out of my mouth, but I refused to allow it, swallowing it back down. I didn't want to give this thing, these people, the satisfaction of seeing me lose my lunch.

The bull backed off Stooge and came toward us.

CHAPTER THIRTY-NINE

I pissed my new pants when the creature stomped toward us. So much for retaining my dignity. I backed away from Dwayne, not wanting him to catch wind of my urine and realize what a coward I was.

The bull went to Dwayne, pushing its muzzle against his nose. Bristly hairs on its snout stabbed into my friend's face and cheeks, leaving behind fine, red welts as the animal breathed in his scent.

I shouldn't have worried about the smell of my piss because the stench of the beast was overwhelming this close. It was so strong my eyes watered, running down my cheeks like tears. I'd given up on salvaging any pride and let it happen.

Dwayne was full-on sobbing when the beast opened its mouth and let its long, pink tongue tumble free. I rushed back to them, using my meager strength to try to push the bull away from him, but I couldn't budge it an inch.

The bull, annoyed by my actions, kicked out with its hind leg. The hoof caught me square in the sternum, so hard all my wind was knocked out of me as I tumbled backward, going ass over head and coming down face first in the grass.

All I could do was lay there, wheezing and gasping as I tried to remember how to breathe. It wasn't an easy task as pain radiated through my torso in crashing waves.

I managed to roll onto my side just in time to see the beast run its tongue up Dwayne's face, starting at his jawline, trailing up across his cheek. His skin was pushed aside the way a fish displaces water in a placid pond.

The bull licked up Dwayne's tears, then dragged its tongue across his eyeball. He struggled against his binds, tried rocking from side to side, but the bull had straddled him, pinning him between its legs. There was nowhere to go. No escape.

When the bull's tongue hit Dwayne's long, curly locks, the creature withdrew its muscle back into its mouth. Then its jaws closed, and it whipped its enormous head to the side, ripping free a large shock of Dwayne's hair.

Dwayne yelped, eyes bulging as a trickle of blood ran down the side of his face. He strained harder against the ropes to no avail. I managed to look away for a moment to check the crowd and saw frantic, mad glee on their faces. They looked like spectators at the Colosseum, watching a wildcat tear apart a helpless victim.

"Help him!" I screamed. I didn't expect anyone to rise up and lend a hand, but the plea seemed an obligation. "Someone do something, you freaks!"

Not a single person gave me so much as a glance. Their eyes were on the show and, upon realizing there was no way out of this, so were mine.

The bull butted Dwayne with its snout, knocking him backward and off the bench. Then the beast used its antlers to lift and toss the bench itself out of the way. The seat flew a good twenty feet before crashing down and splintering.

As the creature pushed his head towards Dwayne, my friend raised his arms to fend it off. It was the natural thing to do but a very poor decision.

The beast chomped down on Dwayne's right hand, closing its ragged jaws over his wrist. It didn't have enough teeth remaining in its mouth to sever it in one quick bite, but the strength of its jaws smashed the bones with an audible crunch.

Dwayne shrieked with pain. He kicked with his feet, floundered with his other arm, pounding against the creature to no avail. The bull's jaws worked back and forth, side to side, as it slowly masticated the skin and muscles and tendons.

With a sloppy tearing sound, Dwayne's hand separated from his arm, and the bull swallowed it down in a single watery gulp.

Blood spurted from Dwayne's wrist like water from a drinking fountain. He reached with his remaining hand to cover it, but the bull was faster. It bit down on his left hand, wrenching his arm sideways, and I heard a sickening *pop* as his shoulder tore loose from its socket. Then came the nauseating crunch of his ulna and radius shattering. And then, just like before, the bull chewed through his flesh, separating his hand from his arm and then swallowed the hand down its gullet.

I never heard screams like the ones that came from Dwayne, and I longed to plug my ears so I didn't have to keep hearing them. I wanted to avert my eyes so I didn't have to see this massacre, but I felt I owed it to him.

He was there because of me. He was dying because of me. The least I could do was force myself to watch what I had caused.

"It's killing me! It's killing me," Dwayne shrieked. His eyes found mine, desperate and pleading. "Run, Benji!"

I pushed myself to my knees, my chest still throbbing, my lungs still trying to fill themselves with air.

Running wasn't an option, even if I was physically capable. I crawled toward him, wanting to provide some solace, some compassion in his dying moments. But a heavy boot came down on my back and flattened me against the ground.

"Be still, boy," Conal said. "This ain't your business no more."

I could barely hear his words over Dwayne's screams, which were so loud they echoed through the valley. So loud I thought they might shatter my eardrums. I almost hoped they would. I'd rather have gone deaf than hear his agony.

I craned my neck to see what was going on. The bull pressed a few of its keen horns tight against Dwayne's chest. They penetrated the material of his baseball uniform, and red halos of blood spread and grew across his torso.

The beast grunted, its hot breath a fog drifting from its nostrils as it pushed its head against Dwayne. The horns and antlers and tusks sunk deeper into my friend's body. Blood mixed with saliva bubbled from Dwayne's mouth, and his screams lost some of their intensity.

I didn't wish him dead, but I wished his pain to be over. Tragically, they were one and the same, and one couldn't happen without the other.

With Dwayne impaled on its antlers, the bull raised his head and simultaneously lifted Dwayne off the ground. His hand-less arms dangled, leaking blood. His legs had gone limp. His head hung down, loose on his neck. And still, he stared at me, unable to speak. But I knew what he was thinking.

Your fault.

I couldn't watch anymore. I surrendered and closed my eyes.

There were more noises. Grunting, groaning, whimpering cries. Wet, ripping sounds. Anguished moans.

Maybe I should have kept watching because what my mind

conjured up and associated with those noises may have been worse in reality. Or maybe reality was worse. Yeah, I think that's it. Reality is always worse.

"That's about enough now," an old voice crowed. It sounded familiar and made me look.

The old woman from the shack, the one Conal had called Brighid, stood at the end of the clearing. She wore the same gray sack of a dress and carried a pail in each hand. She set them on the ground and surveyed the scene. When she shook her head, her impossibly long, thin hair dragged across the ground, picking up fallen leaves.

"Well," she said. "About time to get on wit it, is not?"

Several men from the village came forward and pulled Dwayne off of the beast's horns. A pained cry escaped his lips, and it surprised me to realize he was somehow still alive. To my shameful relief, he saved me the indignity of looking at me again. He was delirious or unconscious or some lost place in between.

The men laid him on the ground and Brighid reclaimed her pails and went to him. She looked down at his battered and bleeding and maimed body, touched her forefinger to the center of her forehead, and then she spat on him, sending a phlegmy wad onto his face.

Next, she went to the bull, which stood on all fours, its body heaving from the stress and exertion of the attack. It seemed unsteady on its feet, as if it might collapse at any second.

Brighid grabbed onto the bull's tusk, the one that curved under its jaw and held it steady. She set the pail underneath its head, and, in one quick motion, she pulled a knife from somewhere within the folds of her dress, brought it up, and sliced open the beast's throat.

Blood poured from the creature, filling the pail within

seconds. So much blood came that it spilled over, saturating the ground around it and turning it to crimson mud.

Brighid tossed the knife aside and pressed her hand against the beast's snout. She leaned her face in close, so close they were touching, and whispered words I couldn't hear. All the while, she ran a hand across its face as if consoling a long-lost friend.

Slowly, gradually, the beast bled out. It managed to stay afoot, even after the blood stopped pumping, but not for long. It took one wobbling step backward, raised its head high, gave a mewling grunt, and then collapsed onto its side.

Brighid looked to the villagers, tears glistening against her aged cheeks. "Who's got the saws?" she asked.

CHAPTER FORTY

Several men came forward, carrying a variety of saws and blades. They went to work, cutting off the beast's antlers and horns and tusks. They made rough work of it, sometimes taking off large swaths of skin along with the protrusions. But the animal, or whatever it was, was dead, and it didn't mind.

As the men excised the antlers from the creature, Brighid gathered them together and took them to where Dwayne lay in the dirt. She arranged the horns in a seemingly careful manner around his head, as if she were putting together some macabre, intricate puzzle.

When the last of the antlers had been removed and Brighid had them all placed where she felt they needed to go, she used the same blade she had used to kill the beast to cut off Dwayne's shirt and pants. His head lolled and his eyes fluttered as he looked at her. His chest hitched as he drew in a quick breath, and she put her hand over his mouth.

"Easy now," she said, and he again succumbed to semi-consciousness. Brighid retrieved a pail and brought it to him.

After setting it on the ground, she dipped her hands into the bucket, sinking them up to mid-forearm.

When she retracted her hands, they came out cerulean blue. She smeared her claw-like mitts across Dwayne's chest, painting his torso. She repeated the dipping and painting action over and over again until not a speck of unstained skin was visible below Dwayne's neck.

Once completed, Brighid turned her attention to the villagers. "Turn your backs," she said. "This ain't meant for your eyes."

The villagers obeyed and did as told without quarrel. Conal had removed his foot from my back and sat on the ground beside me. He gave me a pat on the head, pointed to Dwayne, and said, "He belongs to you. You must see."

But I didn't want to see. I squeezed my eyes shut, like a toddler who had just seen the monster under his bed and believed it would cease to exist if he didn't look at it.

With a tired sigh of exertion, Conal pulled me into his lap and grabbed my head with both of his hands. He used his fingers to pry my eyes open and whispered into my ear, "See."

Brighid traded pails, switching out the one with paint for the bucket filled with the bull's blood. She plunged her blue hands into it, cleansing them of the paint, and they came out scarlet. She straddled my unmoving friend like a newlywed preparing to consummate marriage and used her bloody hands to pry open his mouth.

"The great horned god, Cernunnos, requires an earthly vessel. He has chosen you, boy. Now, become one with him," Brighid said.

She tilted the bucket of blood carefully, letting it ooze over the lip of the pail and drain into Dwayne's open mouth. He coughed once, gagging up a bubble of plasma, but then his body gave in and the still steaming blood ran down his throat as he swallowed and swallowed and swallowed.

When the pail was finally empty, Brighid set the bucket aside and closed Dwayne's mouth. She looked at Conal and said, "The corn."

Conal slid me off his lap and went to where the men had separated the corn stalks. He grabbed a large tobacco basket heaped full with the golden brown leaves. He returned and handed it to Brighid, who then carefully spread them across Dwayne's body, fully covering him from head to toe.

When he was completely out of sight, she set the basket aside and wiped off her hands on her dress. "Now it's your turn," she said to Conal.

The old man turned to the villagers, looked at his people, raised his hands above his head, and clapped them. Everyone turned to face him.

"Come," he said. "Place me in my bundle."

While they came to him, he undressed. The sight of his body, so frail, so pale, shocked me. He'd seemed so spry and virile while wearing his costumes and clothes. Now, bare and exposed, he looked like a man who was hours, maybe minutes, away from a face-to-face meeting with the Grim Reaper.

All I could do was sit and watch as the men and women of the village used the blades from the corn stalks to wrap up Conal. They weaved them carefully, like they were making a fine blanket meant to be passed down through generations.

As they worked, they created something like a cocoon of corn leaves. And by the time they were finished, all that was visible was Conal's face.

I was so caught up in my shock over what had just happened to Dwayne and this bizarre dressing of Conal in corn that I didn't notice the covering atop Dwayne had begun to move. Rustling whispers drew my attention. The scratching noise of the brittle corn blades brushing against each other. The heap undulated, growing, rising.

I scrambled toward it, thinking Dwayne was coming around, believing he was somehow going to emerge from this alive and salvageable. But Nora appeared behind me and grabbed me around the waist, dragging her feet against the ground to hold me back.

"No, Benji. You'll die."

I was surprised she cared.

Gradually, the golden pile covering Dwayne began to fall away as the contents underneath rose up. The first things to break clear were the antlers. They were firm, immovable, attached. Then more corn leaves fell away, and the bull's head emerged.

Bits of Dwayne, small vestiges of the boy who'd once been, remained behind. His chin, so square and strong, stood out beneath the snout of the bull, but it was already sprouting brown fur.

On his chest, a four-inch scar where his dad had lashed him with the stick on that camping trip from hell was still there, just above his left nipple. But, as I watched, the paint spread across his skin seemed to melt into and become one with his flesh. And the scar faded away.

The holes put into his torso by the bull's antlers sealed shut and left behind nothing more than dimples. As he rose to his feet, his legs grew longer and taller. His thighs thickened, rippling with muscle, turning into the haunches of an animal, no longer a boy's legs.

His forearms, which after the maiming had ended in ragged stumps, elongated. The bones grew and stretched, mutating together. Turning into cloven hoofs.

My mouth opened, and it was my turn to scream. Screaming was all I could do, and I was helpless to stop. I screamed until my throat was raw and continued even when all that came out was a raspy, croaking wheeze.

The thing which was no longer my friend dropped onto all fours and gave a full body shake. The remaining detritus flew off him, then drifted back to the ground. He made an awkward, clumsy turn, coming to face all of us. Then he threw back his head and unleashed a cacophonous, bestial bellow.

Dwayne had become the great horned beast, and whatever bit of sanity still lingered inside my head went on hiatus.

CHAPTER FORTY-ONE

When I reemerged from my break in reality, I saw the bull far off in the distance, stomping toward the forest. Angry sounds continued emanating from its mouth, a toxic mixture of misery and hate. Before disappearing into the cover of the woods, it took one look back.

My breath froze in my throat as it looked directly at me, singling me out amongst the crowd. And while the eyes were black and bulging and so much like those of an animal, I couldn't miss the familiarity in them. They were still Dwayne's eyes and seeing them made me want to sob.

Then it turned away, pushing through the thickets and brambles and became lost to me.

"Take those two to the hogs," Brigid said.

The sledge and draft horses were on the scene, awaiting their load. All of the men from the village, save Conal, worked together to drag the dead beast's body onto it. It was a struggle that took several minutes.

Once finished, they went to Stooge, tearing the ropes holding him upright from the ground and unlooping them from his body. Then three of the stronger men, men not too exhausted from moving the bull's carcass, grabbed onto Stooge.

One grabbed onto his feet, the others his arms. When they got him to the sledge, they swung him back and forth, building momentum, then simultaneously let go, and my friend landed on top of the bull.

There was a new addition to the meadow. A wooden pole, seven feet high and thick as a tree trunk, had been planted in the ground. It stood out starkly against the flat ground, all alone, but that was about to change.

Seamus and Ewan carried Conal, wrapped in his casing of corn, to the beam. He was a willing subject, not struggling in the slightest. The only reason he needed to be carried was because his legs were tightly bound.

The twins fastened Conal to the pole, tying him in firmly but not so tight as to cause pain or discomfort. All the while, the old man wore a tranquil smile.

When he was secured, the twins left, and Nora went to his side. She now wore a crown of Indian Corn, the deep reds and rusts and oranges circled her head, her hair pulled up and braided. She caressed Conal's face, gliding her fingertips across his weathered, wrinkled skin. They were speaking, but too far away for me to hear, so I managed to stand and moved closer.

"I'm so proud of you, dearie," Conal said to her. "You did everything I asked of you and more."

She touched his lips with her index and middle finger. "I did it for you. Always for you."

"I know. And I love you so." Conal kissed her hand, such a small gesture but one I found unusually intimate.

"As I you." She stood on her tiptoes, and she kissed him. Not on the hand, but on the lips. "I still worry, though. What if something goes awry?" she asked.

Conal tried to shake his head, but the corn binding him was

too tight, and his face only shifted a few millimeters side to side. "It won't. Brighid has never let us down before, has she?"

Nora broke eye contact with him for the first time, her eyes searching for Brighid. Instead, she found me. She inhaled sharply, maybe surprised to see me up and moving or upset I was close enough to eavesdrop. Either way, she backed away from her grandfather.

"I was wondering when you'd return," she said.

I closed the distance between us, unconcerned over interrupting their formerly private moment.

"Glad to see you up and around, young Benjamin," Conal said to me with a painfully genuine smile. "We've been waiting for you."

The man looked as innocuous and gentle as Santa Claus. It would have been easier to accept all of this if he'd looked like a monster, like a crazed killer, but he was so far removed from either that I almost struggled to hold onto my anger against him. "Am I next?" I asked.

"Next for what?" Conal inquired.

"To die, I guess," I said with a shrug. "You've already had Stooge and Dwayne killed. You're not going to let me leave after everything I've seen. So, am I next to the slaughter?"

Conal cast his eyes toward Nora, giving her wordless instructions. She sidled up next to me and took my hand. I was too exhausted, both physically and emotionally, to shove her away, and let it happen.

"No one's going to die, Benji," she said. "I promise you that."

I was trying to come up with a response that promise, something harsh and biting, but Brighid's voice beat me to the punch.

"Circle 'round," she said. "Everyone."

One by one the villages came forward. They formed a tight

ring around Conal, then doubled up, adding in a second row, and then a third. Nora and I were front and center, about ten feet from the man and the pole.

Brighid had not joined the circles, but she was amongst the gathering. She stood behind Conal, her gray dress swaying in the breeze. A gust lifted her hair which danced around her like semi-transparent filaments. In her hands she clutched a round piece of glass which must have been at least a foot in diameter. She stayed silent, allowing Conal to lead.

"I've known most of you my entire life," he said. "I've held your newborn babes. I've helped tend to your fields. I've been at your side during both the good times and the bad. And let me say it has been an honor!" His voice boomed, strong and confident with not a scintilla of fear.

"Our lives may come across as unorthodox to those who don't know our ways." He steadied his gaze on me. "But even those outside our covey can learn and understand, in time."

Realizing I wasn't going to be killed should have been a relief, but knowing he intended for me to become one of them was almost as terrifying. I couldn't imagine spending another day in this perverse, horrid place, let alone months or years.

Nora squeezed my hand, drawing my attention. She gave me one of those stunning, beatific smiles as she leaned in closer, pressing her lips to my ear. The feel of her breath made goosebumps break out all over my body. "*This* is why I brought you here," she whispered to me.

Conal resumed his address. "We are not mere neighbors, we are kin. And I thank you, my brothers and sisters, for being here for me today and watching as my old life is expurgated."

He was crying too, but they were the tears of a man so mad he believed his own lies. I didn't want to take part in this ritual, this charade, and tried to pull my hand loose from Nora's grip, but she held firm. Then the man at my opposite side, a hulking figure who looked strong enough to stomp me like a worm, grabbed my other hand.

All of the villagers held hands, uniting with one another as Brighid held the glass high above her head. She tilted it perfectly to catch the rays of the sun, which hit the glass, and focused their heat on Conal's back.

Conal went on. "I have been blessed with a long and fruitful life. One with more joy than I deserved. I have loved heartily and been fortunate enough to find the woman with whom I shall spend eternity."

The last sentence was directed at Nora, and when I checked her reaction, tears streamed down her cheeks.

Brighid stood unmoving as the heat built up and intensified. All of the sun's energy was directed at one small spot and, after about a minute, a puff of smoke drifted into the air. Brighid stayed still, and the smoke grew from a puff to a wisp. Then it morphed into a full-on cloud.

The people behind Conal saw the fire first. I didn't notice it until the flames reached above his back, licking at the air, using the breeze for fuel. The old man's face twisted and contorted in pain, but he never lost his smile, not even for a moment.

The corn leaves wrapping Conal were dry and brittle, and it didn't take long for the fire to explode. Soon, his entire body was ablaze, save for his face, which had been uncovered. There, his flesh blistered in the heat, the skin bubbling then bursting.

The show lasted under five minutes in total. The flames burned away the corn, burning themselves out in the process. The ropes which had held Conal to the pole also melted away, and he collapsed to the ground.

Some of his flesh had been incinerated, but most remained intact, albeit ruby red like he'd just been submerged in a vat of boiling oil. His hair had been cooked off, and the stink of it hung heavy in the air.

Conal, still alive, curled into a fetal position. The man beside me released my hand. All of the villagers broke apart. A few of the women grabbed sheets from the wash barrels and rushed them to Conal, draping his body in their heavy wetness. He gave a small nod, and I saw what remained of his lips move. "My thanks to ya," he croaked.

Of everything I'd seen since arriving in Carrick Glynn, this seemed the most arbitrary and nonsensical. Why had Conal just allowed himself to be burned at the stake? Yes, he was alive for now, but surely, he'd soon die from his injuries as there were no hospitals to treat his wounds. If he didn't succumb from shock, infection would surely take him in the coming days.

I turned to Nora, wanting to demand an explanation, a real explanation this time not the confusing bullshit I'd been fed so far, but she was no longer beside me. The woman holding my hand was Brighid.

She closed her fingers tightly around mine, her barbed nails puncturing my skin with small bursts of pain. She brought her other hand to my face, pushing her fingers into my hair and grabbing a fistful. "Come forward with me, boy," she commanded.

Although she looked fragile and ancient, I was helpless to fight her off as she led me to Conal, who lay on the ground, shivering under the makeshift blankets. "Kneel," she said.

That time, I did try to resist, refusing to bend my knees. She jerked my head backward and leaned in close, expelling a rotten breath into my face. "The future is already written. Nothing you do will change it. Now, kneel."

Still, I refused. Behind me, someone kicked me in the back of my thigh, the impact buckling my legs. I dropped onto my knees, beside Conal. The smell of his charred skin reminded me of barbecuing on my dad's charcoal grill. It was savory, in a sickening kind of way.

Conal looked at me with bloodshot, watery eyes. Somehow, despite his condition, despite the agony that must have been coursing through his body, he grinned. He reached out with a quivering hand and pressed his palm against my face, then he repeated the action with his other hand.

I tried to pull away, but too many people had hold of me, pinning me in place. I was as helpless to get away as I'd been when I was under Brighid's spell.

"Young Benjamin," Conal said. My name had never sounded so raw and horrible. "I am honored to take this journey with you."

He leaned in closer, his charred, weeping face inches from my own. I tried to pull back, to break free, but their numbers were on me, and escape wasn't an option.

Then Nora was at my back. She wrapped her arms around my chest, hugging me tightly, a lover's embrace. As she rested her head against my neck, her hair rained over me, the delicate softness of it comforting despite all that was going on.

Her voice, barely a whisper, drifted to me. "Even before I knew you, I saw the pain living in your heart, Benji. You were lost, abandoned by your mother. I brought you here to show you love is eternal."

Having her body pressed against my own somehow pushed away my fear. I'd missed and needed this kind of feminine touch. She wasn't my mother but, in her arms, I felt protected and loved.

Conal touched his face against mine. With dawning horror, his mouth opened and pushed against my own. All the while, Nora held me firmly, but now, her arms felt like steel bands rather than my mother's warm embrace.

Brighid began to chant. It could have been gibberish or some foreign language, but it all sounded like nonsense to me. Whatever words she was saying were repeated by the villagers, their voices reaching a deafening roar as the intonation was repeated on a loop, louder and louder each time as it screamed to a crescendo.

I closed my eyes, not wanting to see him kissing me, as my struggling resumed, but it was too late. Conal used his mouth to force open my own. His tongue pushed past my lips, rough yet slippery like some live thing exploring. Our faces were locked together as Conal breathed into me, an outbound gale entering me.

I tried to bite my way free, chomping onto his tongue. The coppery taste of his blood electrified my tastebuds, but the man didn't pull away.

He breathed out again, his exhale so forceful my saliva dried up. Then came another exhale.

And another.

And another.

All the while, the villagers chanted.

Dizziness overwhelmed me. My head felt on the verge of floating away, like a kite in a storm. But it wasn't just my head that felt like floating away. It was... all of me. As if I was being pumped full of helium. If I opened my eyes, I was certain the view I'd see would be from far above, looking down on the goings-on like some omniscient presence.

If I looked and saw such a sight, I knew my mind would snap, so I kept my eyes closed. The chanting voices were so loud my eardrums burst and hot wetness drained from my ear canals and dripped down my neck. All the while, the floating feeling, the pushed away feeling, grew stronger and stronger.

My body was going limp. Only the hands holding me, Nora's arms around me, kept me upright. My thoughts came slower and slower. I began to wonder where I was. Who I was.

I was falling, not physically but mentally. Plunging down the Grand Canyon, hitting the rocks below, but not stopping.

Still falling. Falling. Passing through the ground. Passing through rock. I felt on fire, ablaze and roasting, as I neared the Earth's core.

Falling.

Falling.

Falling.

And then I stopped.

"Deireadh!" Brighid shouted.

At last, I opened my eyes.

And I saw myself.

CHAPTER FORTY-TWO

When I regained consciousness, I was in a featureless, windowless stone building. There was no furniture save for the stone slab upon which I laid.

Upon trying to sit up, a miserable, deeply entrenched pain overwhelmed me. It felt like my insides had been liquified, and every nerve in my skin was exposed and misfiring. I wanted to cry out in pain, but a hand covered my mouth.

"You came 'round sooner than I expected," Brighid said. "Bad luck for you as I wasn't finished applying your nostrum. Now, you'll have to suffer till I'm done."

And suffer I did.

I stared at the ceiling, wanting to cry but unable to cry, as the woman slathered some type of oily, gel-like salve all over my body. She didn't miss an inch, even working the ointment into my groin and orifices without shame.

Despite the humiliation of the acts, whatever she'd applied to my body turned the agony down to a dull ache. She wrapped my waist in a large cloth, covering my loins and saving me a small amount of modesty.

When she finished, she ran her hand over my head, cooing, "You done good, boy."

Something about the way her hand passed over my skull startled me. I could feel the texture of her thin, papery skin pressing against my head where hair should have blocked sensation. Had they shaved my head? Why?

I tried to rise into a sitting position but was unable, my body was too tired. I'd never felt so exhausted and... used up. Rolling onto my side was more successful but still required tremendous exertion.

I let my legs fall down from the table, my feet hitting the earthen floor. That surprised me too because the table was three feet off the ground. My feet should still be dangling mid-air.

The skin on my legs glistened with the salve. Beneath the thick substance, I could still make out burned, reddened flesh. Then I shifted my attention from my legs to my arms. They, too, were burned. Burned, as well as long and frail. The arms of someone very old.

I stood, took an awkward step. Every part of me felt foreign and outsized. I'd lost my coordination, and even standing took great effort. I almost collapsed.

My balance steadied when Brighid appeared at my side and put her arm around my waist. "Easy," she said. "You're gonna go through an adjustment period. If you ain't careful, you're apt to damage yourself."

She eased me back into a sitting position on the table, our faces aligned. I caught a glimpse of something - someone - in her milky eyes but couldn't get a good look before she turned away.

"You stay here, boy. I'll fetch Conal and let him explain."

The woman left me, disappearing out the building's only door. She left it open, and moonlight spilled in. I wondered how much time had passed since the afternoon in the meadow. Hours? Days? Longer?

I stood again, taking my time and ensuring my footing was solid before I took a step. The second try went better, marginally, but I no longer felt like I was going to fall. I tried another, then another.

I'd made it within a yard of the door when a shape appeared, backlit by the night. The person looked to be about five feet tall - my height - only now I was looking down on it. I told myself I was mistaken. The door was taller than it seemed, or lower, or maybe the floor inside was raised, or the person was standing in a hole, or... anything. There had to be a reason.

The shape stepped through the doorway and into the room, and I found myself looking at... myself.

It was the face I'd seen every morning in the mirror. The body I'd dressed each morning and undressed each night. It was a carbon copy of me.

"Hello, young Benjamin," the person said, using my voice. "Why don't you join me outside? It's a glorious night and seems a shame to waste it." It turned away and left me.

I was certain I was dreaming and tried to pinch the skin on my arm, but the slick salve made it impossible to get a grip. I resorted to slapping myself, which stung, but the effect was numbed by Brighid's nostrum. Regardless, I didn't wake safe in my bed back in Sallow Creek. I didn't even wake imprisoned in some stall or cell in Carrick Glynn. Because I was already awake.

It seemed I had no choice but to follow.

The night was cold, below freezing, and the grass underfoot crunched as I walked to the other version of myself. Its back was turned, but as I approached it turned, giving me a smile and nod.

"It's a shock, even for me, and I've been through this so many times I've lost count," other-me said.

I opened my mouth, but it was so dry I couldn't form words.

"Almost forgot. Brought this," other-me said, pulling a flask from the pocket of the jacket it was wearing. It removed a cork from the lid and passed it to me.

I accepted, noticing how long and slender my fingers looked as they wrapped around it. I was bringing it to my lips when my reflection appeared in its silver shell.

But it wasn't my reflection looking back at me. It was Conal's burned, charred face.

The flask fell from my hands, the contents spilling into the frozen turf. The other version of me hurriedly bent and scooped it up before all the drink could escape.

"Too good to waste," it said, taking a nip for himself then offering it to me again.

I shook my head. "What's going on?" I asked. Of course, it wasn't my voice that passed through my lips. The voice coming from inside me was Conal's.

The body which had once been mine reached out and took my old man's hand. "Let's have a sit, shall we?"

He led me to a wooden bench, and we sat side by side. I was trembling all over, either from the cold air, terror, or, more likely, both.

"You stole my body," I said.

He cocked his head, a crooked smile - my crooked smile - tugging at his lips. "Don't know if *stole* is the right way to say it. I gave you mine, after all. Seems more fair to call it a trade."

My mind raced, struggling to find a rational explanation where there was none. I didn't want this old man's body. I wanted to be me. I wanted to be young, even if it meant living out my days in this awful village.

"I want it back," was all I could say. It wasn't much of an argument. There was no debate team in my future.

"I reckon you do. Such feelings are normal, but that's not how this works. Don't take my stubbornness for ungratefulness, though. I'll be forever appreciative of your sacrifice."

My entire body shook, my teeth chattered. I felt as if I was going to shake to pieces. In some ways, it might have been a relief. Instead, the man inside my body put his arm around me and pulled me in tight, sharing his warmth.

"It's not all bad," he said. "You'll have food and drink. A safe place to lay your head at night. Many aren't as fortunate."

I wanted to pull away from him but needed his body heat. I also didn't want to let go of myself. If I held on long enough, maybe I could find a way to reclaim it, to force my way back inside.

"It will be hard at first, as you adjust," he said. "But you're strong, young Benjamin. You might be with us for a good long while."

He stood, taking my hand. I rose and followed, trance-like, as he led me back to the keeping room. When I passed across the threshold, he remained outside. "Get some rest. You'll find you need much more sleep than you're used to. One of the curses of an aged body. But there are worse fates."

He closed the door in my face, and I stood there for a very long time.

CHAPTER FORTY-THREE

It's been a few months now. The burns on my new body have healed. Sometimes, when I look down at my skin, I can even work up enough humor to think of myself as a Freddy Krueger knockoff. But humor is rare.

Most days, I sit inside this cottage, eating and drinking whatever they bring to me. Oftentimes, Conal delivers the food. I won't say I've accepted what's happened, but I'm getting used to seeing him wearing my body as his own.

This new form my soul and mind inhabits is a far cry from what I'd had before coming to Carrick Glynn. My back aches, my knees throb. Climbing up and down from the table leaves me out of breath. The nights are long and sleepless, and on those rare occasions when sleep does come, I dream about my friends and their deaths and wake up with this old skin soaked in sweat.

With each passing day, I seem to grow weaker and more tired. There's a gnawing pain somewhere deep inside my torso, like some small wild creature eating away at my insides. When I cough, which is often, it's common to bring up blood.

Yesterday, Nora came by. She cooked me a steak and mashed potatoes and brought enough for the both of us. It was the first time I'd seen her since that day, and despite everything, I felt a bit more spry with her around.

We chatted most of the afternoon. She told me about life in the village, the goings-on of the people who lived there. I wasn't very interested, but I listened. It was nice having her around.

When she was ready to leave, she leaned over and gave me a long hug. I held onto her, not wanting to let go. With my arms around her, I could pretend I was still fourteen years old with my life ahead of me. Maybe a life with her. With my arms around her, I was young and immature and never had to grow up.

Eventually, she pulled away, and I became an old man again. She quickly turned her face from me, but I'd spotted the wetness on her cheeks. Her show of emotion gave me the courage to ask questions which had been gnawing at me for months.

"Conal isn't your grandfather, is he?"

She bit her lip. The sun shone through the open door, silhouetting her figure, which had become more womanly since I'd last seen her. The sight made the old butterflies that lived inside my belly come back to life and flutter about. I suppose some things are eternal.

"No." She took a long pause. "He's my husband."

I'd suspected as much but hearing it out loud made my head start to throb. "For how long?"

"Too long to count. Centuries."

I looked past her, suddenly unable to look at her emerald eyes. "So, you..."

"Went through the same ritual? Yes. I claimed this body last year on Samhain."

"What happened to the real girl?" I asked, but I already

knew the answer. I was a smart kid, after all. "Was she the woman who had her head chopped off in the meadow?"

Nora nodded. "She was."

"Is that what's going to happen to me?"

Nora traced her fingers across my bald, scarred dome. "Don't fret about what the future holds, Benji. It's only February. There's a long time before harvest."

CHAPTER FORTY-FOUR

Most days, I sit in silence, passing the hours with writing. But now, my story is told, and I don't know what I'll do to occupy my time.

It's so lonely here, and the days are so long.

When night comes, and I toss and turn on my stone bed, and one question lingers.

Will I live to see another Halloween?

AFTERWORD

First, let me thank you for reading my tale of murder and mayhem in the woods of Pennsylvania. I've started writing "Carrick Glynn" in Nov of 2020 and it took me almost a year to finish it up. I hope you enjoyed it!

I'm a lot like Benji in that Halloween is my favorite holiday. I love everything about the season, but maybe most of all the pervasive spookiness which seems omnipresent. Fall, with its shorter days and darker nights, feels like home to me and I hope I was able to capture some of that emotion in this novel.

I've been writing stories since I was in elementary school. I read those missives on the school bus and occasionally in English class, but never dreamed my writing would reach an audience beyond that. Now, five years into my writing career, and I've made the #1 horror best-seller list on Amazon (briefly) and have readers around the world.

To say it's a dream come true is trite, because its more than that. It makes me feel whole.

Some of you have been on this journey with me since the beginning, or damn close. Many more have joined us along the way. To all of you, I give my most sincere thanks. I wouldn't be here without your support. Thank you, Dear Reader, and I hope you'll stick around to see what I come up with next.

Much love,
Tony Urban

ALSO BY TONY URBAN

Within the Woods

Hell on Earth

Her Deadly Homecoming

The Land Darkened

Printed in Great Britain
by Amazon